MEMORIES END

GARY PETRAS

MONTAG

First Montag Press E-Book and Paperback Original Edition August 2020

Montag Press
ISBN: 978-1-940233-73-4
Front cover design © Victor Leza
Back cover images © 'tiero', 'Ankor light' & 'AlienCat' via Adobe Stock
Interior design by Niall Gray
Editor - Kate Sargeant
Managing Director - Charlie Franco

A Montag Press Book
www.montagpress.com
Montag Press
1066 47th Ave. Unit #9
Oakland CA 94601 USA

Montag Press, the burning book with the hatchet cover, the skewed word mark and the portrayal of the long-suffering fireman mascot are trademarks of Montag Press.

Printed & Digitally Originated in the United States of America
10 9 8 7 6 5 4 3 2 1

Memories End is a fantastic fable of foes, freaks, friendship and freedom. Moe and Bazil are an odd couple for the ages, seeking after the self-realization of their own sentience and a redemption for their animalistic sins. Escaping from a circus where the Hermaphrodite leader of the freaks performs bizarre experiments for his/her freakshow, our chimp and elephant duo find more than they expected. They discover love through fellowship, and also their own humanity along the way to...*Memories End*. A page turning story that leaves the reader pondering: What does it truly mean to be human?

> — Ed Bonilla- Author of *5 Clones* and 2020's first place
> winner of the Kelly J. Abbott Short Story Contest

Friendship, like love and hate, cannot have just one standard definition; instead, it has as many definitions as there are people in the world. And I was pleased to read Gary Petras' definition of friendship exhibited in his wonderfully creative, fun and exciting story about the journey undertaken by Moe, a chimp, and Bazil, an elephant, to Memories End, all while encountering a number of obstacles along the way. So, if you are a fan of buddy stories that will keep you engaged in the fate of the characters and cheering for them throughout, then you will definitely enjoy *Memories End*.

> — Jonathan R. Rose, author of *Carrion*, *The Spirit of Laughter*,
> *Gato y Lobo* and *Siempre hay un lugar, Siempre hay un Tiempo*

For Michael F. Petras, Jr.
Who Found Memories End
And Bruce Rosenberger
Friends do not get any better than him

.

"Sabu was sad the whole tour stunk
The airline's lost the elephant's trunk"

— Sabu Visits The Twin Cities Alone, by John Prine

"The freaks will stay together
They're a tight old crew
You look at them
They look at you"

— Devil Baby, by Mark Knopfler

CHAPTER ONE
Unjust Rewards

Moe the chimp hopped the ringbank and scurried toward the back door of the big top. In his haste he unconsciously used his hands for balance, going three or four paces before returning to his upright gait. His expression never wavered. His hair had suddenly fluffed out at every exposed area, making his dark narrow eyes and tightly pressed lips only appear more intense within the crown of his black coat.

Moe fixed his attention on the loose sidewall between the rows of occupied seats, blocking out the eyes and laughter that followed his exit. Once he hit the backyard where the dressing tents and living quarters were located, he snatched the pink bonnet from his head. The thin spaghetti-like strap had cut off his oxygen, locking his breath and voice inside, so after his first deep inhale, he let out a *hoot*. The sound startled him, but he quickly regained his composure and swaggered away from the loud applause that drowned out even his departing curses.

The night air was crisp and cool, especially after performing under a stuffy canvas, but Moe had no time to linger and enjoy. Soon, Amelia and her other chimps would finish their bows. In fact, from the sound of the rippling laughter, that time was just about now. The clowns were taking over inside the tent, their antics covering the preparations for the next performers, a high wire act. Moe's finale was a parody of that act. The very thought of it, coupled with the ever increasing laughter, renewed his anger.

By the time he reached Amelia's dressing tent Moe had torn the pink and frilly dress from his body. Crushing it into a knot, he heaved it into the first convenient corner, then hurriedly dressed in an outfit more befitting a fellow of his stature. He pulled on a light shirt, a vest and trousers before stumbling back into the night air, trying to walk and tie his shoes at the same time.

He paused in the shadows of a nearby trailer to straighten his attire and to watch Amelia herd the other chimps into their cages. Soon she would enter the dressing tent, find the tattered dress, and then try to find him. She would lure him with bananas and the threat of Slade's threat of confinement. But Moe wouldn't stand for it. He drew his Chicago Bears cap from his back pocket and pulled it down over his ears and eyes as he slunk toward Slade's living quarters.

Moe found the trailer locked up tight as a drum, but he was not easily beaten, especially when it came to cigars. Grabbing the doorknob and pulling sideways, he managed to open a quarter inch gap between the door and jamb, revealing a portion of the lock. With his free hand he groped for his pocket knife. Using his teeth to open it, he inserted the blade until it pushed against the locking mechanism as he pulled harder on the doorknob. A sudden *click,* and he was inside.

Slade would be announcing the high wire act at the moment, giving Moe ample opportunity to poke around, but the place reeked of cheap aftershave and alcohol. It reminded Moe of the sideshow which, next to the cages and Slade's, was the only place at the circus that distressed him. The freaks looked at him like they knew who and what he was. They saw him as just one more of the oddities. They tried to link him with all those misfits that drowned in their cages, but Moe would rage until his last breath at that vile canard. Those mishapened chimps did the world a favor by meeting their demise at the might of the big grey brute. Fortunately, there was little of interest to him at the side-show, so he could avoid it like the plague. Cigars were a different story. For them, he'd risk unpleasant odors and unpleasant threats.

He sniffed out the humidor, plucked two fat Cuban stogies, and split---no sense being greedy. One for now. He flamed his Zippo and took deep puffs. And one for after the banana bunching.

CHAPTER TWO
And Unjust Desserts

Slade had fifty-three years on this earth. He was fat, balding, sweating and looked three times his age. Most of Slade's professional acquaintances thought of him as the boiling hothead of the Slade Bros. Circus and Sideshow. The title was a somewhat inside joke known only to Slade, and he thought that by letting everyone believe he was an only child and an orphan to boot, it created instant empathy. No one was certain if Slade was his given name, adopted name or one he acquired somewhere along the way.

He intercepted Amelia Boone as she was leaving the dressing tent. "If you're looking for that damn ape of yours," he snarled, "someone just saw him leaving my trailer."

"Who?"

"What does it matter 'who'? And what's that in your hand?"

Amelia clung tightly to the tattered pink dress.

"Destroyed another one, did he?" Slade let loose a low growl, removing his top hat and mopping the perspiration from his brow. "This is the last straw."

"I can fix it. Besides, I've wanted to change the costume anyway." The woman put on her best conciliatory smile.

"This is hardly the time to push for more money."

"When have I ever asked for anything?" Amelia asked shyly. She was overweight and looked it, even in her loose-fitting blue robe. Nor could she hide her rising blood pressure. It showed over her face, and if Slade had ever taken the opportunity to look deeper into that face, he would have seen something else there. A touch of defiance perhaps. Something she was learning more of as the years rolled by her. "I've always paid for my acts."

"And I suppose you're going to pay back everyone for the stuff's been stolen from them," Slade said, still sweating.

"Everyone's so quick to blame Moe. Maybe this is just a circus of thieves, each using Moe as an alibi."

"Well, when you find him, lock him up. Then you'll have your answer." Slade blinked the stinging sweat from his heavy eyelids.

"It's not that easy." Amelia suddenly looked very old and sad. Cages seemed so cruel, especially for Moe, who had never known them. From the moment Louise first placed the infant chimp in her care, Amelia knew he was something special, and if she hadn't kept him separate from the other chimps at the time, he would certainly be just another dead animal now, murdered by that big, dumb raging elephant.

"It was a mistake," Slade said knowingly, "my allowing you to pamper that ape. He may have become a star performer, but I'm beginning to think that now he's slowly killing the entire act. You're purposely holding back the others."

"It takes time to train a whole new group of animals," Amelia said sadly. "And don't try to tell me any different because you didn't have that elephant, Bazil, destroyed for that very reason."

Slade wiggled his hat back into place. "Well, time proved me right about Bazil, but it's running out for Moe. He's getting older, and bigger. Too big to handle soon. And then..."

Amelia closed her mind. When Slade talked like that, she wondered what she had even seen in him. They both walked away, going in different directions. In the back of Amelia's mind she felt the sun beginning to set on her career. She was only thirty years old and things were all but over and done. If she could just get Moe to behave and join the program.........it was the biggest *if* of her life.

CHAPTER THREE
King Of The Beasts

Moe moved attentively among the menagerie cages, keeping one watchful eye on the chimps. A song kept running through his head but he could not place its source. It was pleasant enough and as he sang a bit out loud it seemed to sooth the savage beasts.

> *"Cheer up, Sleepy Jean, oh what can it mean,*
> *To a daydream believer and a homecoming queen."*

He exhaled large puffs of smoke from his dwindling cigar between lyrics while he watched Amelia distribute the last of the evening bananas. It was a ritual whether the show went well, or in the well. The latter seldom happened with Moe as the star attraction. And because of that, he felt he deserved more—*much* more—than his fair share of the rewards.

Amelia continued to chitter and chatter with each chimp, always looking around furtively. Moe knew for whom. But he kept his distance, moving laterally until he came to the lions. They were the next attraction. Already the metal, cage-like run-way was strung from their wagons to the big top. Moe could hear more covering laughter being perpetrated by the clowns.

Here, Moe stopped to torment one large male cat in particular. His name was Baron. A lazy, scarred, and disagreeable sort,

Baron lay practically motionless, except for an occasional swiping action of his tail. Numerous flies crawled around his head, but he paid them no mind. He was set in a stare; cruel yellow eyes were riveted on Moe, who had moved close to the bars of the wagon.

"Typical," Moe said, blowing smoke from the corner of his mouth. "Shit and honey are two of the best ways to attract flies. And there's nothing sweet about you, you ugly brute."

Baron growled deep in his throat.

"Who are you trying to kid?" Moe laughed. "This is the real you, you lazy ass. Not what goes on in there---" Moe pointed the lit end of his cigar at the tent. "All those suckers should come out here if they want a true look at the king of the beasts."

Baron's growls grew in intensity and soon spread to the other lions. Moe looked up and down the line of wagons as he drew heavily on his cigar, then he blew the smoke into Baron's face, setting the flies into a buzzing frenzy and Baron into a roaring rage. He lunged head first at the metal bars. Expecting it, Moe calmly took one step backward and released his cigar with a flick. The lighted end hit Baron's nose with a sizzle, igniting another lunge. This one was accompanied by a sweeping paw, but Moe again anticipated the action.

The amused chimp used the momentum from his backward jump to carry him away from the aroused cats, making his final gesture an obscene one and saying: "Typical. All talk, no action."

Moe could still hear the roaring as he came to the smaller chimp cages. They were arranged in a tight U-formation, two animals to each of the three structures. Moe's appearance started a series of *hooting* sounds from the six occupants.

"All together now, gang," Moe said, holding up his arms," what time is it?"

The noise changed to a soft scuffle of excited chimps trying to hide their caches of bananas. Some went to chewing furiously on the wads already in their mouths.

Moe walked from cage to cage, shaking the bars and shouting: "What the hell is this, you stupid apes? You want those fuzzballs you call heads squashed because of a few bananas?"

Everything stopped; then a chimp named Sally crept toward Moe and deposited a banana in front of him. Moe picked it up and examined the pitiful specimen. It was half overripe. He peeled the skin until the dark mushy area showed, then broke off the firm white section. Stuffing it into his mouth, he tossed the other half back at Sally and said, "This will cost you three tomorrow." He looked long and hard at the others. "That goes for the rest of you mush brains."

Sally scooped up the remaining piece of fruit and carried it to a corner of the cage. She conferred with her companion, who rose momentarily and offered three bananas to Moe.

"You think this gets you off the hook, huh?" Moe said with a sneer, watching while the bananas appeared in the other cages. He collected nine in all, three short of his usual quota. He stuffed them in his pockets and inside his shirt before adding, "Out of the kindness of my heart I'm letting you get away with this out-and-out thievery. *This time.* Because I know you're all stupid, as stupid as baboons. But this is the last straw."

Moe made a threatening face, one he knew they would understand. "I'm going to make sure you don't take advantage of my good nature. Old Bazil will be with me next time. And in case you don't remember, Old Bazil was the one who handled the last group of apes who dared to cross me. He crushed their heads like empty peanut shells."

Moe peeled the one banana remaining in his hands and stuffed it into his mouth. Walking away, he knew the time for words of warning had long passed. If he was to continue to dominate these chimps, he needed action. Tough action from Bazil was the only way for Moe to regain respect. How could apes have respect for a male chimp who wore a dress? Only baboons would be that stupid

CHAPTER FOUR
Images

"Lay-deees and gentlemen..." Benjamin Slade crooned his introduction above the roar of the lions. As he pumped anticipation and excitement into the crowd, he kept an eye and an ear on the behavior of the huge cats.

"...world's greatest...lion tamer..." Usually Daniel Carr tamed his animals with sedatives, as he tamed his own rages with alcohol. But as Slade caught a glimpse of him now, Daniel appeared to be sober, standing outside a large cage. Daniel was sixty if he was a day, with a bad toupee and bloodshot eyes. Reams of loose skin splayed out from different angles and body parts, testament to Daniel's unending bouts with weight loss. He was losing on points in every round. The unflattering outfit he wore suffocated and tamed the folds of skin, caging them beneath the creases of the garments. Whether the appearance was a figment of the cats' behavior or one of Daniel's own imagination—the one that went with his regaining his old bravado and success—Slade was not certain. Nor was he certain about the behavior of the lions. Had the roles been somehow reversed? Had the lions taken to the booze while the sedation went to...

"...Daniel 'Wild Man' Carr..?'

Slade drifted off in a wave of applause which deposited him in the shadows of the bleachers. Supporting himself against their cold, metal frame, he watched with interest the reaction of the crowd. Apparently they hadn't picked up on the slight question in his voice; their minds had already been focused inside the cage, two steps ahead of Daniel. Something else soon became apparent: the lions needed little inducement from their tamer, besides his appearance among them, to act in a scurrilous manner. They snarled, swiped and roared with belligerence as well as gusto. Slade would have liked to see more but his concentration was broken by the appearance of Arthur Curry.

Slade ushered the younger man with the neatly trimmed beard and stylish haircut outside with a final backward glance at the lion's den as if to say: *"I know what you're feeling."* Beyond the tent, Slade looked and felt a bit ridiculous in his top hat, red coat and black jodhpurs and boots; particularly in the presence of the impeccably dressed Curry. Curry was the show's advance man, and out of necessity was all things to all men and women. He was handsome enough, young enough and slick enough to pull it off. In that capacity he was perhaps the greatest performer of all. Slade knew it, and so did Curry. He was young to those who admired the drive and enthusiasm of youth, and old to those who respected the wisdom of age. He could alternate between handsome and homely, meek and aggressive, weak and strong where the situation called for a particular trait. He read people quickly and accurately.

To Slade he said directly, "Louis assured me that everything was in order."

His tone muted Slade's opening question and made a reply or need for affirmation irrelevant. Lost for words, Slade went to a slow and silent pace.

"What is there to worry about?" Curry reassured rather than asked. "The freaks guard their privacy as if it were diamonds."

Given the opening, Slade replied, "That's what worries me." He pulled the top hat from his overheated head. "That chimp's been roaming around, more than ever it seems now." Slade stopped and gave the grounds a perfunctory examination.

"So what can a chimp do?" Curry looked amused.

"Hell, can't you people see it?" Slade displayed the opening of his top hat. "There's no magic to what we're doing, or to how we're keeping it a secret. In her own naive way, Amelia said it just moments ago." Slade was enjoying his little performance, even if it had the distinction of being for a captive audience of one. "The chimp's been snooping around in all the trailers, pilfering this and that. Everyone knows it. So suppose just one person gets it into his head to do a little stealing of his own."

Slade paused for effect and nearly lost the initiative when Curry immediately filled the gap with: "And what better place than the--"

"--freaks." Slade jumped back in quickly and continued to press his point. "Where the hell can they go and spend all their money which one figures would have accumulated into a tidy sum over the years? That's what I'd be thinking, wouldn't you?" Slade ended there and tried to bow out gracefully by ducking back into the big top, but Curry followed him to the sidewall.

"You figure our would-be thief would know what he's seen when he sees it?" Curry asked doubtfully. "What are you think-ing? Moe's going to come across one of the log books for the master plan, figure out the blueprints and blackmail the circus? What's he going to ask for? A lifetime supply of bananas? Or maybe he'll decide to open up a freak show just around the corner. Louis made him smart, I'll give you that, but he's not that smart."

"Maybe not him," Slade replied, "but someone else may be."

"His trainer? She's more tamed then he is."

"Why take the chance?"

Slade placed the top hat on his head and turned away to end the conversation and the growing pain in the middle of his stomach.

*

Curry walked through the grounds as careful as always. He had had enough of wiping elephant dung off his brand new shoes every time he had to talk with the boss or collect his thoughts. The smell was enough to choke a horse, or in this case, an elephant. One time he had even walked away before noticing he was missing one of his shoes. When he returned to the scene of the crime, he found his expensive loafer stuck in a pile of pachyderm droppings. Needless to say he changed his shoes. As he walked he brought forth a lightly perfumed handkerchief from his pocket, and though he knew it made him look a bit like a dandy, he didn't much care. He had to mask the smell somehow, and anyone who thought him something other than what he was, was, like his shoes, full of shit.

He had found his calling. He slowed down a bit with age, though he was still relatively a young man, but his mind was always racing toward the next town, the next payoff, the next performance. He was very good at his job, and he hated everything about it. He had a long ago dream of one day being a famous actor, but that dream, like most things in his life, ended before the fade in. In some ways he was still acting. He never got that breakthrough role, that moment in the spotlight, but he knew all his lines and he knew how to make others feel like they were the lead in the blockbuster.

His real name was Arthur Currytucket and he hailed from Joplin, Mo. He was an only child and he left home and began rolling his own at age thirteen. He shortened the sir name to Curry shortly before the acting bug bit him. He always thought it rather amusing that he had given himself the same moniker as the comic book character Aquaman. It hardly came up in conversation, so he left it alone. The truth be told he would have preferred Barry Allen--The Flash. He never quite lost that ambition of being an actor, but those dreams, like most of his bit parts, found themselves on the cutting room floor. He became a stuntman, but his fear of heights, getting hurt, and hard work put an end to that sideline as well. He left Hollywood in a hurry and under the guise of a scandal as his affair with a Hollywood starlet was discovered by her mobster boyfriend, and Curry thought that a broken heart would heal much faster than two busted kneecaps. He bummed around from town to town until he came upon an ad in a small town paper about a traveling circus insearch of an advance man. 'What the hell', he thought, I'll run away to join the circus and see the world. Little did he realize that the world of the circus was mostly vacant lots and one shady small town deal after another. He grew to despise his own vacant lot of a life, but stuck to the routine until he was barely trying. He ended up drinking too much, trying to forget even more. The advance man would take on the rubes and try to convince them that a circus and sideshow was just the thing to liven up their lives and the lives of the residents of their town. Bordom was like a weed that grew into dissent and mischief, and the clowns and animals would be a breath of fresh air, sort-of-speak, to the townsfolk. He had to pour on the actor's charm like a cheap dimestore aftershave, and the women, and sometimes men, filled the nights with something he lacked during the daylight hours. But even they had grown rather tiresome. He gave up the drink before he gave up the ghost, and his new found celebacy was out of ennui rather than necessity. It had all come full circle and now he was trying hard to break out of the rut that was his life. He had learned long ago to adapt to whatever circumstance presented itself to him at any given moment in time. And here among the elephant shit he found it.

Arthur Curry moved further along in quiet contemplation through the circus grounds, wondering who would play him in the story of his life. He often thought that his only equal among the unwashed of this unholy life was that odd little man with the spark of intelligence behind his eyes. Perhaps in another lifetime they could have been friends. He saw him once comforting that killer elephant. What was in that tragic man's soul to do such a thing? August Purefoy was one very big little man.

Curry hurried along, unaware of the huge pile of uncertainty that lay in his path, and that he would soon be stepping into it once again.

CHAPTER FIVE
Elephant At Stake

Bazil was chained to a metal stake. This single line of confinement seemed terribly inadequate when measured against the awesome size of the mighty gray giant. He stood more than nine feet tall and weighed in excess of four tons, but none of it was inclined to test the restraints. As Moe approached him, Bazil simply swayed from side to side, eyes closed, trunk weaving back and forth, sampling the smells in the air. It stopped at the height of its arc when Moe bopped it with a banana. Bazil rumbled inside like a large, well-oiled motor and his mouth opened as if in a yawn. Moe deftly flipped the fruit into the beckoning darkness. Bazil scooped in a bit of hay, then proceeded to chew leisurely, all without opening his eyes.

"Such a noble beast," Moe said, patting one pillar of a leg and studying the chain and the stake. "It's a shame, I tell you. A goddamn shame. Someone of your stature given only so much space."

Moe indicated the distance with outstretched hands as Bazil cracked one large almond-colored eye. Moe looked up at it and continued, "Not even the opportunity to walk around the grounds like, say, after a performance. You know, to sort of unwind. Before they chain you up for the night."

"Forget it, Moe," Bazil replied in a voice much softer and gentler than his size would suggest. "And I want you to stop threatening those poor animals with me."

"Exactly what I had in mind. Stroll with me by the chimp cages tomorrow and show them what a wonderful, lovable guy you really are, Baz. Show them they have nothing to fear." Moe patted the large leg again. "What do you say, big fella?"

"What's in it for me, besides grief?" The elephant's ears swayed in the night breeze.

"I'm talking basic freedom here and you're worried about a little grief. Hell, you walk by, set the chimps free from fear, and yourself free from all that guilt. It's about time to let it go, isn't it? Well?"

Bazil tucked more hay in his mouth and grumbled thoughtfully.

"You've paid enough for that little incident," Moe said. "And it wasn't entirely your fault in the first place. If those dummies that set things up around here were more responsible—why, they were the ones who left the chimps in their cages near the pond."

"I really don't know what came over me," Bazil blinked several times as if trying to clear his mind.

"What does it matter? No one else was locked up because of it. You didn't see any of those men locked in their trailers." Moe hoped that Bazil wouldn't nitpick about elephants having been chained in a similar manner long before the mishap.

"I did try to stop...No, I hit the wagon. And knocked it... down the hill." Bazil saw himself standing beside the pond watching the wagon sink out of sight as he trumpeted desperately, helplessly, mournfully. "They didn't understand then and they won't now. They only punish me. Maybe..." Bazil swallowed, and then whispered, "maybe they'll kill me."

"So, you're going to let a little thing like a threat stop you." Moe paced directly in front of the huge pachyderm.

"No, not forever. Just until..." Bazil let the thought drift away.

"Well?" Moe looked annoyed.

"Until I go to Memories End." The big brute let the thought drift back to him softly.

"Hell. I should have known." Moe planted his hands on his hips, stopped pacing and shook his head. "Here I thought you were preparing to go out and bash a few heads and all you want to do is go to dreamland without getting in one lick."

"Don't talk like that, Moe. You're the only one I can confide in anymore." Bazil placed a weary eye on Moe.

Moe quickly looked away. "Yeah. But what's in it for me... besides grief?"

"Freedom, Moe. Basic freedom. You can use a little of it too. The Monster/Man said so."

"The Monster/Man. How many times do I have to tell you, he was just a flunky?" Moe became agitated as he paced back and forth before the giant eye of the elephant. "A little beastie doing Slade's dirty work. He told you all those stupid things to calm you down, keep you in your place, and get you to do their bidding all over again. You did—and do—the work of twenty men around here. Slade couldn't afford to have you destroyed. Then or now. Think about it, you big jerk. Sleep on it tonight." Moe flipped another banana, then turned his back, waved, and said, "I'll see you tomorrow, after the show."

"It won't do no good, Moe." Bazil closed his eye and returned to his gentle swaying with the words of the Monster/Man softly spinning around his brain: *"A heart filled with hatred is left only to contemplate and seldom commiserate but never to tolerate a soul so full of love."*

CHAPTER SIX
Between Man And Woman

"You look terrible, my dear."

The words broke the spell and Amelia smiled at their speaker. "You haven't seen him?" She asked hopefully.

"No, sorry. But the little rascal caused quite a ruckus among the animals tonight. Come sit here."

Amelia seated herself beside the large body of Louis, or Louise as Amelia preferred. The billing at the sideshow tent read: '*See The Half-Man/Half-Woman*'. Had that billing drawn you in, what you would have got for your money, time and curiosity was Louis/Louise the hermaphrodite, who lived happily amid the confusion that overcame those who thought they knew her and what to expect. It was the unknown events and situations in life that so often left her unhappy.

"That simian gives you such a time, dear." Louise laughed before continuing, "But nothing near the time I hear old Daniel had earlier this evening with his cats, especially that old brute, Baron. Another Daniel in the lion's den come to judgment. However, I heard the old tamer was never better." Louise laughed once again. "Poor dear, I'm afraid he wasn't quite prepared for his newly acquired panache. He is going to have the world's greatest hangover when and if he wakes in the morning. But I would have liked to have seen his performance."

"Not me," Amelia said dejectedly. "I pray everything goes smoothly because if it doesn't, they always blame Moe."

"You must admit, dear Amelia, he's growing into quite a problem." Louise chuckled in her rolls of fat." He acts too human for his own good and it makes people nervous. Not to mention it gives you a bad reputation. Perhaps---for the good of your act---you should put him in his place."

"You're beginning to sound like the rest." Amelia rose to leave.

Immediately Louise patted her back into place. "I was referring to the sideshow. He could be billed as the man-ape or Moe The Apeman."

"That's awful." Amelia swallowed hard after the words passed her lips, then looked at Louise and said, "Sorry."

"Don't let it worry you, dear heart, I'm quite accustomed to it. All of us---freaks---are. Why do you think we quarter away from the rest of the performers? You thought it was in deference to their insults, right?"

Amelia nodded sheepishly. Actually, she hadn't really given it much thought at all. Once the circus landed on a spot the entire scene became a solid, blurred tapestry. Everyone set their stakes and dug in their heels until the grasses around them turned from green to brown, and everything else became the color and texture of dirt. The wagons and trailers, and the bright colors of the tents, all long ago faded into a certain kind of neutrality. Everything and everyone was separated---human and animals, everything in its place and a place for everything. She never gave much thought to the reasons behind it all, but now they washed over her clearly and unpleasantly. The circus and sideshow were even more closed off than she had wanted to believe. It did not paint a pretty picture for herself inside her mind. Saying sorry came up way too short in the end.

"Au contraire," Louise said proudly. "We really don't blame them for resenting us. It's their ignorance---born out of self-righteousness—that we can't tolerate. They're quick to acknowledge that their talents and ours—such as they are—come from the same place: a creator, if you will. But their resentment comes from the fact that they must work hard to keep their talent perfected. Their ignorance comes from their belief that it isn't very difficult to be what we are. In truth, we work at it twenty-four hours a day, and it never seems quite enough—for anyone.

"Now, if anyone has the right to be resentful, it's us. We should resent God for being so lackadaisical about his creations. He—or she, if you prefer...I myself think God is both and neither. Anyway, where was I? Oh, yes, God should have paid a bit more attention to what he was baking. Just because you throw all the right ingredients in a pan that doesn't mean the cake will come out perfect. You have to spend some time mixing and what-not.. you do bake, don't you, Amelia?"

"No," Amelia said with a shake of her head.

"I don't believe I can either. Oh well, so much for that analogy. What I do believe, however, is that half the battle is accepting one's lot in life and learning to live within it. Even if it means simply choosing to live apart as we do. You, and that remarkable chimp of yours, would do well to adopt a similar arrangement."

Louise put on a friendly smile and patted Amelia's hand. "My dear, this whole mess is just another version of the question, can God make a rock that even he can't pick up? I mean, there are some things over which we simply don't have any power."

Some of those things, Amelia knew quite well, were her parents and her upbringing. Her mother and father had been a high wire act. Life was all big time, big top, until her father had a stroke. He retained only slight paralysis, but enough to suspend the act for an indeterminable amount of time. It might as well have been forever since her mother was at the top of her form and not about to waste days or months, let alone years. In the interim, she joined a rather prestigious European circus. Amelia's father understood, but he could not bear to stand by and watch. So, with Amelia in tow, he rolled into Slade's winter quarters with the hope of regaining his old form and re-establishing the act, this time with his growing daughter. But Amelia only grew fat. Too late, she grew determined to change things after the fact.

"Like my glandular troubles," Amelia finally said. "I used to take this medicine; I actually believed it was some kind of miracle cure. Every night I'd go to bed telling myself that everything would be all right in the morning. Then when morning after morning passed, I began to realize I was just kidding myself."

Amelia, with tears in her eyes, paused to stare across the road. There she was faced by rows and rows of aluminum-sided houses, mostly white and mostly the same at every stop along the way. Sometimes she would watch the people coming and going. They'd run their power mowers, plant flowers, chat over fences. Kids would laugh and scream in play. All those acts, being played out on rectangular carpets of green grass, had direction and meaning to someone. Didn't they?

Amelia shrugged to herself and said: "There may be a miracle for me out there but it doesn't matter anymore. Not since I killed my father."

"Your father died of a cerebral hemorrhage, and don't you forget it." Louise's voice was filled with agitation. "And don't look at me that way." She cleared her throat and bought her composure time to resettle. With a big smile she added, "You're not in the company of some ignorant freak."

"I didn't mean to say I literally caused his death, it's just that I feel I had let him down, just like mother, and he gave up after that. He didn't seem to want to go on anymore. With the act, with me, or with living." Amelia had tears in her eyes.

"It's everyone choice to live or die. You did not provide the rhyme or reason. Don't always play the victim, my dear, sooner or later you will tire of it all as well." Louise stood and waved Amelia to do the same. "Come with me...come on."

They had been friendly for several years now, but this was the first time Amelia had been invited to enter the sanctum sanctorum. It wasn't so strange because that was the way it was with most folks in the small circus; space was rare, so they valued what very little they could call their own.

Louise's trailer looked like a public library. Books were scattered everywhere, including some rather unorthodox places: cupboards, the sink, the stove top. Large stacks of them reformed the shape of the rooms, running from floor to ceiling, sometimes precariously.

Louise cleared a space for Amelia to sit on a stool and said, "Once I entertained the thought of becoming a doctor." She chuckled while she put some water on for tea. This simple operation called for further rearrangement of books, some of which found their way into an already over stacked oven. Louise wasn't lying about her inability to bake, unless she had intentions of creating a new dessert from several bound volumes of Shakespeare and Nietzsche.

"Entertained is a good word for it," she said while her back was to Amelia. "I also entertained thoughts of becoming a lawyer. An astrophysicist. Perhaps a professor of English literature...oh, dozens more. "She flicked all thoughts away with her hand, as well as a loose strand of platinum-blond hair.

"I can't picture you as..."

"As anything more than what I am? It's quite alright, my dear. I am perfectly aware of the way people envision me. In fact, I encourage it most of all. Now, that's our little secret." The teapot whistled her to a stop. She rattled around the kitchen for a while, then said, "I'll tell you another little secret. I *am* a doctor, of sorts."

For just a fleeting moment something odd appeared at the corner of Amelia's eye in the shadowy corner of the room. At first she thought it to be some sort of deformed butterfly, but before she could form a more complete picture, it was gone and so, too, was the thought from her mind.

She wore a broad smile as she carried a tray of cups and saucers into the room. "I'll bore you with that story some other time. For now, just remember that if people get what they want from you, they'll generally leave you alone after that. Particularly if you let it be known that that is all you have to offer." While she poured the tea, she added, "Oh, I've had to sacrifice a number of things—all those occupations to say the least. Then there were some valued friendships..."

She handed a cup to Amelia and settled in with the other one in a heavy wooden rocker. "But they never touched what's really up here." Louise pointed to her head. "Never surrender that, Amelia dear. I perform brilliant operations in my head, and defend the falsely accused, visit the furthest star..." Louise suddenly grew silent, rocking gently and sipping delicately, and watching Amelia over the steaming rim of the cup. It all made Amelia feel uncomfortable. It was nice to have someone to confide in, although who was confiding in whom and why it should be now, after all the time that had passed since her father's death, she was at a loss to say. Nor would she ask, for she remembered those days when she quieted her sobs of grief in Louise's large bosom. And she remembered the little chimp that passed from Louise's large but delicate hands into hers. Maybe this receptiveness was the price she had to pay for past kindnesses and small price it was, because Moe was worth any sacrifice of her past.

"Psychology is a new field to me," Louise said between rocking and refreshment, "but I don't believe it is too healthy to remain fixated on the misfortunes in our lives. If we can't work them out to our advantage, then we must lock them away. Do you understand what I'm trying to say, dear?"

Amelia nodded slightly and placed her half-empty cup atop a small stack of Edgar Rice Burroughs hardbounds. She was ready to leave but Louise had intercepted the signal. Moving straight from the rocker, Louise halted the departure by clasping Amelia's arm gently and saying sweetly, "We don't fail others, Amelia dear, we only fail ourselves—often by allowing them to drag us down. And that goes for apes as well." Louise's hand worked up and down along Amelia's arm. "Put him in his proper place. Let go of everything that's holding you back."

Amelia could feel her entire body stiffening. The sensation had started in her head and was working its way down to her feet. All she knew was that she wanted to move before it reached there, but she couldn't; she was too confused to know forward and back.

"Let...go," she heard herself saying nervously, "...perhaps I should," and she found that she had backed herself into the door. "I could blow up to four hundred pounds and become the jolly fat lady."

"Why not?" Louise said with a Cheshire grin, "If it makes you happy."

Amelia was out the door, missing a few steps on the way down and out of the trailer.

CHAPTER SEVEN
Saving Face

Moe was waiting in her trailer when Amelia returned from Louise's.

"Where have you been?" she scolded as she entered her small but cozy trailer. She sounded more relieved than angry, even if some of the relief was registered for her own safety. The conversation with Louise hit too close to home. She wasn't used to opening up old wounds. Even if some of them were more likely self-inflicted.

Moe made a show of scratching beneath his cap and looking quizzical, then leaned back in the soft, high back chair and crossed his legs as if to dismiss the matter as too trivial for further consideration.

"You can't keep this up, Moe," Amelia said, lifting his cap and stroking his hairy head. "I don't know how much longer I can go around patching things up." She hugged herself as if she had just received a chill. "No one really believes me anymore, anyway. And not knowing where you are half of the time makes it hard for me sometimes. To believe. In anything." She looked at him but his expression hadn't changed. "You don't understand a word I'm saying."

She replaced his cap and noticed for the first time the pile of banana peels on the small end table near Moe. "But maybe you'll understand a little punishment. Nothing too severe or drastic as locking you up—" She gathered the peels. "—Just no more bananas if you don't learn to behave and follow the rules. How would you like that?"

Moe understood every word perfectly. He just didn't care. It wouldn't matter if the plot he was hatching came to fruition. So far he had invested eight bananas in the hope of getting back many more. Two had gone to Bazil for naught, but a while later Moe gave six to the youngest elephant, an imp named Pinky. All of those were from the nine he had collected from the other chimps. He didn't like stealing from Amelia, but it was necessary—for his plot—to have a dozen or more at his disposal. And he couldn't resist disposing of a few himself.

"...you wouldn't like that at all, would you?" Amelia was saying from the tiny kitchen, hers free of books and clutter. "But everyone else around here would. They'd just love to see me lose my trust in you and you in me. Oh, I know their game...I see it now."

She came back to the room and faced Moe. "You better stay inside today. Until it's time for us to go on..." She went over to her sewing machine and sat down with her back to Moe. "I remember Ben Slade played up to me when I was training with Papa. And, later, when I got you and we started the act. He had no real interest in me; he was just playing it safe. First, figuring I might be as good as my mother. Then, that you might be something special... well, at least you didn't disappoint—"

Moe slipped a large wooden box from beneath his chair, quietly opened it, and began to poke around among the contents and keepsakes, selectively setting aside certain items.

"---always telling me how I'm going to hit the big time. Work hard, Amelia. Work your way to the Big Top. And all the time I was working for nobody but him. It would serve him right if I did turn out like my mother after all---and ran out.

"I couldn't do it alone though. But together...Benjamin Slade may own those other chimps, but you are mine, Moe. We'd have to show everyone first. How disciplined we are. So if he tries to give us a bad name or reputation, it won't work. No one will believe him."

Amelia concentrated on her sewing for a moment, making sure her seams were straight before continuing, "I'll contribute these nice new costumes and you'll be on your best behavior. You'll give 'em what they want." Her eyes adopted a faraway look. "You'll knock 'em dead. You'll get up on that wire, looking frail and feminine, and vulnerable. You'll make them see what they expect to see---a death-defying act. The little lady risking life and limb. Maybe we could add some more visible danger? Like fire. I remember when my mother used to..." She turned away from her work and thoughts to glance over at her, hopefully, captive audience. What she saw caused her mouth to drop open and remain that way for several speechless seconds.

When she regained her composure, she said, "Alex will kill you for that."

Alex Hornbill was the clown known as Zippo. He, like most of his kind, put his makeup on upside down so that when he smiled it would appear to the audience as a frown. It was done mostly for sympathy, and Alex used a combination of whites, reds and blacks for his desired effect. Moe had duplicated the sad-face frown of that particular clown to perfection by mixing the right amounts of white and red grease paint with his already black fur. If clowns had one prize possession it was their faces. Some went as far as trademarking the look. Moe stared across at Amelia from beneath the purloined makeup and face.

Amelia stared silently while her own face turned slowly to a grin. "I can always count on you, can't I, Moe?" She produced the new pale blue costume on which she had been diligently working all evening and held it up to him. "And this should put a smile back on your face."

The hairy clown just stared.

CHAPTER EIGHT
Bananas

Moe performed beautifully. He took his bows with Amelia and the others and waited patiently while she caged the rest of them afterward. He even wore the pale blue dress she made for him back to Amelia's trailer where he changed and seemed to settle in for the night. Of course, it was all part of a greater act.

The night threatened to storm. No rain had fallen yet but the wind was increasing steadily and gearing up for the best performance of the night.

"It's a John Robinson type of night," Amelia said standing in the doorway and watching the dust swirls. "Get the crowd in, give 'em a quick show, and get 'em out. Without a single refund."

Moe tugged at his ear and yawned.

"I'm going to the cook tent for bananas," Amelia said as she pulled a sweater around her shoulders, "Moe, do try to stay awake."

*

"I only have a minute," Slade said as he shielded his eyes from the biting winds.

"You mean you're actually allowing the acts to run that long," Louis answered above the roar of the wind, and pushing aside the tent flap.

Ignoring the comment and invitation, Slade added, "I don't know what you told that girl but that chimp was really in line tonight."

"I told her everything."

Slade snorted. "If it were only that easy."

"You're getting soft, Benjamin. Soon this whole business is going to mash you. Then all you'll be good for is our little sideshow here."

"Might as well, you're running the show anyway." Slade peeked at the crowd. "Nothing keeps them away." He shook his head. "They must crawl out of the woodwork."

"Curiosity is as difficult to keep in line as that chimp," Louis said knowingly. "But they're both important to us, aren't they?"

Slade continued to stare at Louis who, noticing, added, "These are grotesque times. Not that they're really any different from other times, but we happen to be living in these times. To those who have the opportunity to see others who are worse off than themselves, to see how far they have come in these trying times, all the better. Even if they know the difference is only trickery."

"But we know better," Slade said without glancing at the half-man, half-woman oddity before him.

"But it's enough for them, it always has been and always will be...as long as they're treated to an *authentic*-looking trick. The electronic media has made that much mandatory."

"So you're saying as long as they think we're good makeup artists, we'll be okay?"

"A plastic banana's as good as a real one until you try to peel it."

Slade shrugged but was not amused, while Louis looked to the darkening skies.

The wind howled through the Big Top.

*

As soon as Amelia closed the door, Moe was up. He went quickly to a large trunk in her bedroom and pulled out a bunch of bananas, then slipped out through a window in the trailer.

Bazil and the other elephants--Pinky and Bernice---were set to perform. All that remained was for them to be unchained and led, trunk in tail, across the grounds and into the ring where they would go through their usual routine: they would all do a headstand; while one adult stood upright the other would rise on its hind legs and plant the front ones on the other performing pachyderm's backside; young Pinky would do a few circles before following suit; a young girl would then lie upon the ground and Bazil's foot would hover threateningly over her head; Bernice would balance herself on a tiny platform by standing on all four legs, then lift them one at a time; etc.

Before any of that happened, Moe strolled up to them. He paused in front of Bazil, who was intently drawing a crude map of intersecting lines in the dirt with his trunk. Sensing Moe, he looked up and said, "The road to Memories End."

"Shit," Moe grumbled and moved over to Pinky. He fed the small one two bananas and then drifted away.

His actions produced the desired squeals from the runt. They grew steadily louder but where swallowed by the howling wind. Moe was likewise swallowed by the shadows, and none too soon. The handlers showed up a moment later.

*

On their way to the Big Top Louis commented on the sudden slackening of the wind. "The calm before the storm."

Slade examined the sky and made an observation of his own. "I must have been crazy to let you talk me into this."

"I'm not noted as a person of few words but as I recall only three suffice in your case: money, fame, revenge. And not necessarily in that order."

"We're alike in that respect."

"And in the way we treated poor Amelia."

"She just read too much into my attention," Slade said. "It was all business."

"And I suppose you show equal interest in all the losers that find their way here." Louis gave a slight wink.

Laughter rippled from out of the Big Top and Slade patted his top hat in place. "She came from better stock and you know it."

Slade held the sidewall apart, but Louis made no attempt to enter. "Like I said, it was all business. Sometimes a show can rise with the popularity of one really good attraction."

Louis interjected. "And what happens to my poor souls?"

"Souls? That's a strange word coming from you." Slade took his cue and entered the tent.

*

The elephants were being paraded toward the tent, Bazil in the lead, Bernice at his tail, and Pinky conveniently bringing up the rear with the taste of bananas still in his mouth and on his mind.

As they turned a corner and began their entrance through the back door, Moe rushed to Pinky's side and shoved a banana at him. Pinky wheeled quickly to grab it, breaking his hold on Bernice's tail. She disappeared into the tent and Moe moved in haste in the opposite direction, baiting the young elephant toward the chimp area. Pinky, with ears flapping and trunk stretched out before him, came squealing at Moe's heels.

Moe managed to reach the chimps just a few strides ahead of the elephant and tossed some loose bananas into the first cage. He had time for nothing more than a hair's-breadth escape because Pinky arrived in a frenzy, hitting the cage head on, toppling it, and nearly crushing Moe in the process.

All six chimps began to shriek in wild unison while Pinky shook at the metal bars and sniffed around the cages like a vacuum cleaner. For his efforts he got one squashed banana and a cut on his trunk.

The injury was nothing serious, but the sting of it brought him to his senses. He stepped back and swirled his trunk from side to side, taking in the scent of fear and panic. His trunk snaked upward like a cobra, his ears began to flap, and he turned and ran toward the Big Top.

It was about this time that his absence there was discovered by the handlers, by Slade, and by Bazil and Bernice. Everyone seemed confused and the show was brought to a sudden halt. Even the clowns, who were still parading around the bleachers, stopped to catch the inaction in the center ring. The world paused for a moment, then Pinky burst on the scene. His only intention was to get back to Bernice and the familiar routine, but his way was now blocked by the clowns and their props.

The former scattered and the later were shattered, much to the delight of the audience. The clowns failed to see the humor in it. Gaining composure and courage, they started yelling at Pinky, but their antics served no purpose except to draw more laughter from the crowd and stir up some maternal instinct in Bernice.

The female elephant began to put on a show of her own. First she twiddled her trunk and flared her ears while pawing at the ground with one massive foot, then all these movements dissolved into one ever increasing tic of her body. As the crowd and the clowns grew more hectic, her motion took on speed, until she could stand no more.

Trumpeting loudly, she bounded forward, and the entire place became instantly aware that there was nothing funny about six feet and three thousand pounds of anxious elephant. En masse, people poured from the bleachers and rushed toward the exits, trampling as they went. The old canvas began to burst at the seams, spouting pandemonium from its sidewalls. Individual expressions of enjoyment transformed into one solid roar of panic.

CHAPTER NINE

Of Apes And Apemen

Miraculously, no one was seriously injured in the stampede. The only real casualty was Moe. At least that was how he saw it. He began his death act the moment a new order descended on the circus.

"He was seen slinking away just before the elephants were set to perform," Slade said, twirling his top hat with knotted fingers that worked feverishly to abate his anger.

"It's a lie as usual," Amelia answered. "I happen to know that Moe was in my trailer when--"

"When you were with the cook. Don't lie to me, Amelia. You were seen too." Slade spat his words at her.

"You're so determined to get him that you've taken to spying on me. Go ahead then, put him in a cage. What does it matter? We're obviously on constant display as it is." Amelia tried hard to hold back her tears.

Moe went without much of a struggle. He even gave up his clothes without as much as a show of teeth. He was not the only one to submit that night. Because of the elephants' antics, the entire circus was forced out of town.

"It'll cost us three weeks' box office," an even angrier Benjamin Slade said, "but at this point I think it's best to get out ahead of the publicity. I put away one snoop; we certainly don't need any more around."

"But to get there," a disgruntled Curry said, "we have to go deep into God's country. You know what happened last time we played in that area."

The last statement was meant for Louis, who remembered the area quite well. It was wide-open farmland, tucked between rolling hills covered with dense forest. There were a smattering of small towns joined by a state highway, numerous winding back roads, and Providence. Unfortunately, this divine direction saw fit to lead its people away from Louis and his fellow freaks. Because of their damnation, Louis and the freaks were forced to spend a non-performing eternity there while the rest of the show went on, doing four weekends at the height of a summer much like the current one. Louis suspected that not a great deal had changed, except for the rain, or lack of it, this time around. It never materialized that night; in fact, it hadn't rained in the area for quite some time, much to the consternation of the local farmers.

"Ben might be right," Louis said.

"Thank you," Slade replied.

"No, seriously. There may be a need for distractions up there. I know something of droughts... They're bad for temperaments as well as crops. So a circus---freaks and all---may seem a godsend."

"Then it's settled." Slade turned to Curry. "Get us at least one booking and we'll go from there." Slade left the two of them alone.

"This must be a first," Louis added to the still immobile advance man. "Hurry Curry dragging his feet."

"I'm hardly looking forward to dealing with people who see only good and evil, and nothing in-between." Curry did not like how the conversation was going—not in his favor.

"I should think that would make your job easier. Simply sell them the circus the way they've been sold heaven: something to keep their minds off the fact that this miserable life is all they have, and there's no guarantee that it will ever get any better." Louis said. "We all have a tendency to rise to the level of our own incompetence."

"Too bad that creepy little friend of yours, the Monster/ Man, isn't still around anymore," Curry spat, making a face and turning to leave. "He'd be perfect for the job."

Louis angrily watched the smug young man retreat while Slade celebrated the move by directing the collapse of the Big Top.

Meanwhile, Moe made little progress out of his depression. He barely stirred as the circus folded around him, nor did he eat during the sojourn, which took a day longer than anticipated because of some engine trouble with one of the long haulers.

The engine trouble brought a worried look to Slade's face, but in his present state it hardly affected Moe. He was playing the same tune, barely aware of his surroundings, when they finally arrived at their destination. He remained alone, scrunched up into a corner of the cage while the circus took shape around him.

Bazil, working as if possessed, was responsible for most of that. He unloaded the trucks; lugged the materials to their proper places; and, once the canvas was unrolled, helped to raise it, much to the delight of some of the local youngsters. They hung around while the guy ropes were stretched from the tent poles and secured to stakes in the ground, and moved off only when the activity there became more mundane. From there, they found their way to the menagerie wagons and Moe.

"Look at that monkey." One red-headed boy of ten rapped on the bars of Moe's cage but Moe gave no sign that he was seeing or hearing the youngsters. "Let's see if we can get him to fling some shit."

"I think that's Cheetah. Oo Oo Oo." Another boy of twelve, with a buzz cut and freckles, jumped up and down, his lips in full pout and each hand scratching his armpits.

"Yeah, good old Cheetah. Ah Ah Ah Ah Ah." The third boy, the youngest of the group, and with torn jeans and an unruly mass of dirty-blond hair, pounded his chest with his fists. Moe did not stir.

"Oo Oo Oo Oo Oo Oo Oo Oo Oo."
"Oo Oo Oo Oo Oo Oo Oo Oo Oo."
"Oo Oo Oo Oo Oo Oo Oo Oo Oo."

*

Amelia had a plan. She wouldn't use Moe in the act. He couldn't perform well while caged. It took something out of him, and out of the act, and, therefore, out of the circus, and Slade's pocket. But she had no idea how long it would take for her plan to show effects. Would Moe give in first? Would she?

She couldn't bear to see him this way, which was the reason she only came by at feeding time. "You have to eat, Moe," she said for the umpteenth time. She continued to try to entice him with all sorts of goodies. "You can't just give up and let them win. You need to eat, you need your strength. We both do. Don't you see? They want us to give in. Don't you...

"Of course you don't see." She stepped back and kept receding with backward steps. "All you see is them. And I'm one of 'em."

*

From the first sign of darkness, Bazil went into renewed action. First, he pulled up stakes, literally. The elephants were chained front and back now, one foot on either side. The double security measure was not particularly a double inconvenience for Bazil. He simply wiggled the front stake free with his trunk, then yanked it out of the ground by moving backward while stepping side-long into the rear stake, which he then freed with one sudden jerk of the tethered leg. Finally, he smoothed the motion into a slow lumbering walk to ease the *clang* of the chains as they were dragged behind him.

The big beast sidled up to Moe's cage and said, "Did you see it, Moe? All that glorious space...and the trees. Lush, glorious green. Miles and miles of it...It's just like the Monster/Man said it would be."

Moe uncurled slightly and grumbled, "Go away, you big oaf. Leave me to die like your stupid Monster/Man."

"But he's not dead--he's at Memories End. And that's where I'm going. Didn't you see it when we passed by on the way here?"

"I didn't see a damn thing." Fully in the act, Moe kept his mind closed tight.

"Then come with me." Bazil swayed back and forth in front of him.

"Sure. Only one problem." Moe slapped the nearest bar of the cage.

Bazil nodded knowingly, then wrapped his trunk around three of the bars and squeezed the outer two tight against the middle one. Moe stared in disbelief at the opening, and said, "You think it's that easy, huh?"

Bazil remained silent.

"Okay...okay, I'm going. But only because you've given me no choice." Moe slipped his head through the gap in the cage. "The only way..." then a shoulder, "you're going to get this..." his still rounded stomach came next, "Memories End nonsense...out of your mind," followed by the rest of him as he hung on the small ledge outside the bars, "is for me to prove to you that there's no such place."

Bazil stepped aside and Moe bounded to the ground. Without another word he shot straight to Amelia's trailer, entering through an open window. He took his usual outfit, a pair of jeans and his favorite Grateful Dead concert tee-shirt, along with his high-top sneakers. Moe dressed outside, pulling the Bears cap tightly over his ears and nodding to Bazil, "There, that's much better. The real me. Now I can face the world."

Before Bazil could say a word, Moe was off again. He slipped into a few more trailers. When he returned, he was carrying two sacks stuffed to the limits.

"What's all this?" Bazil asked.

"These are other reasons why I'm going along." Moe set the sacks on the ground. "You think food grows on trees out there?"

Moe took a set of keys from his pocket and went to work on the padlocked bands around Bazil's legs.

The chains were set aside and the food sacks were placed on Bazil's back. Moe scrambled up the elephant's left leg and settled in behind the ears. Moe balanced the stuffed sacks there and rode off like Tarzan.

CHAPTER TEN

Wise Guys And Otherwise Guys

They skirted the nearby towns. The circuitous route led to a railroad track which just happened to be heading in their direction, making the going easy. Bazil immediately took this as a good sign even though the footing was sometimes treacherous. Moe grumbled continually. The food sacks seemed more of a burden then a necessity. They shifted from side to side, threatening to fall to the ground with each faulty step.

He wasn't much more content when the sun and a morning freight train caught up with them, forcing them to slip off into the cover of the woods. After breaking through a narrow thicket, they came upon a small clearing where Moe and the sacks slipped to the ground.

Moe found himself a spot against a smooth tree, propped his feet up on one of the sacks, and began to fill his belly with the contents of the other. As he ate, he studied a large, plump rat that rooted among some old, rusted tin cans. That type of rodent always fascinated him. They had always given him the impression of being as much a part of the circus as the lions, elephants, or chimps for that matter. Here was one looking ever so at home in this wilderness.

Moe tossed a near-empty jar of strawberry preserves to the rat and said to Bazil, "Well, here we are—Memories End. Eat the leaves off the trees and drink the cool, clean water from the streams and wash your mind clean of all your trials and tribulations. Only the leaves are black and there isn't any water, not even a mud hole, so how are we supposed to forget about the last few days? Or even that stupid ride, wrestling these?" He kicked at the sacks of food.

Bazil, sitting dog-like in the shade and waving his ears to catch any available breeze, reached above his head with his trunk and plucked some leaves from the overhanging branch of a sycamore. After a brief sampling, he finally spoke, "You're right about the leaves, probably because of the trains, kicking up the dirt as they roar on by to their destinations. I can't fix that, except to remind you that there are no trains at Memories End." Next, he grabbed a sack with his trunk and spilled out the remaining contents on the ground. "But I can do something about all this."

Bazil began to flip the edibles into his large, open mouth. Moe watched for a moment, then asked, "Now that we had our little picnic, what's next?"

"I'm pushing on," Bazil said, chewing deliberately. "But if you've had enough, you can go back. Maybe you're ready now to jump at their commands, do unrewarding work just to have a place to sleep and eat. Get sprayed with a hose or occasionally rubbed down with oil. You can go back and be me, Moe; the old Bazil."

To his mind, the choice wasn't as clear cut, but when Bazil leaned over, Moe did a fork jump to the elephant's back. It was simply an easier ride going on with Bazil for now. As they left the clearing, Moe looked back at the rat standing among the mess they left behind. "Maybe we should have asked him for directions."

*

Finding Moe gone left Amelia with mixed feelings. First there was shock, then a touch of relief. At least he was fighting back. For a time she was more happy than sad because she expected him to show up in her trailer at any moment, and she never once considered the possibility that Benjamin Slade would not be far behind.

As it turned out, neither one made an appearance. Amelia finally opened her door to Alex, who still had traces of white grease paint in the edges of his sideburns. She seemed a bit disappointed, and let her face show it.

"It's all over camp," Alex said, his expression somewhere between a grin and a grimace. "How did they manage it?"

It was hard for Amelia to get used to him without his make-up on. "So what are you doing here?"

"Seeing that it goes no further," the clown replied.

"For Mister Slade's sake, or mine? Does everyone think I had something to do with it?"

"For the sake of the show. You know what rumors can do, Amelia."

"Very well," she said smugly. "But why did Slade send you?"

"He thought you would take it better coming from me. You know—not doing anything just to spite him. We all want to know if you had anything to do with it—you know, the show must go on and all that. Besides, I'm one of the only ones who hasn't had anything stolen by that...well, you know..."

"If the clown only knew," Ameila thought to herself.

"I suppose Mr. Slade believes that Moe stole that elephant? That Bazil?"

"For what it's worth, Amelia, I never believed that that monkey of yours stole anything. Actually, I don't see how anyone can accuse him of some of the outrageous thefts and still keep a straight face." Alex broke into a frown, and Amelia could see the clown beneath the man. "And just because he's temporarily among the missing, there's no reason to keep such a long face."

Amelia's expression never changed and Alex added, "If you persist, I shall have to accuse you of stealing my trademark."

Amelia showed the clown the door. On his way down the steps of the trailer he thought he heard her say, through the closing door, "Moe *was* the show."

CHAPTER ELEVEN
Greener Pastures

Down time was something that Louise was never really comfortable with. Too many bad memories haunted her daydreams. She knew from the start that she was not prone to a multiple personality disorder, but she could certainly use both sides of her being intersex to some advantage. She was well aware at a young age that being both male and female could work in her favor. She would just have to learn when and how to use these traits. The first memories that flooded her were those from childhood. From birth both her parents turned away from, her. She was shunned from the moment she took her first breath. They could not understand nor love the "freak" they had borne. The only human touches she could recall were from the back of her father's hand striking her face repeatedly. Icy stares of condemnation were her mother's contribution to her upbringing. Coldness and indifference turned to ridicule and loathing on both sides.

Louise took her first chance to move out.

When she told Amelia that she only dreamed of becoming a doctor, she wasn't being entirely truthful. As a matter of fact, she studied for almost three years, and medical school was a balm of salvation in a turbulent existence. If becoming a doctor was the dream, then medical research was her passion. She often told herself that even Victor Frankenstein was a medical man long before the trappings of sanity began to slip from his grasp and the *madness invaded* his mind, sending him off on the unholy quest to become a deity.

Louise was surprised when her parents let her Uncle Philip finance what they referred to as 'her folly', when he agreed to fund her dream and her passion. She often told fellow researchers that she and her mother and father came to a mutual understanding, and she was paid to stay away. She was more than happy to comply and never return home again

Louise didn't have a name for the type of research that took hold and became the obsession. The closest she could come was "radical genetics." She looked inward on herself, and figured if she was female and male, in one body, there must be a way to cross other species: mix and match and see what came into being, or perhaps even see what was the dominate of the two. She wasn't sure she really wanted to rid herself of her male appendages or persona. She had given it a name—that would work well much later in the sideshow when Louis could emerge more fully to deal with the more male dominated side of the circus. Their neanderthal brains would find it hard to accept a female as an equal. She could learn to play both sides against the middle and come out on top, to use the manipulation to her/his advantage.--but others might not be so accommodating to their other halves.

She started small, with a frog and a sparrow, to see if one could mix and match and see what became of either one. She tried to grow feathers or sprout wings on an amphibian or turn a sky dweller into an aquatic one. She failed and failed and failed.

She felt like a scientific chef, mixing a little DNA here with a dash of gene splicing there, and then for her own amusement adding a pinch of salt to taste. A year or more into the research, all she could claim as a success was the stunting of the growth of a handful of salamanders. The breakthrough finally came with the first of the abominations.

It was about three years into her experimenting that she decided to run away and join the circus. Someday soon, Louise vowed to herself, she would tell the story of her life to someone she hoped would listen.

The beehive of activity throughout the circus and sideshow grounds brought Louise out of her ruminations. All everyone was talking about were the two escapees and their daring attempt at a dash for freedom. The escape from the circus of the chimp and elephant brought her much more amusement then it brought to the others. She started to picture the two creatures upon the road and what havoc their sightings might unleash upon an unsuspecting populace. The panic that would erupt upon the sight of the two unwelcomed travelers in their midst made her smile as she played scenarios out in her mind. George and Lenny on the road in one of her favorite books: 'Of Mice And Men.'.

Would they believe their own eyes when seeing what they thought they saw on the road?

The stretch of interstate was boring, just four lanes of black top slicing through rows and rows and rows of trees. The forest ceased to be a source of wonder many miles and hours ago. Sharon Ungurian had tried to interest her children in a game of naming the different animals that might be roaming those very woodlands, but like all the other games designed to keep young children occupied during long car trips, this one failed miserably. Soon the inevitable squabbles returned. With her husband Hank white-knuckled behind the wheel, she sighed at the prospect of the long, winding road ahead.

The children carried on in spite of the first real break in the scenery for some time. The woodlands suddenly gave way to sporadic farmlands, large open fields of crops drying and dying in the noon sun, and tiny white houses and red barns seen in the distance. Mrs. Ungurian managed to interest the three children in a few choruses of *Old MacDonald* but somewhere between the *oink-oinks* and the *moo-moos* the children's minds wandered off again, and they were not about to return to the old man's farm. It was turning into a regular battle of nerves between her composure and her husband's steadily increasing boil. His last outburst was several miles back and she knew he was due for another, but she had to agree with the kids---dying cornstalks were just as boring as living trees.

Then, amidst a new session of pushing, bickering, humming, yelling, pinching, and droning, six-year-old Cameron Patrick Ungurian exclaimed in an urgent shout: "An elephant! Look, it's an elephant!"

"Where? Where?" his twin ten-year-old sisters, Enid and Erin, shouted in unison.

"In the field...oh, you missed it," Cameron Patrick exclaimed.

"No I didn't," Enid said.

"Yes you did," Erin said with her tongue out to emphasize her statement.

"Did not."

"Did too. If I didn't see it, you didn't see it."

"Did not. 'Cause it wasn't even there. Cameron Patrick's a liar."

"Was too." Cameron Patrick was emphatic in his response.

"Was not," the twins shouted in perfect unison once again.

"Was too. Daddy just drove too fast past it." Cameron Patrick began to show signs of tears and frustration.

"Can we go back, mommy?" Enid asked.

"I want to see the elephant," Erin remarked.

"There was no elephant, sweetheart." Sharon Ungurian pulled Erin into the front seat, past the sidelong glare of her husband. "Cameron Patrick was only making it up."

"See." Erin stuck out her tongue once more. This was her answer to everything.

"Was not," Billy whispered, looking back longingly at the rows and rows and rows of corn.

Enid joined her twin sister in the showing of tongues, aimed spitefully at their younger sibling.

It was the sound of her own laughter that brought Louise back to the sideshow from her daydream miles away. Scenes like that made her glad she decided against a family and a normal life. What could be normal for her anyway?

She did hold onto some contacts from her research days, those who found the love of money was not so evil after all, and were not inclined to ask too many questions about the ongoing and questionable research of a dropout. She could always count on them to send her whatever equipment or samples she requested. The makeshift lab in the shed among the tents and trailers of the sideshow provided the convenience and the cover she desired, affording her the privacy for her experimentations.

However, the urge was growing within her to let those secrets out and let the cards fall as they may. What good was it to try to change the world when no one knew it was you? A man named Tesla could testify to that. She knew who she would like to tell, but how to tell her was an entirely different matter. She remembered the last person she tried to confide in about the ongoing research and experiments. August Purefoy shut her down before she even started, and a week or so later he up and disappeared into the night.

That's why the ruckus surrounding the circus was a much needed distraction for now. Louise believed that the search for the two animals would either bring them all closer together or tear them further apart. Either way, she would be there to pick up the pieces and experiment on the remains.

*

Bazil stuck his tongue out as he placed another cornstalk in his mouth. He plucked them very deliberately, choosing the greenest, shaking each lightly, and inspecting the results with a very wary eye.

Meanwhile, Moe was peeling a few ears of corn and testing the kernels. "These things are as hard as rocks."

"But as a whole," Bazil said, "this is not too terrible." His munching drowned out the drone of bees nearby.

"Oh, I can see you're enjoying this." Moe threw the ear of corn aside and the bees buzzed dangerously close. He swatted, and they zigged and zagged on their way.

Bazil's foraging stripped a large section of the field, forcing Moe to stay in the elephant's shadow to keep out of the blinding sun. It was tricky business at best, keeping from being trampled underfoot.

"Having to eat an enormous amount of food each day," Bazil said, "it's a great idea not to be too fussy."

"Sure, fifty pounds of this. A hundred pounds of that." Moe spit out the corn he was trying to chew before it chipped a tooth.

Bazil drifted to the edge of the field. "This is a lot like the Monster/Man's description of Africa: A sea of sweet green waving grass, where a thousand elephants and other animals come to graze."

"All that eating make you colorblind, too?" Moe asked as he ducked out of the way of a large, hind foot.

Bazil studied the sky with a worried look. "The sun beats down the same way but there's always a lush forest or a cool lake nearby. An elephant could lounge in the shade, or roll in the mud. Heavenly...Memories End is a lot like that. The next best thing. As close as either of us will ever come to rediscovering our birthplace."

"What the hell are you talking about?' Moe said while keeping pace. "Africa? I was born in a field outside of Allentown, Pennsylvania. And you were--"

Bazil had moved off to greener pastures.

CHAPTER TWELVE
All's Well That Ends Well

Amelia read the local newspapers and listened to the radio for any word. How long could an elephant on the loose remain a secret? Something that big, that obviously out-of-place, could not stay hidden for long.

Moe was a different story---she knew he could disappear for good. Forever. And she couldn't really blame him. But, even on the chance he was not with Bazil, the sighting of the elephant would break the secrecy and allow her at least a kernel of hope. She'd know where she might begin her search for Moe.

She'd give it another day. Perhaps. If her nerves lasted that long. God, she'd adjust to keeping him in a cage. Anything. If only she could get him back. Goddamn that elephant. She tried to occupy her mind by putting the other chimps through their paces, but the real thrill of performing was gone. It was out there somewhere in the wide, wide world.

*

Moe complained about the heat, but it was Bazil who was falling prey to it. Moe suffered somewhat needlessly because he refused to depart from his clothes. The Grateful Dead tee-shirt and faded jeans clung to his fur. Bazil's problem was a natural one: his hide was an inch thick with no sweat glands, so his well-veined ears were his only cooling system. In a real pinch, he could stick his trunk down his throat, draw water from his belly, and spray them, but he was working on a less drastic plan.

He had grazed his way to a strip of shade trees that separated the open fields. Here there was a dried creek bed which he proceeded to excavate with his front feet. When he finally hit upon a favorable spot, he used his toenails like shovels and a nice sized hole began taking shape. He continued this way until it came down to some finer work, for which he used his trunk. He curled it and pushed the loose dirt on top of it with the side of his foot, tossing the now-moist particles aside, often nearly hitting Moe in his preoccupation.

"Watch where you're tossing that stuff, Baz, I'm trying to catch forty winks here." Moe yawned.

Shortly, Bazil stood back and watched as water seeped slowly into the hole. "There ya go," he said proudly.

"What the hell is that?" Moe shook an annoying fly from his ear.

"A mud hole. Can Memories End be far away?" Bazil sniffed the free-flowing liquid with his trunk.

"Don't try to humor me just when I'm getting used to being depressed," Moe said as Bazil siphoned off most of the seepage. He held it in his trunk for a moment before spraying his ears; then stood there motionless except for the billowing of those large fan-like appendages, prompting Moe to ask, "You trying to take off? Disney beat ya to it, Dumbo."

"In time," Bazil said, undaunted. "But first, it's your turn."

Moe peered over the edge of the water hole. "You expect me to drink that sludge?"

"You have a better suggestion, Moe?"

"In time."

In time Bazil sprayed his ears again and waited patiently for the hole to refill. He found respite from the sun, but the insects found him. The perpetual motion of his ears kept them out of his eyes and off Moe, who had climbed aboard and sprawled across Bazil's head to catch the only available breeze.

*

In the dead of night the two freewheeling wanderers stood outside a large building in the center of a dead-end town. Several streetlamps, the bulbs broken by rocks or perhaps a BB gun, stood like silent sentinals watching over the vast empty stores and the ravaged thoroughfare in between.

Moe had guided Bazil to the one place in town that showed any signs of life, drawn to the glow of security lights that lit up sections of the grocery store. Moe slid off the elephant's back and took a careful peek through the doors of the store. What he saw captured his imagination and began to sooth his growling stomach.

"It's a regular cook tent." Moe informed Bazil on his way back to the shadows of the alley where the big beast stood. Moe sniffed the air and caught the scent of something foul and familiar.

"Sorry, Moe, I got a little nervous stomach," Bazil said, a bit embarrassed.

"No worries, big guy. It's all natural." Moe was careful where he stepped as he took Bazil by the trunk and led him from the alley.

"What are you going to do?" Bazil asked, still a bit nervous about being on the streets of the town.

"Just need a little muscle," Moe said, walking the two of them from the alley and around to the back entrance of the place.

"You're going to break in?"

"That's the general idea."

Bazil began to slowly pull away.

Moe held tight and nudged the big lug forward. "Now, now, big guy, don't get shy." They both stood a trunk's length from the shop, and Moe looked upon Bazil with big, soulful eyes. "For me..."

Reluctantly, Bazil stuck out his trunk and grabbed a solid hold of the handle on the door. "Do I really have to do this, Moe? It's...stealing."

"Don't think of it as that. Think of it as borrowing. We can even leave them a note and tell them to charge it to the circus," Moe said as he patted the big gray beast.

Bazil tugged, pulled, wrenched, and the door gave way. It was a little too much damage for Bazil's taste. He took back his trunk as Moe slipped past him into the semi-darkness of the store. "I'll wait here," Bazil said.

"Good." Moe was already down an aisle. "Keep watch."

The place was like a buffet, and Moe acted like a kid in a candy store. He didn't know what to touch or take first. He was thirsty---he drank some milk, then tossed the container and popped the top of a Pepsi. He headed for the snacks. He ate some cupcakes, and found some bags of peanuts, stuffing them in the pockets of his vest and jeans, to give to Bazil for his watch dog routine at the door.

Bazil waited nervously at attention. "Hurry up, Moe, before someone sees us." The elephant had stuck his head inside the shattered doorframe. He sniffed air that brought him a tapestry of smells. His mouth watered, but he decided to back it out and wait his turn.

Meanwhile, Moe ravaged several boxes of Slim Jims and had a regular feast on some shoofly pie. He bounded to the front of the store, took hold of several paper bags and some plastic ones as well, and began to stuff them to the brim. That's when he spotted *them*. Bananas. More bananas then he had even seen in his life.

"So this is what Memories End must be like," Moe said as he gathered up much more than he could carry.

When he left, with the sacks upon his back, he bore a striking resemblance to a gentleman with a white beard and red suit who carried a bulging sack once a year---only Moe was hairier.

"Get what you needed?" Bazil whispered in the dark outside.

Moe popped a few bags of peanuts into Bazil gaping mouth. "I didn't forget you, you big bundle of joy." Moe carried the sacks to the top of Bazil's head. He settled in and belched. "Ready when you are."

Bazil hesitated momentarily. Moe thought it may have been the peanuts, but it was really just a sense of caution. Moe took the lapse in movement as a sign for yet another banana break.

"You know something, big guy, if I find out that there are no bananas in heaven," Moe said through a mouthful, "then I am going down below."

Bazil turned and made his way back into the shadows of the alley. He was about to step out into the light once again when Moe squeezed his legs a bit tighter around the elephant's neck.It was a signal for Bazil to halt. They both looked off to the street just as a police cruiser was meandering down Main. The cop car shone a light that wandered from one side of the street to the other, illuminating the empty storefronts. There was no traffic—foot or vehicle—this time of night as the black and white patrolled, inching its way along at what Moe thought was a snail's pace.

They both watched from their hiding place in the shadows of the alley until they were certain that they'd seen the cruiser make a left onto Depot Street and the car's tail lights faded in the distance. Bazil walked out from the alley, and together he and Moe rode off just like Butch and Sundance.

CHAPTER THIRTEEN
Headlines

GROCERY RANSACKED
By Martin Mulberry
County Call Staff Reporter

Sometime in the wee hours of the morning, Dan's Market, at the corner of Main and Freemont Streets, was broken into by what local police believe to be a bunch of juvenile delinquents. Chief of Police Desmond Brophy admitted that there have been a few isolated incidents of vandalism in the area over the past three months, "but nothing as severe as this."

He went on to say that he has a few suspects under surveillance, but does not plan to make any immediate arrests at this point in time. Dan Schinko, owner and proprietor of Dan's Market, discovered the damages when he came to open for business at seven this morning. The back entrance used for deliveries had been battered "like someone rammed it with a truck."

Schinko went on to say, "It's really weird. Our alarm system went on the fritz just the other day and I was told it would be another week before it was back in working condition. I was thinking about hiring a night watchman until then, but I figured if we just kept it a secret and went about business as usual, no one would be the wiser."

Schinko also said that he never had any trouble before. But Chief Brophy does not rule out the possibility of an inside job. He did say, how-

ever, that he leans more toward one of the employees having a loose tongue rather than masterminding the break in.

All the employees are currently being interviewed and it is not known at this time whether any have mentioned the faulty alarm to anyone outside the store. Schinko has operated the market in town for twenty-five years and most of his employees have been there with him for ten of those years or more. Some have even been there from the very beginning when Schinko first took over the produce selling business from Oliver Stern. Stern, who died last year at the age of eighty-five, started the store in his family residence. It wasn't until the late 1920's that he moved it to its present location. When he retired, he sold the business to Schinko, who was the manager of the market at the time. Dan is proud to say that he went from 'bagger to boss' with hard work and gumption.

"Business has always been good," Schinko said with pride. "Even this here drought hasn't really slowed things down. So I doubt if this little bit of trouble will have any lasting after effects. After all, I'm still the only market still standing in the neighborhood."

Schinko turned serious and said that he did not understand why anyone would want to do this or why or if he may have been targeted. This is a very quiet area where everyone knows everybody else. Most folks are related in some way or another. After a quick inventory of what had been damaged or stolen, he added," I still don't have an answer."

Suffering the worst damages were the dairy and fresh produce sections. Several milk containers were emptied. Large puddles were still visible on the floor of the aisles in the store. (Pick up on aisle five). Nearly all the fresh fruits and vegetables vanished without a trace. There were no signs of bananas anywhere.

"Obviously a gang of milk-hating vegetarians who like to relax afterwards with some good cigars," Schinko said, referring to all the items involved in the break in.

The one unexplainable event, if you can call it that, was the large pile of feces left behind in an alley adjacent to the store. Local veterinarian Jeanette Goodfellow said that it looked to her to be a large pile of elephant dung. After the entire scene was cleared by police, Ms. Goodfellow proceeded to remove the pile, and said that she would dispose of it properly. "I'm going to be able to fertilize my rose bushes for a year with this s--t."

CHAPTER FOURTEEN
Ups And Downs

Louise held on tentatively to the newspaper. "I think this will be of some interest to you, my dear." Amelia read the story and Louise watched for some sign that would prove her intuition correct.

"So..." Amelia said, returning the paper. "Oh, I should have known. Once a thief, always a thief."

"I didn't mean for it...I thought it might cheer you up. You've been looking so distraught, walking around like a lost child." Louise started to reach out, reconsidered, and just let her hand flop awkwardly against one of her own meaty thighs. "Anyway, I'm not the only one who has surmised that Moe and Bazil were responsible. The door smashed in, fruits and vegetables missing, and most of all---cigars."

"You mentioned something about others making the connection?"

"Our show's intrepid advanceman, 'Hurry' Curry, is at this very moment heading toward Fairmount."

"So?"

"Fairmount is back the way we came. The show is booked in the other direction." Louise looked intently serious. "And, for the piece de resistance, Curry took along a couple of burly handlers, who handle guns as well as animals."

Amelia slumped on the steps of her trailer.

"I realize I'm placing you on an emotional rollercoaster," Louise said, "but I'd just like you to know who your friends are in times like these, dear...friends who can help you out of these low points in your life."

Amelia looked up pleadingly.

Louise smiled triumphantly through her fatty cheekbones and said, "There's nothing that says the two of us can't go up to Fairmount ourselves for a little look-see."

*

Bazil lumbered along a back road, guided by the light of the full moon. Moe was having a hard time staying aboard the elephant's back and dodging low-hanging branches at the same time. After receiving several leafy slaps in the face, he took to bending down like a jockey on a race horse. During one particularly low lean, he shouted into Bazil's ear. "Do you know where you're going?"

"It's a bit of a detour, but we'll get back on the right track soon." Bazil moved forward with his eyes to the trail beyond.

Soon was not to be for another lonely mile, along which their only company was a few panicky rabbits, their mealtime foraging disturbed by strange noises and scents. Direction and distance weren't Bazil's only concerns. He was also considering the promised, relentless heat of another day.

By first light he foraged along a dirt road while Moe slept fitfully in the shade of a tree, the species of which, Moe was certain, held out a special invitation to the noisiest birds in the world. He only escaped the wrath of the other end of the songsters by covering himself with the broad leaves of some skunk cabbage. It was one of the only pieces of vegetation growing nearby that Bazil hadn't devoured, and Moe knew why, for when he broke off the leaves from the ground, their pungent odor sent his nose into a tailspin. He could guess why and from whom this gross plant got its moniker. No exaggeration, it stunk to high heaven.

By noon, they were stalled in a pine grove. Bazil's temperature had risen dangerously, so, in spite of Moe insistence, Bazil refused to move.

Without recourse, Moe reluctantly slid to the ground again. He lit a cigar, took several puffs, then held the stogie at arm's length and said, "You take the pleasure out of everything, you ornery beast." Moe began to pace. "Just when I fall asleep back there and begin to digest my meal, you wake me and force me to go on again. Then when I'm hungry and want to find some food, you decide it's time to rest. Who put you in charge of this, whatever it is, anyway?"

"That food," Bazil softly said, "that's what's been worrying me."

"I could see that. Hell, you only managed to eat about seventy-five pounds since then." Moe puffed, paced and would not relent.

"That was terrible what we did last night. And we're sure to be punished for it." Bazil waved his ears to try to create any sort of breeze. He also felt remorse for having to defecate in the alley just outside the store.

"What are you talking about? Who's going to punish us out here anymore than we're suffering already? Or is there some sort of rule at this Memories End of yours that says a guy can't look out for himself in any way he sees fit. It's tha---"

"---Quiet!" Bazil turned quickly to a whisper. "What's that?"

"What's what?" Moe stopped in mid-puff on the cigar.

Bazil swished his trunk from side to side trying to catch a scent of impending danger. "The smell of pine is too strong. You'll have to go see."

"I don't hear anything." Moe finished his puff and blew a smoke ring or two before he choked on an extended inhale.

"Maybe you could climb that tree there?"

"And maybe you can go to hell, you dumb elephant."

Moe plopped himself onto the ground but Bazil quickly plucked him upright and nudged him along with his trunk. Moe was conducted to the base of a tall pine where Bazil said, "From my back you'll be able to reach those fatter branches...maybe you should take off those shoes?"

Moe threw up his hands as if in surrender and said, "An elephant's telling me how to climb a tree."

Bazil lowered his body, resembling a bow and allowing Moe to scramble aboard. Once there, Moe grabbed the nearest branch and pulled himself into the tree. Bazil straightened and took a few steps backward, craning his huge head for a better view.

"Look back the way we came," Bazil said, "I think..."

Moe managed to traverse two branches before his footing gave way. He went backward with a jolt, became startled, and lost his handhold. In what amounted to half a somersault, he bounced off a lower branch, then off Bazil's forehead, and finally landed on his back on a floor of dried pine needles.

Bazil let out a gasp to Moe's groan.

"What was it?" Bazil frantically asked. "What is it?"

Moe lay with his eyes closed among the pines. "About the lowest point in my life."

"That's okay, it's gone now, whatever it was," Bazil said.

'Along with my pride," Moe didn't move an aching muscle.

CHAPTER FIFTEEN
Stages

"Well, will you be back in time for tonight's show or not?" Slade had to follow Louis into the sideshow tent for an answer.

Louis knew the question must at least seem important to Slade, but he couldn't resist a bit of procrastination at Slade's expense, knowing how uneasy the sideshow made the man feel of late.

"Well..?"

Louis halted his inspection of the premises in front of a small stage marked: *Australopithecus*. It was empty except for some debris on the floor. Louis reached through the bars and picked up a piece for closer inspection. "People are becoming so insensitive. They don't even have respect for their relatives."

"That's nothing compared to the flak I've been getting," Slade said. "One night and the discontent are lined up at my door."

"You should be happy. You're the most popular attraction once again." Louis suddenly went pensive. "Perhaps I should install some Plexiglas."

Slade was distracted for a moment by some groans emanating from behind the row of stages. Each stage had a back door that led to a more permanent looking structure attached to the rear of the tent. When his attention returned, he saw Louis had moved farther down the line. "You'll be lucky to keep this going at the rate I'm paying off people." Slade learned a long time ago to grease the palms of policemen, politicians and anyone local in authority that could make or break a weeks run.

"Then I'll have to be certain to return in time," Louis said. "I certainly want everyone to get their money's worth."

"Why do you have to go anyway?" Slade asked as he followed Louis through the early primates.

"All the world's a stage."

"You think you can do a better job than Curry?"

"That shouldn't be too difficult,"Louis said, amused, "because Curry won't find a thing. That chimp is smarter than he is."

Slade listened to the groans again, then said, "Maybe that ape's smarter than us all. Getting out while the getting's good. Before he ends up like the others." He paused, but when Louis didn't acknowledge his statements he added, "I think their drowning was perhaps the best thing for them. They were stunted in more ways than one."

"As I recall,"Louis said, no longer finding things funny, but without looking at Slade, "I warned you about two things at the time we started this. First, that there was a risk of mental degradation that went along with the physical growth stoppage. Now, that type of thing may have its advantages if you're a freak. At least, that way, you won't have to be constantly thinking about your predicament. But it can be a hindrance to those who are expected to learn and do things beyond what's natural---and that goes for men or animals."

"So I've found out. The hard way. By paying for your mistakes as well as my own." Slade looked, sounded, and felt angry. "How many biscuits you have to burn before you hit on the ones that are edible?"

"My second warning covered that, dear Benjamin. You can't afford impatience or a conscience in matters experimental. We're changing the natural order of things. Change takes time."

"You really worked us all over, haven't you, Louis?" Slade said, fingering the mesh that covered the stage of the prosimians.

"Except for that chimp. Amelia's made him what he is. That silly little girl did it, without all your scientific mumbo-jumbo. And that makes you mad, doesn't it?"

Louis tried to look harshly at Slade, but the expression lacked sincerity with Amelia on the mind.

"What's this?" Slade asked, "Do I detect a trace of human emotion in you? Are you suddenly becoming human while the rest of us go in the opposite direction?"

Louis brushed a strand of loose hair from his forehead. "One man in time plays many parts."

As Louis made his exit, Slade was once again assaulted by the moans and groans coming from beneath one of the stages. He was making his way toward them when the sounds abated and two side-show performers, both with so many piercings that they jingled and jangled as they walked, moved out of the shadows. He couldn't be certain if the moans had been amorous or the two had simply locked piercings and finally escaped. He wasn't about to ask.

*

Ben Slade sat alone in his trailer staring at a half-empty bottle of scotch, trying hard to convince himself that it was actually half-full. It was a losing battle for him for long ago pessimism had infected his heart like weevils into a field of alfalfa. He let his concentration on the bottle wane and began to examine his limited options. What if he just up and left in the middle of the night, leaving the circus and sideshow to sink or swim on its own? He no longer felt in charge of anything significant. His "Master Of Ceremonies" duties could be handled by anyone in the crew. He was not one of those people who thought that no one could fill his shoes. After all, his were just an ordinary size ten. What impact had he had over anyone or anything these days?

It was clearly a younger man's game. He could leave the circus to Curry and be done with it. Just for spite he could hand over the keys to the sideshow to Louis, and then let the two of them go at each other like rabid animals. He would love to have a ringside seat as they both tried to get in the last word. Someday, perhaps, he would be ready to cash in his chips and call it a day, but not quite yet. There was a power struggle brewing and he was holding his cards close to the vest for now. Time would catch up to all of them. Every show he had ever worked with had either sold out or collapsed its tents under the weight of debt. He was under no illusions about the Slade Bros. Show. He knew what was coming, and that they would not be the exception to the rule. It was becoming more and more apparent that not only time but the whims of a fickle audience would inevitably bring about their demise. Anyone who thought differently never read the writing on the wall. Perhaps that was what brought the three of them together in the first place, hatching this plan to save the circus and sideshow. They were made for each other. If he, Louis and Curry were to go their separate ways, each would take something from the other and never be whole. Was it all worth it in the end? Like all birds of prey he was very territorial. What was his was his, and what was yours was his if you could not hold onto it. He knew that most people, himself included, were all the same, and that the things they were thinking were not necessarily the things that they said. In the end he would be forced to up and sell or liquidate or just walk away. Perhaps one day he could travel the world, seeing the sights and dreaming of a better life. Maybe, just maybe the old saying was wrong and you could go home again. But what would be left for him there?

He was neither an orphan nor a Slade, but he had been born with the given name Benjamin. Both his parents were performers of sorts. They would set up a small show tent in any vacant lot they came across through the many small towns they traveled through. While his old man sold bootleg whiskey, his mother would dance, revealing as much or as little as the puritanical zoning laws of the towns would allow. If his father had bribe money available greasing the right palms would allow his mother to perform free and easy and without retribution.

For a time it was just the three of them. Then his younger brother James was born several months prematurely, and with multiple birth defects that made him a prime candidate for any sideshow attraction. His father ignored the newest member of the family, while his mother tried her best to be motherly. All James could manage to do was cry. Hunger, pain or soiled, it was all the same to him. Day and night the old man took to drink, his mother wept along with her youngest, and Benjamin would stuff his ears with whatever he could find to dampen the misery that surrounded them.

One night the crying stopped. He saw his mother go catatonic as his father carried out a small, pathetic thing, wrapped in a blanket, into the cold of the evening. His brother James was never to return. After that his old man stayed drunk and belligerent. His mother turned morose and remorseful. He, himself, was mostly unconcerned with it all. It was only years later that he began to wonder if his father had taken it upon himself to end James' suffering. If he did, he didn't hold it against the man. He had contemplated it himself on several occasions, but he was either too scared or too much a coward to go through with it. He didn't blame his father. The man did them all a favor.

How he survived his own childhood he did not know. The horseshoe that his father always hung above the door of the different hovels they'd call homes finally ran out its luck. His parents drifted apart, and he drifted away. His father faded into obscurity and his mother into a sort of madness that she embraced with an open mind.

He never knew what eventually became of both of his parents, but he was certain that they had now joined his brother James in whatever afterlife that was afforded to them. It wasn't much of a comfort, but it was all he had.

He drifted from place to place, with no particular destination in mind. As fate or dumb luck would have it, a small circus was passing through the same town at the same time. Gathering up his courage, he asked for a job. The next day he was shoveling shit and trying to convince himself that it was sunshine. He was eager to learn the ins and outs of the life, but mostly he saw the push and shove of the underbelly of it all. The small shows had a shelf life, and that life was shorter and shorter as the years went by. When the final tents were struck and the assets sold off, Benjamin moved on along with the performers and animals to the next show. It wasn't until he attached himself to the Harry Slade Circus And Sideshow Extravaganza that he went from shovel, to trainer, to advance man. Old Man Slade was only interested in one thing:the box office tally. A good show meant a good cash flow. It was from the old man that Ben learned the tricks of the trade. They had to deal with everything from temperamental performers, to price gouging vets, to politicians and police officers whose hands were always reaching out for a donation from the till. Paying off the right people meant that the show could go on. And to old man Slade the show was everything. The old man weighed in at the far side of three hundred pounds, with a nasty-looking nose and a permanent sneer on his fat face. He drank too much, ate too much, and never took a day off in his life.

Then, as fate or dumb luck would have it once again, Harry Slade died of a massive heart attack while enjoying the many delights of the bearded lady, and no one spoke or stood up to take the mantle from the old man. No one, that is, but Benjamin. He filled the old man's shoes. His first order of business was to change his own name to Slade, and add the Brothers to the circus and sideshow billing. He got rid of the Extravaganza part because he thought the rubes wouldn't know what that meant, and that these small town types expected their shows to be entertaining and their sideshow freaks to make them feel uncomfortable but not to the point of disgust. He greased the right palms, and spread the right attitude among the towns. The crowds came out in droves, but only for a limited time. Things dried up and they drifted through towns like tumbleweeds. For several years he kept them one jump ahead of the law until, almost at the same time, Louis and Curry made their appearances. Things began to take on a more interesting turn, and got a little bit weird, but Benjamin Slade still felt that the sky was the limit.

For some reason his mind drifted now to the little man. August something-or-other was a hard man to forget. He practically saved their bacon after the rogue elephant went wild, tearing up the grounds and killing those chimps. He thought the big beast would have to be put down, but up stepped the little man. He actually talked to the beast as if it understood. Well, I guess, one monster to another. They were a sight to see.

He remembered once asking the dwarf for his opinion, without revealing any trade secrets to him, on the infusion of new blood and tactics into the circus and sideshow. His rather cryptic answer was something about a time just before the surprise attack on Pearl Harbor. One lone Japanese General stood up against all the others to let them know of the folly of waking the sleeping giant—America. Benjamin Slade wondered what 'sleeping giant' was about to be awakened by them. The little man answered: "God."

A knock on the trailer door brought him back from another time and place and into the present.

"What?" Slade said, annoyed.

"Sorry to disturb you, boss." It was one of the grounds crew. "We got a situation."

"What it is now?"

"One of the clowns is refusing to go on. He says he's just not feeling very funny tonight."

"Son of a bitch."

CHAPTER SIXTEEN
Traveling Hopefully

Moe uncurled and brushed the dried pine needles from his clothes. His hands came away sticky from the pine sap, and full of needles of their own from his having slept in an awkward position. He was wide awake now but his arms were still fast asleep. He stood and shook the blood into them and attempted to stretch the kinks out of the rest of his body. He swore softly as he awoke the ache in each muscle, particularly the ones along the left side, which had broken his fall.

"Climb the stupid tree, he tells me. That big one there will do—damn near did me in--what was that?" Moe did a quick three-sixty. "Didja hear that..? Hey..?" Moe reached out and punched Bazil on the foot. "I thought you were standing guard?"

"Hmmm?"

"You big, dumb..." Moe searched the darkness, adding the glow of his eyes to those that watched back. "How can you sleep at a time like this?"

"It's night, isn't it?" Bazil opened one eye to look around. "And you were right. There's nothing out there but my guilty conscience."

"Does your conscience have eyes?"

"Oh, those are just animals."

"Just animals? I suppose lions are 'just animals'?"

"Lions don't run wild here, Moe. They're from Africa."

"We're from Africa and we're here."

"Hmmm, that's interesting. I never thought that there might be lions at Memories End. But I can live with that." Bazil closed the eye for a few seconds, then opened both of them to add, "And you can too. The Monster/Man told me that apes sleep in trees."

"I already smell like that junk Amelia uses to clean her toilet. Upwind or downwind, pine scented, and they'll find me in the dark no matter what."

"Then may I offer my back for your protection?"

"No, thank you." Moe rubbed his own sore backside.

"Are you trying to tell me that the only place you'll feel safe again is in a cage?"

Moe sniffed. "I happen to have first-hand knowledge that chimps in cages aren't always safe, huh, big guy?"

"It wasn't intentional," Bazil said.

"That's not wh---" Moe took a quick inventory of the staring eyes in the woods. "Never mind. Maybe killing those missing links wasn't intentional on your part, but I believe those creatures out there have a different outcome in mind for me."

"Would you feel better if we just moved on?"

Moe agreed and Bazil rambled off through the pines, talking from the very first step. "You just go along stumbling in the dark, with no real direction, like in a dream almost. Until one day you awake and take a good look around you and realize that you got yourself nowhere. It was just up and down; up and down. And suddenly you know you just have to escape. Go in a different direction. So you charge off without any plan, you only want to get away, out of your rut. It sounds crazy, even feels strange, but you understand the need to do it and that's enough for you. Unfortunately, that's not enough for anyone else. All they think is that you're going crazy. Gone nuts. And all your actions serve is to prove them right. Because the only thing you find out is that if you don't know where you're going...there's no place to go. And you come away thinking that there's nothing out there for you. You were better off in the dream world..."

Up and down they went. Moe lay low, ducking branches and remaining silent, giving no sign of listening or hearing. Bazil continued to highlight the trail with night vision and insight. "But now that you know that, it's hard to go back. Because they keep after you, prodding and pushing to put you in your place. And the more they push, the more you resist, until you can't take it no more and you begin to push back. Not to hurt anyone, just to get them to leave you alone. To let you find your own place. Your own way back...

"The Monster/Man assured me mine was a normal reaction. He said African elephants do it all the time. It's a natural response whenever they feel threatened—pawing the ground, flapping their ears, trumpeting loudly. Charging, only to stop before the actual contact. They don't want to hurt anyone. I guess I was just out of practice..?"

Moe looked back at the dark woods, then ahead at the brightening sky and said, "I think we're safe now." He didn't sound too reassuring, even to himself.

"Just remember, Moe, like the Monster/Man always said: 'Tomorrow is a gift as yet unspoiled by chaos'."

"Yeah, swell, but that still leaves today as a steaming pile of horseshit."

Bazil lumbered on a few more paces before reciting, "A broken bottle shines just like a diamond ring."

"More pearls from the dwarf?" Moe added with a snip. "Do you even know what that means?"

"I think he said it was from a song he heard and that it meant that not all things are as they appear to be."

"Let's see, we're lost in the woods, plodding around in circles, searching for someplace that doesn't exist...I'd say that things are *exactly* what they appear to be."

*

Amelia leaned out of the morning sun. The bench seat of the old pickup was drawn back as far as it could go to accommodate Louise's bulk. She was the owner and operator of the vehicle.

Amelia considered that this must be how a small child feels. So helpless. So left out. Yet it was a purely physical affliction, for mentally she had not felt this good since Moe was first placed in the cage.

They were a day behind Curry and the handlers, but Louise had salved Amelia's anxiety all the while. Louise was a self-proclaimed expert on small town life and lore. She claimed to have been born and *razed* in such a place.

"Curry will go to the authorities who will double talk him as much as he them. They deserve each other. We, dear Amelia, shall go directly to the people. They'll be more than happy to give us the facts, the fiction, and everything between and beyond."

"I hope you're right," Amelia said. "I'm worried that we'll be too late. We should have left yesterday."

"Ah, but the show must go on. Even a mud show like ours." Louise watched the road and the woman beside her.

"I'm just tired of being so helpless and thinking how helpless Moe must be. He's at the mercy of that killer elephant. There's no telling..."

After a moment Louise said, "There was a time when I only saw the worst in a situation, but no longer. Not since August...Purefoy."

"Who..?"

"The Monster/Man, my dear."

"Of, you mean that little dwarf?"

"No, Amelia, he was a giant." Louise paused for composure. "I believe this is the first time his real name was spoken aloud in years. It was something else that became lost along the way for him. But never his dignity. Or his faith. Or his stature among those of us who knew him. If he had been small, he never could have lasted."

"I only meant that he was short."

"I know." Louise's driving was on automatic and so was her memory. "We had some very spirited discussions...about life mostly. Where it all started and where it was going. I believe it's safe to say that August was a Creationist. He believed everything came from God, including that misshapen body of his. He needed no proof, and faith was his missing link—something that he found completely lacking in my arguments. He couldn't believe in evolution because there were no known fossils of transitional forms—say a fish with part fin and part feet.

"He was unflappable. If he died his soul certainly went to heaven, if there is such a place . He never wavered on his beliefs, not for an instant. And I'd never admit it to his face, but he did set me to thinking. I think I heard someone say he died of a heart attack out west somewhere. I say, if that's true, that little heart was just too big for this world. I know they say you can't take it with you, but I believe that sometimes they are wrong, for the day that man left, I swear I woke up that morning and I knew something great was already gone."

Amelia's mind had been racing in the opposite direction. She was already miles farther down the road than the pickup. She actually heard very little of what Louise was saying and understood even less. It wasn't until Louise uttered a direct question that the two of them were once again together in the front seat.

"Do you remember how he calmed that elephant after the... tragedy? That was the direct result of the beast sensing the presence of a more powerful being. Animals will always surrender to authority. If only that elephant could talk. They're said to have great memories."

"I hope the folks in Fairmont can still remember yesterday," Amelia said more to herself than her traveling companion.

"Not to worry. A happening such as the one perpetrated by our Moe and Bazil will be the talk of the town for months to come." Louise let the wipers swipe across the windshield once to clear off a suicidal moth.

With that they both withdrew into their own pensive shells for the remainder of the trip.

CHAPTER SEVENTEEN
Barking Up The Wrong Trees

Mutilated Trees
By Martin Mulberry
County Call Staff Reporter

Several trees were severely damaged recently in a section of woodland owned by Orville Coombs of R.F.D. 5, Fairmont. Mr. Coombs made the discovery himself when he went into the area to lay in some firewood. "I'll go about once a week for a truck load. It's good for the trees to thin them out and good for my heating bill. I got me one of those big country houses...

"Everybody's feeling the pinch these days, what with the high price of fuel. So I've been having some problems with poachers and I expect I will again this fall. They upset me a little but this sort of thing really sickens a fella. I guess I'll have to find out if those (damaged) trees can survive the winter or if I have to cut them now so's they won't rot. I thought the drought was bad enough. Now this."

Most of the damaged trees were left standing, but even the few that were toppled had been peeled to the bark. Some stood naked to the height of seven feet and those that were toppled showed no signs of being cut. They had simply been pushed over, uprooted as if by a strong wind or an act of God.

Local authorities are concerned about what they call "deliberate attempts at pernicious vandalism" because the Coombs property adjoins state animal propagation land. A spokesperson for the state said that although the damage stopped some distance from state land there's nothing to prevent such things from progressing. "We're spread too thin here to patrol a large area so there doesn't appear to be much we can do to stop it. Except get lucky or just hope the appeal of such vandalism wears off."

Experts have been brought in to assess the damage and try and determine the type of instrument used to strip the trees. Meanwhile, one has to wonder what the appeal of tearing large strips of bark off trees was in the first place. Or what anyone would do with the bark once it had been removed. Only small chips have been left behind in the area of the damage.

To further the mystery, it had been learned from Chief of Police Desmond Brophy's office that several farmers have reported crop damage within the past few days. Chief Brophy declined to speculate as to whether the two incidents are related and if they somehow tie in with the vandalism at Dan's Market, which took place around the same period of time as the damage to the corn crops. Apparently hundreds of cornstalks were uprooted in several fields and like the bark were carted away from the scene of the crime by unknown means.

In both instances, the ground in the area was said to have been too hard and dry to contain any real evidence, but Chief Brophy did say that his department was following up on a few leads which may help break the case(s) within the next few days.

CHAPTER EIGHTEEN
Wondering And Wandering

I wonder if he's all right. It's so hard to picture him...

"I'm a mere image of my former self. My clothes just hang. I'm a walking skeleton."

...and it's only been...how long? Just over a week. How long can he survive out there...

"If I don't get some real decent food soon I'll waste away to nothing."

...These folks in Fairmont were a strange lot. So friendly, they seemed phony. So helpful, that they were no help at all. I'll never find him...

"Someone will stumble over my bleached white bones and think they've found the missing link or Bigfoot's baby. And that's about as much as we'll ever find of your precious Monster/Man."

...But Louise has been such a dear, I'm afraid to even think such a thing. She's footing the bill and keeping Slade away from me and I'm being ungrateful. She says that Bazil might well be out there looking for that little---dwarf...and I think, in some way so is she...

"Bazil, old boy, you have a one track mind. You don't care that I'm dying out here. How can I expect any sympathy from someone who eats bark off trees and thinks it's a banquet?"

...Louise seems as possessed with finding Moe as me. And after all her lecturing. Maybe I misunderstood her... then...maybe...

"Aren't you ever going to stop? Are we just going to plod on and on 'till we drop..? Who the hell am I talking too? He sure as shit don't hear me. I'm just along for the ride."

...No one seems to mind that I've neglected the other chimps lately. I don't even think the chimps mind. They've been kind of lifeless. Maybe they miss Moe, too? We don't train anymore. Don't even perform. And no one says a word about it. The show went on without me for the first time in years. It bothers me, but I'm not certain why...The crowds have been good. Louise said so. I can't bear to watch. Good enough to keep the show in the area. Is that the reason Slade doesn't care? Am I through? Or is there something else..?

"You're dead set on Memories End, isn't you, big fella?"

...We're going to wear ruts travelling back and forth over this road. Louise refuses to allow me to go alone, yet she won't miss a performance. All she'll say is that she owes it to the others. She calls them her children. I know she believes that because she has always been like a mother to me. More than my own mother. She didn't abandon me when my father died...I feel bad for still taking advantage of her but I know I'd feel much worse without her...and I don't know what she expects from me...Will anything good ever come out of this?"

"What the hell am I doing here?"

CHAPTER NINETEEN
Unwholly Trinities

"Still watching for your Mercury?"

"Huh?" Slade watched as Louis approached. "Oh, if you're referring to Curry, yes." He watched until Louis was alongside, then he led the way into his trailer, adding, "I see you've returned empty-handed."

"In time for the show as usual, as promised."

"Well, that may be more difficult to keep in the future. I've decided it's time to move on. Our success relies on short, hit and run performances. We've already been here too long...Coffee?"

Louis nodded to the raised pot. "Do I sense a bit of hostility in your voice? Or maybe resentment? You're blaming me for our predicament?"

Slade passed a filled cup. "I don't see us making any progress here. The only thing I'm getting is bigger headaches."

"The evolutionary process is slow. Your bigger headaches are a sign that your head is getting bigger." Louis smiled.

"I'm not laughing."

"I'm not a clown."

"It wouldn't matter. The ones around here aren't exactly funny."

"Then take this any way you like it, but it is my belief that you are trapped by an antimetabole--in a sense. You do the show because the show is all you can do." Louis paused for a sip and effect. "But you have a dream; it was with you before I arrived and unfortunately hasn't changed since then. Although I led you to believe that it would. So you continued to have faith in your faith. Perhaps it is my fault, but only because of my overenthusiasm, and oversimplifacation.

"Stop me if I'm wrong," Louis did not wait but went right on, "but you went along with me because you're ambitious. You came from a big show, should be in charge of one right now, if certain dealings hadn't been uncovered..."

"I took the rap for them sonsabitches and they sold me out." Slade spit angrily. "Grease the right palms and it runs smooth. Other hands got in the pot and I paid the price."

"So you want to get even. Understandable." Louis held up his hand to waylay another interruption. "*Even*, in a sense that you want to get back to where you started. Back to the big time. You'd make a wonderful Christian. You come from God and go through hell, only to go back to the beginning. What's the use?"

Louis paused and sipped the coffee as if tilting for an answer. It never came, so he continued, "There isn't any unless you use the knowledge gained along the way. Don't go around trying to prove you're as good as the gods, show them you're better. Tilt at known windmills, not at imaginary dragons."

"Have you taken a good look around this place lately?" Slade emphasized his question by a spread of his hands. "The gods haven't exactly left me with a great deal to work with. They haven't exactly been...kind. You know the type of people we get here— you couldn't do what you're doing otherwise."

"But that's the perfect atmosphere. The gods will never suspect. They'll leave you alone. And in the end you get them, in your own time and on your own terms. Take the *goods* the gods provide thee, and reshape them."

Slade huffed. "I'll leave the playing of God to you."

"Who's playing? I don't want to be God. I want to make her. Like all the rest. Just another shape along the descent of man.

Nothing special. No higher state. No cosmic arrogance." Louis was on a roll and did not wish to stop. "Besides, I may have seen God, and she's taller and thinner than me."

They heard the sound of an approaching vehicle and Slade went to the window to have a look. After acknowledging Curry's late arrival, he turned to Louis and said, "You may as well hang around. I always get the feeling that we're all here for your pleasure and convenience anyway."

*

Bazil approached the farmhouse from the upwind side, cautious not to step beyond the covering hedgerow. As his motion slowed, Moe became less tense. Relaxing his grip on Bazil's ear, Moe crawled to the edge of the elephant's brow and exclaimed, "Apple."

A sudden tilt of that massive head sent Moe rolling backward. He almost slid to the ground but for his nimble fingers. With those of his left hand he latched onto Bazil's ear again, swinging freely. He thus gained momentum for the upward spring, which he accomplished with accomplished grace. "Be more careful, you big lug, or I'll give you none of that apple pie."

"Sniff again, Moe," Bazil whispered. "There's a dog that goes with that pie."

With that Bazil moved off. Moe asked pointedly, "Where do you think you're going?"

"We want to be on the other side of this place and I'm taking the safest route possible."

Moe started to protest but, with the reason for such action already vacating his sense of smell, his common sense was given room to intervene. Unfortunately, Bazil's sense of anything wasn't in full command either, until it was too late. As they reached the far side of the farmhouse, the dog picked up their scent and with an enormous racket, replete with growls, snaps and barks announced their presence to the world and to an erudite and apologetic Bazil.

The dog's repeated actions, aside from boring the humans thereabouts with the information that another stray animal was nearby and eliciting a chorus of "quiet down" followed by the refrain of "stupid mutt," applied excess pressure to a chain that had steadily grown rusty and weak over years of confinement. Finally, inevitably, this effort broke it at its attachment point to the dog's house, and the dog's sounds only quieted because of the distance he put between himself and the farmhouse.

He was still loud and belligerent when he arrived snapping at Bazil's feet. Immediately Bazil stopped any forward motion and went into a little dance, the choreography of which had Moe hanging on for dear life.

"Stomp it, you idiot," Moe cried.

Bazil misunderstood and said, "Good, Moe, good. Talk to him." *Step! Snap! Step! Growl!* "But don't be insulting and call him names. After all, this is his territory."

It was during that little speech that Bazil zagged when he should have zigged and before he could sidestep the dog had a hold of his trunk. Bazil, more stunned than hurt, halted in his tracks and Moe swung into action. With a well-timed lunge he descended to the dog's back, landing just above the tail and caving the dog's hind quarters. Bazil's trunk swung loose and so did Moe. With the free end of the long chain in one hand, Moe shot upward and grabbed a limb with his free hand, then completed the maneuver with a graceful loop that deposited him on the top of the branch.

He sat there, waiting for the dog to regain its senses and footing, which it did momentarily and reacted in exactly the manner Moe anticipated. With bared teeth, the dog swung in a little circle and leaped at Moe. As it went airborne, Moe effected the opposite and equal reaction by jumping diagonally toward the ground and pulling in the slack of the chain which was now draped over the branch. The completed strategy had him standing on the ground, holding tightly to one end of the chain while an infuriated dog dangled from the other, struggling to keep its hind legs on the ground and not choke to death.

"You got him," Bazil said in amazement.

Moe strained to admit a grunt. "It may look...that way... from...where you're standing..." The chain slipped slightly.

"Don't let him go, Moe." The elephant trumpeted. "Give not that which is holy unto dogs, neither cast ye your pearls before swine for they would trample them beneath their feet and then turn and tear you to pieces."

Moe gave Bazil a look of utter bewilderment. He wished that the dwarf, who had filled the bigger beast with all kinds of nonsense, was standing here right now, so he could kick him in his righteous little ass, or at the least feed him to the dog.

"What do you...want...me to do with him?" The chimp asked when he regained his composure.

"Continue as before. Talk to him."

Moe groaned in physical and mental strain. "He's beyond... reasoning...with. Give me a...hand...or a trunk."

At the mention of it, Bazil flexed his trunk for the first time. It stung a little and there were small rivulets of blood winding their way through the wrinkled gray skin; but he had no trouble in keeping the dog in place.

Freed at last, Moe flexed his aching fingers and arms. "I shall never play the piano again."

Meanwhile, Bazil toyed with the length of the chain, but each time he loosened his grip the dog lunged at him, missing by mere inches, "I think...you're right, Moe," mumbled Bazil. "I'm begin... ning to recognize the...symptoms. Do like the...Monster/Man."

"Me!" Moe was baffled.

Bazil tried to tighten his grip, cutting off a bit of circulation and air to his trunk. "Yesh. Got go...for hish bark...bring the peep...from housh."

"I guess it has to be me," Moe said as he circled to the rear of the dog. "He's got you trunk-tied." Moe grabbed a handful of the furry tail, gave a yank, and snickered, "Nice doggie."

Bazil mumbled something incoherent to which Moe answered, "Just wanted to get his attention. Now, Rover, let's see what we can do about this temper tantrum. Hmmm. How's this? We animals have to stick together. We're all alike, really, we're brothers. Blood bonds us all." The tail of the part-Golden Retriever, part-whatever-may-be had remained in Moe's hand so he gave it a convenient lift. "Right, brothers under the skin. Of course some of us appear to be more clever than others---" Moe looked across at Bazil. "---and some stronger, but there's no need to think that we'd take advantage of you."

"Hmmm," Bazil said as the dog appeared to quiet down. The barks and growls had stopped and so had the tension on the chain, so Bazil relaxed his grip. "Good, Moe, good."

Moe grinned and continued, "If you're angry for some reason, don't take it out on us. If it's the chain, hell, been there and done that. We're just passing through. Right, Baz?"

Bazil nodded and released a few links of chain by saying, "Why not come with us, perhaps we can help you?"

Without warning, the dog used the advantage he had gained from his modified behavior. He twisted, pulling an extra foot of chain from the startled Bazil, and snapped at Moe, who was saved from a painful bite only by his own cynicism. It had served him well up to and including this point. All the dog came away with was a mouth full of its own tail.

"Reel the bastard in," Moe screeched, and Bazil obeyed.

When it was done and equilibrium re-established, Moe fished out his pocket knife and pointed the keen blade at the dog and his sharp words at Bazil. "This is a mixed-breed, you mixed up oaf. You can never fully trust it, because you never know what it truly is. It doesn't even know itself. It only knows what it's been told. And that's probably this brute's major problem."

Moe removed the vest that he put on earlier this morning atop the Dead concert tee-shirt, and began to cut it into strips. "Plus, there are those, mixed or not, who persists in being sons-of-bitches." Moe looked up from his work, holding three strips of cloth about two feet in length. "And we're on opposite ends of one such creature."

Moe braided the strips the way he had seen Amelia do her hair, and snapped them, testing their tensile strength. Satisfied, he grabbed the dog's back legs with his left hand and twisted the mongrel on its side. With his right hand and his mouth he wrapped and fastened the cord and watched for a moment as the dog tried to attain a three-legged stance.

"Every mongrel needs a dog beneath him in order to feel canine," Moe snarled.

After knotting the chain back around the base of the tree, Moe began to lead a relieved Bazil away by the trunk.

"I hope someone finds him soon," Bazil said. "Before he gets hungry or a storm comes up.

"I hope he wraps that chain around his throat and--"

"Don't talk like that, Moe. We are all God's creatures."

Moe grunted but did not deem it worthy of a response.

After a short distance back into the woods, Bazil turned to his traveling companion with praise. "I like that part about 'blood bonds us all'. You sounded just like the Monster/Man."

"Yeah, well, I read it in a Superman comic book." Moe searched his pants pockets for a cigar and his Zippo.

*

"It appears our beloved Hermes has become Cassandra," Louis said as Curry entered the trailer.

"That's one thing I'll admit that you can do better than me." Curry swept aside the remark.

"Let's keep personalities out of this for once," Slade intervened. "What kept you?"

The advance man flopped into a chair and opened a small flask he retrieved from his hip pocket. One long pull and he was ready to spill. "The police in Fairmont got a call. Somebody hog tied a watchdog, out on this farm. Sounded just stupid enough to be true..." Rummaging through another pocket he produced a pocket knife. "I found this at the scene and slipped it into my pocket. It's mine, the one that's been missing for more than a month now."

Slade examined the knife. "There are probably hundreds of those around. Every kid's got one to skin fish or play mumbly-peg. I had one when I was a kid."

"You were a kid?" Louis could not help himself.

"They also found a vest. The police have that. But it's the same one I've seen that chimp wearing around here." Curry took a second pull from the flask. "It's where he keeps your cigars."

"Damn," Slade said. "But the animals got away? The law's not suspicious?"

"Yes and no." Curry remained vague.

"Golden opportunities," Louis chimed in.

Undaunted, reluctantly, Curry continued. "They're still out there, but I had to tell this Sheriff Brophy fella."

"Damn." Slade remained a man of few expletives.

"Nothing I could do. He's not as stupid as he looks. The bumpkin saw my interest and was about to check up on me. Hey, don't worry, we look like honest citizens now and he wants the same things we do. Get this over with the least amount of hassle... There is one condition though."

"This bodes some strange eruption to our state," Louis recited gleefully.

"Oh, knock it off," Slade shouted from mid-pace of the trailer.

"Now is the summer of our discontent made miserable winter by this son-of-a-bitch," Curry said, pointing a finger at Louis, who laughed even louder.

"This is just great." Slade threw up his hands in surrender. He paced, stopped, and paced more until he settled a few paces from Curry. "What is this condition?"

"The sheriff wants the show to stay in the area." Curry stretched his back to work out a kink or deflect the '*kill the messenger*' vibe that had just been sent.

"Damn, this just gets better all the time." Slade started, and stopped pacing once again. He looked directly at Curry. "Where does he expect us to go? And what am I supposed to do while we're there?"

Curry shrugged. "He didn't specify, but I figured we could move in the same direction as those two animals. Wherever they're going." He added after a safe distance. "It would save me some driving."

Slade stepped off again as his weird little dance continued. "Damn."

"A man of few words." Louis rose from his chair, allowing his large frame to re-establish his domination, then cleared his throat and said, "I believe there's a way to turn this whole mess to our advantage."

He departed without elaboration.

Slade looked dejectedly at Curry.

"As this entire mélange loses vision the empire will fall." Curry was serious.

"And you'll be around to pick up the pieces?"

"What makes you think I'd want to?"

"Half the time I don't know what the hell you or that freak are talking about!" Slade turned away with anger.

"And the other half?"

Slade ignored the comment and glowered after Louis' bulk lumbering into the night.

*

Later that evening Louis returned to his own trailer, and within its domesticated confines he felt at ease enough to shed one skin for another. As Louise emerged from the bedroom, in robe and slippers, she eased a look in the bathroom mirror and saw the face that she believed she had now grown to deserve.

She was growing weary of playing both sides of herself against the middleman. She knew that men the likes of Slade and Curry would never allow a woman into their hierarchy, so she had Louis to speak for her. He was well equipped for the task at hand. She used that masculine side to stand on equal footing with their kind. She would revert to her feminine wiles only to sooth and charm someone like Amelia. A softer, gentler approach was necessary, and Louise was well suited for that. Playing both sides of the same coin was taking its toll, and she wished for the chance to flip that coin high into the air and let it fall where it may, where she could take on the role she was always meant to play. Maybe someday she could just be the woman she always thought that she was meant to be. Oh, how God had played such a cruel joke on her, leaving it up to her to decide who or what she was. So, she thought it only fair that she try to improve on his little experiments. But somewhere deep down was that woman. August always said, "Just be yourself, my dear." Easy for him to say, he knew who and what he was supposed to be. Lately, she had been waking in the middle of the night trying to figure out not where but who she was.

Louise settled her substantial girth into a much smaller chair, and sat there with an unopened book and a breathing bottle of wine. One or the other would give her the most comfort in an otherwise lonely venture into the arms of Morpheus. She closed her eyes and wandered away for only a moment when a slight tug at the sleeve of her dressing gown brought her back from her journey beyond the trailer.

Louise opened her eyes and smiled brightly at the young woman standing now at the very end on the arm of the chair. She stood all of one foot tall, and dressed in a gossamer, golden-laced outfit complete with beautiful and colorful butterfly wings. It wasn't the diminutive size of the tiny creature before her, nor the odd-looking outfit, that made Louise turn away slightly to hide her sadness, but rather the distortion of facial features. The entire symmetry was off perhaps half an inch or more. The forehead drooped, as well as the eyelids and the corners of the mouth. The ears, if one could properly call them such, barely covered the sides of the tiny, conical head. And what could be thought of as hair would be a mistake on anyone's part. The nose was two slits and the teeth resembled Chiclets. But one feature that could not be hidden nor ignored were the bright and sparkling blue eyes that shone beneath the heavy lids. They burst, projecting outward, like any star in the night sky. They told of an intelligence and wonder hidden beneath the grotesque mask that the young lady wore.

"Momma," the young thing said with a melodic tone that was hardly above a whisper, "when may I venture out beyond these confines and visit the outside world?"

Louise had to replace her sadness with motherly advice, as she said, "I fear that the world is not yet ready for the likes of you, dear Evangelina. Your beauty is much too captivating for the cruelness that awaits."

"Is it because I am an abomination?" The ugly word seemed much too harsh for the angelic voice.

"Where did you hear that?" Louise sighed heavily.

"I hear the whispers from the others."

"Then I will have to have a talk with those *others.*"

Louise looked to the young girl, and with one chubby finger, she reached out and gently stroked the left side of her face. "My darling one, you are the brightest star in an otherwise mournful and empty sky. Your smile lights up the universe and sets God to singing."

The tiny figure pirouetted on the arm of the chair and the wings nearly took flight. "Maybe I could one day fly around the world and see the lights and the buildings and the people. Wouldn't that be grand, momma?"

"That is what all these books are for, dear heart. To let you experience the lights and the dreams." Louise tapped the cover of the unopened tome beside her.

"But those are someone else's dreams. Someone else has seen them before me. I wish to see it all for myself." Evangelina clapped her tiny hands together. The sound barely registered above a soothing, soft breeze. She closed her eyes and hugged herself, lost in a dream of her own making.

Louise watched and shook a small but frightening thought from her spinning mind. When the tiny creature awoke from dreamland she looked to the enormous woman on the chair and saw a tear falling, lonely, down the side of her face. Louise's corpulent eyes tried hard to hold back the sadness.

"Do not cry, momma. It is not a time for tears," the young girl said with a flip of her butterfly wings. "Let me sing for you and brighten up your sadness." The tiny voice soon filled the room with the harmony of angels.

"I asked heaven to send me a dream
I asked heaven to make it come true
I asked heaven for just one thing
And heaven sent me you

I asked the moon and the stars above
I asked what they could do
I asked the moon and the stars for love
And they sent me you

I will love you for a thousand years
I will cry with you every tear
I would walk a million miles
Just to see you smile

I asked love if it could grow
In a heart that sorrow knew
I asked love to save my soul
And love sent me you"

As the singer continued to bring heaven a little closer to earth, Louise could not help but return to the thought that had plagued her ever since the experiment went terribly wrong. As she felt the words of the song strike her soul over and over again with a sledge-hammer of sorrow, she knew what had to be done. It was what she had had to do so many times before to the so-called *mistakes* she had created. And although it meant that she would never hear the singer nor the song ever again in this lifetime, she convinced herself that it was the only thing to do; the right thing to do.

And the one thing that succeeded, that one bright shining gem, she could not ever take credit for.

Suddenly, painfully, she felt quite old and useless. She tried hard to remember what the little man with the big heart used to say to her at times like these. *"Age does not define us, it refines us."*

As she sat back and tried to listen one last time to the singing, Louise now only heard, over and over in her troubled mind, the words of Benjamin Slade back when they both started their descent down the slippery slope. Were they words of wisdom or some profane attempt at stopping her in her tracks? "Don't you feel any remorse? Regret? Pity? Or are those emotions for us mere mortals?"

The song inside the trailer and the one inside her head merged into a single, mournful dirge that she could not escape.

CHAPTER TWENTY
Daydreams/Nightmares

Bazil tried vainly to convince himself that he should be feeling better. They were back on the right path, and the day had grown quite overcast while the air held the scent of rain. That dog had placed more of a strain on his system, both mentally and physically, then he had realized at the time. Now it was difficult to suppress some unsavory memories. It played out over and over again between his ears. That man, the one they called Blackie, he always used a bull-hook, the long stick with the sharp, ugly hooked-spike at the end. He prodded and probed and liked to bring them to the very edge of exhaustion and temperament. The hook hurt. Scars and blood. Scars and blood. Prodded one too many times along the back end of the left foot, Bazil heard loud trumpeting, and it took him a moment or two to realize that it was coming from deep inside of him. A reservoir of pain and emotions that welled up over years and years of the hook spilled over, no longer contained. He finally had enough.

He just wanted the man to stop. He wanted to stop the man. But all he saw as he ran, bellowing into the night, were the cages and the body of water beyond. Who had placed them there and for what reason? The chimps were somehow malformed not-chimps. But they were still living and breathing beings. He wanted to stop. He tried desperately to stop. He could not stop.

The memories faded but the fuse was still lit.

Bazil had once seen one of the circus trucks overheating, steam belching out from beneath its hood, and now he had an inkling as to how that truck might have been feeling moments before the final convulsion.

He wondered if a similar feeling might have overcome the Monster/Man at some point. Bazil couldn't picture it, but he had a clear insight into what might have been the aftermath of such an ordeal.

The dwarf appeared all pressed together, back bowed into a hump, his forehead so protruding that it nearly obscured his penetrating, smoke-gray eyes. The ponderous forehead gave the appearance of being too heavy to be supported by the lower part of his face, which seemed to have already collapsed from the weight.

In reality it was all an illusion perpetrated by the slant of his features, which receded quickly from the hooked nose to the nearly non-existent chin and neck. Those two bottom-most features were more or less buried between his round shoulders as if he were in a permanent hunch. In spite of it all, his voice was always calm and cheerful.

"You can't help the way you act, Bazil, anymore than I can help the way I look. We have to accept that and go on believing it has a bigger purpose, even bigger than an elephant. Because look what they've done to you. What they've made you do. They just take from you and leave you nothing to live for. But I'll tell you a secret. There is something they can't take. It's kind of a place. They can't take it because they don't know how to find it. It's up here, in the head. It can be like Africa. I told you about that place, Bazil. Remember..? But it really just makes all the suffering okay. It helps to carry a picture of it though. Like these tall and perfect people standing...Only for you if would be elephants. Great beasts standing knee deep in green grass, in front of a large clear lake, surrounded by trees. Trees and elephants that go on and on forever. These great beasts have no names given to them by humans. Their minds are free, and their

memories are all their own. Someday, big fella, you will shed that name of yours, and you will be free and at peace. Your terrible memories will come to an end, and, by the grace of God, you will return home. Keeping faith is easier that way. And lord knows we need all the help we can get before we reach..."

"Memories End," Moe said as they reached the tip of a small glade. "This has to be it because I'm going among those trees and falling dead asleep."

*

Moe weaved thin flexible branches together until they formed into a small mat which he placed in a small hollow in the ground. Then, after a series of stretches and yawns, he squirmed into a comfortable prone position. "In the beginning there was nothing, and then God said: 'Let there be light', and there was still nothing, but as least you could see it." Moe looked up toward Bazil, "See, big fella, that little man ain't the only one who knows stuff."

Bazil chewed on similar branches and watched curiously. Once in place, Moe said to his captive audience, "I've got to hold onto some bit of civilization out here in the wilds, where I'm forced to gnaw weeds and suck mud. Our whole existence out here consists of walking around, looking for food. Walk and look. And eat. Walk. Look. Eat. I don't even have time to pick and choose. What I wouldn't give for a banana."

He stretched, then snuggled deeper into the hollow. "I can still smell that apple pie." He yawned and smacked his dry lips. "I'm so tired. Too tired to put this thing in a tree where I'd be more comfortable. Not that it matters much. Either up there or down here, I'm sure I'm only one step away from death." A second yawn escaped. "And I'm too tired to care if I fall down it...or if I'm dragged down by one of those hungry beasts out there in the dark...behind all those hungry yellow eyes...ah...yellow. My favorite color...What I wouldn't give for a banana..."

He peeled back the skin but, before he could take a bite, Pinky came squeaking at him. Moe ran off, running in no particular direction, just trying to get away to eat in peace. But the faster he ran, the louder the squealing behind him grew until it became so loud, a rushing roar, that Moe had to chance a look.

Pinky had become part of a larger stampede of animals led by an angry Slade. Moe immediately recognized several other humans from the circus and sideshow. Those freaks freaked him out the most, but he went on searching the onrushing crowd. He spotted Baron the lion and Bernice the elephant before he thought to watch his own hurried steps. But it was too late. He slammed into something hard and unyielding. What stopped him was a cage. He struggled against the bars but they wouldn't give; he couldn't get inside.

The angry shouts were getting nearer and nearer. In desperation, Moe ripped off his clothes and squeezed through the bars. He huddled in a corner and a cold chill darted up his spine as the cage became ringed with ugly cries and distorted faces. The next moment the crowd parted and Slade appeared at the center of the opening. He was carrying a large gun which he proceeded to point directly at Moe.

Moe closed his eyes and waited for the report. But before there was any sound of gunfire, a shadow, so dark Moe even saw it behind his closed eyelids, fell across the scene. Under the mysterious darkness, Moe's innate curiosity got the better of his fear, and he unscrewed one eye to take a peek. He recognized Bazil the very instant a loud noise went off inside his head...

Moe awoke with a shriek. Seeing Bazil standing over him, Moe said, "It was---you---were..."

"I know," Bazil replied, as his ears followed the sound of thunder still ringing across the valley.

*

Robert 'Blackie' Morrison the elephant handler had always been a bully. From a young age he always picked on those weaker and more timid and therefore less likely to fight back. As he grew, his sadistic tendencies grew as well, and that's why he took to the 'bull-hook' like a fish to water. He wanted to cut the big beasts down to size. His size, for Blackie stood just a hair over five feet but every inch was built upon pure hatred for others. He was born to a prostitute mother, and he was told his father was anyone from a handful of her clients who walked in and out of her life, and her body, without so much as a kind word or thought. A twenty dollar dad was his own way of joking about his heritage. He was grateful for one thing from his mother, that she left him upon the doorstep of the 'Sisters Of Mercy Orphanage' just outside of Modesto, California rather than drown him in a sack like some unwanted puppy. The only thing was is that the so-called 'Sisters Of Mercy' had shown him no mercy what-so-ever. They tried to beat him into submission while espousing the fear of God and the wrath of everlasting damnation, emphasized by every punch, kick and pull of his hair. As payback, on his thirteenth birthday he stole the cash from the 'children's fund' and took off for a better life upon the road.

One other thing he was grateful for upon leaving behind the orphanage was his nickname. 'Blackie' was anointed upon him by one Sister Mary Angelica, who was often times heard, in consternation and not biblical amusement, referring to the boy as having the darkest heart and blackest soul of anyone she had ever encountered in her life. He started to incorporate this new found stardom into his acts of violence. Just before pouncing upon any unsuspecting prey, he would let them know right before delivering a painful blow, that this was a 'gift from Blackie'. He lived up to his name throughout his tenure at the home. He lost count of the countless black eyes, busted lips, broken bones and blood he had left behind as his legacy. He wore it as a badge of honor to be referred to as: 'The Monster' of the orphanage. All the times he would defy the Sisters and sneak off to some horror movie marathon, where he would sympathize with the creatures and hope that at least once they would win out at the end, but they never did. This should have come as a warning to him but he did not heed the circumstances that led to the demise of all the evil monsters in the movies. What he loved more than anything was to scare the new recruits that entered his sanctum. He would hide beneath their beds at night, snarling and growling, and in his spookiest voice conjure up images for the impressionable young minds about being eaten alive if they dared to take one step onto the floor. If he could get them to wet the bed, which would bring on a beating from the Sisters, then he felt he had accomplished what he set out to do. He was the boogie man of their nightmares. He was Dracula, the Wolfman and the Frankenstein monster all rolled into one. He would carry these roles into the next phase of his life.

But he never could quite catch on to the whole religious fervor, nor latch himself to the holy roller war wagon. He just wished that for one time someone could have lain out all the angelic clues upon a table so that he could sift through all the biblical mumbo-jumbo and decide for himself. But it all came with such a high price to pay for leaving it all down to blind faith. Too many inconsistencies about the 'big picture' and some of the puzzle pieces just didn't quite fit for him no matter how hard he tried to believe. He remembered asking Sister Mary Angelica once that if her God was such an all powerful being, why did it take him six days to make this soap opera, and then on the seventh day he had to take the whole day off to rest up. That didn't sound like any 'Supreme Being' to him. That was no more than any other ordinary Joe he had ever met with a six pack of beer and a job. And what a mess he had made of things. He recalled the Sister trying to explain that the Almighty was not responsible for all the woes of this sorrowful world. That was mankind's own doing and downfall from grace. He thought about that very carefully before offering up that it was rather convenient for the big guy in the sky to have all the reward with none of the regret. Sister Mary Angelica tried to beat the religious conversion into him. He still had the tiny scar over his left eye from where the huge wooden crucifix from around her waist swung left and right with ever blow, and caught him just above the eye, taking out a huge chunk of skin. From then on it was his own blood on the nail at the feet of the man on the cross. He also came to learn just how to push the Sisters Of Mercy's buttons. He recalled with a smirk how on one particular frozen winter in the chilly orphanage he asked if he could pray to Jesus to come down from the cross because they could sure use the wood for the fireplace. Needless to say that the only answer to that prayer was a fist.

Blackie grew up alone and mean. He had once upon a time fancied himself a prizefighter, but he was really nothing more than a street thug and brawler. He was soon disqualified and banned from the ring for biting off the nose of one of this opponents. He drifted around from state to state aimlessly, blaming everyone and everything for his bad luck and current predicament. If at all possible he grew even meaner with every twist and turn in the road and his life. Like the song said: 'he shot a man in Reno just to watch him die', but this particular man was not co-operating, taking a bit too long to find his demise, and when the sirens blasting in the Nevada night were approaching ever closer and closer, Blackie hightailed it out of town. He never did know if the man he shot had lived or died. It was the one great mystery he would have to take to his own grave.

Early on Blackie had learned that one thing that provided him with great pleasure and evil joy, even more so than fighting or bullying, was to see two others going at it in a knocked down, no holds barred, free-for-all, and his being the instigator was more than half the fun. He could often be found in the seedy bars and dives in any town he was just passing through. He would pan the interior spaces of the shadowy, low-lights of the barroom for two complete strangers. He would then sidled up to one of them, telling them in hushed tones what the person at the other end of the bar thought of them in no uncertain terms, and how he had just happened to have overheard them talking trash about them to the bartender and anyone in earshot. While the first stranger was in the early throes of seething anger, Blackie would then slither on down to the opposite end of the bar to put the bug in the other person's ear about the steaming man down the aisle. He would then sit back, nursing a beer, watching as the two drunken forces of nature, like rampaging rogue elephants, roared with anger and collided in the middle of the sawdust-filled floor.

If the moment moved him to it, he would make his way to the jukebox and select a tune that was fitting for the pending conflagration. A Johnny Cash song always seemed appropriate for every occasion. As punches, kicks, claws and chairs were being thrown the man with the dark heart and black soul would be grinning from ear to ear. And if the warring factions just so happened to be two women, so much the better. The pleasure of seeing the inebriated dames do battle was enough to last him until he was either thrown out of town or walked out with a chip on both of his shoulders.

In one such town, one such seedy dive, the entire ploy back-fired on him. He was beaten to within a inch of his life by two men he decided would be his next victims. They pounded the holy hell out of him in an alleyway, and to his surprise, they had seemed to pound some sense into him as well. He never again tried to instigate a war between the lowlifes, deciding then and there, around the time of the sixth or seventh kick to his groin, that there had to be a better way to fill his sadistic impulses that would not have him ending up in a fetal position on the cold ground and taking a beating that hurt like hell.

When he healed, he moved on, and somewhere along the line, by sheer luck or last chance, he fell in with the Slade Bros. Circus and Sideshow extravaganza. The freaks freaked him out, but the animals stirred within the building attraction of pain and suffering. Theirs—not his. He worked his way up from lowlife, shoveling shit, to elephant handler. For some unknown reason the owner of the place took a shine to him. Perhaps they were kindred spirits or something. He had finally found his place in the world, and it was right next to the biggest, goddamnest beasts he had ever seen in his life. He had to meet them on equal terms and show them right off who was bigger, badder and better than them. When he found the 'bull-hook' he found his calling. The thing was like an extension of a much smaller appendage, and he took full advantage of its power and might. He even modified it some by adding and sharpening to razor edge a large spike at the very tip of the hook. This way he could jab and prod and draw first blood. He was going to beat them into submission if he had to kill them to do it, and he owed it all to the wonderful training from The Sisters Of Mercy. He thought to himself, every time he used the instrument of torture on the tame beasts, that God truly did work in mysterious ways.

CHAPTER TWENTY-ONE
Barnstorming

They were awakened by the rain. It peppered them like large pellets fired from a warring sky.

During the night Moe's clothes became entangled in the branches of his bed, and when he sprang up, the right sleeve of his tee-shirt was left behind along with some strips of material from his pants. He managed to retrieve his precious cap, but while he searched for it, he misplaced Bazil.

It was still too dark to make out even such a large shape at any appreciable distance and the rain and thunder made calling out his name futile, but Moe tried it anyway. When no answer came, Moe staggered off in what he thought to be the right direction. All it did, however, was put him in direct line with the shifting curve of the rain. He pulled the Bears cap down tighter and felt his way forward, continuing to call out into the howling winds until the elements deafened even his own ears to the pleas. He was about to panic, but a little voice from the back of his head kept telling him he would soon wake up, high and dry, from this nightmare.

A few more blind steps and his blind faith in the voice was put to the test. Moe slipped over the edge of a precipice. He was airborne. If this was a dream, he would wake before hitting the bottom. He always did.

As it turned out, it was a short fall, but a long slide and an even longer tumble to the bottom. Once there, water swept him up in its current, bobbing him off the hard ground and bouncing him against rocks until he grasped reality in the form of a tree limb and dragged himself clear of the onslaught of the swollen river.

Moe hunched against the tree, awake, alive, and miserable. His head bowed forward to keep his face out of the rain. The stream from which he had emerged was beginning to swell around his dangling feet. He would have to move soon, but in which direction? It was a difficult choice, having such freedom. He raised his head, squinted, and tried to study his surroundings. The rain slackened so he could see far enough to make out a gradual clearing just down-river.

He leapt from the precarious safety of the tree to the soggy ground, and followed the brown churning water into a cornfield, the sight of which made his heart leap into his throat. He skirted the edge of the field, looking for a break among the steady rows. In several places there were stalks that appeared to have been trampled but the damage never went deep enough for Moe to alter his course of action.

Eventually, his search brought him to a barnyard. The large farmhouse was still dark and quiet; the squeaking sound Moe heard was coming from the swinging barn door, which somehow matched that of his sneakers. Cautiously, Moe peeked inside the barn. Bazil stood in the middle of the floor, dripping mud from his huge frame.

*

"Connor, what on earth..?

"There's an elephant in the barn, Mom."

"You're dripping all over the carpet."

"What is it, Angela?"

"It's Connor. He's been out in the storm."

"I just wanted to see the elephant, Pop."

"Uh huh."

"On the one morning your father and I decide to sleep in."

"But I think it's hungry, Mom."

"Take off that raincoat and hang it in the kitchen to dry."

"But, Mom..."

"Connor, do as I say."

"But, Mom..."

"Connor."

"But it's hungry..."

"Now, young man."

"Uhhh. For Christ's sake, Angela, find out what it likes and let the kid feed it."

"Oh, boy, thanks Pop."

*

"Thanks for leaving me out there to die."

Bazil looked up from the hay bale he was tearing apart with his tusks. At the circus they were kept short and blunt, but Bazil had left between croppings and the tusks were beginning to take shape alongside his trunk. "You look rather well for a dead ape."

Moe took inventory. Miraculously, he had kept his cap; his shirt was in shreds and his pants weren't far behind in that department. He was wearing only one shoe. He had no idea where or when the other had been lost. He had just assumed earlier, when he heard them squeaking along with the barn door, that they were both intact. After taking it all in, Moe stripped it all off and laid each article of tattered clothing over a wooden stall. He set his precious cap aside to dry. Meanwhile, Bazil returned to the hay.

"That was my favorite shirt." Moe patted the remains as he offered the eulogy. "Where in the hell did you run off to?" He asked with a sharp turn in position and tone.

"It was you who went running off into the night, Moe. I was perfectly content to stand there and soak up the wonderful wet rain."

"You should have yelled or come after me." Moe was angry and annoyed.

"I wasn't in any shape..."

"You were in damn good enough shape to find this place, you big liar."

"In my own way and time. Same as you found it. No lie, just fact."

"I found it by dumb luck."

"Instinct."

Moe heard a noise and climbed quickly into the loft.

"Instinct." Bazil chewed his breakfast twice.

*

"Why must you encourage him?"

"For Christ's sake, Angela, he's five years old. Let him be a kid while he can. Soon enough he'll be too damn tired working the place to even think about elephants."

"Well, you don't have to clean up after him."

"How big of a mess can he make?"

"Just listen...Connor!"

*

Moe had exited through a loft window, slid down a rope, and slipped, unseen, into the house a few strides behind Connor. He hid outside the pantry until the youngster was finished, then Moe did a bit of rifling himself, gorging himself on all kinds of assorted goodies. He rushed through honey, jam, fruits and vegetables, bread, and things he didn't even bother to identify with more than a glancing sniff before stuffing them into his mouth.

*

"Mom...Mom..."

"Slow down now. Catch your breath."

"He said...he liked shredded wheat or fruit loopers. Just like me."

"Did you have to go outside to ask him?"

"He's in the barn, mom. And he's kinda muddy. So I'm gonna take this new box of cereal out to him."

"Connor...Connor!"

"Let him go, Angela."

"And where are you going?"

"To see a man about an elephant."

*

Moe cradled a cache of fresh fruit in his arms and waited until Connor rushed past him. Then Moe stepped off the porch and hurried to the shelter of a small shed next to the barn. There, he gorged further on the booty. After stuffing in the last morsel, he tried to rise. A sharp pain grabbed him around the middle and pulled him back to the ground. He wrapped his arms around the pain and groaned into his chest.

*

"What the hell?"

"What's wrong, Ryan?"

"How'd that kid open the barn door?"

"Maybe you...my God--it's an..."

Bazil walked out of the barn, sniffing the air. The rain was still falling but the sky appeared brighter.

"Connor. Connor!"

"Connor boy."

Bazil's ears were pulled straight back. He saw the man and woman in the window--

"Connor..."

---then only the woman. Bazil turned and walked to the shed where he scooped up Moe in his trunk.

"My God...Connor!"

CHAPTER TWENTY-TWO
Elephant At Large

ELEPHANT SIGHTED
by Martin Mulberry
County Call Staff Reporter

Yes, folks, you read it right. An elephant has been sighted and not at a zoo or circus. The large male pachyderm was seen two days ago at the farm of Ryan and Angela Jessup, R.F.D. #3, Fairmont. (That's 'Rural Free Delivery' to all you citified folks.) It is reported to have escaped from the Slade Bros. Circus which had been performing over in Farley. Soon, the show will be setting up for an extended engagement right here in our fair town.

Chief Desmond Brophy confirmed that his department has known about the elephant since its escape but figured to apprehend it before it got into too much mischief. "I was assured that the beast isn't particularly dangerous." Brophy stated. "It's just big and hungry. We didn't want the knowledge of its escape made public to avoid a panic. We wanted to avoid having folks hereabouts running around, looking for the beast, and maybe getting hurt."

Looks like we could use some help from Sabu The Elephant Boy, from all those late night movies on TV, on this one.

The Chief's advice to anyone sighting the stray elephant is to call the local authorities immediately. DO NOT ATTEMPT TO AP-

PROACH THE ANIMAL OR FEED IT! THIS MIGHT CAUSE
THE ANIMAL TO PANIC.

However, Chief Brophy had nothing to say concerning the circumstances which surround the leaking of information to the press. This newspaper heard about the elephant at large only after several national broad-
casts about the sightings. (Remember those droppings outside the grocery
store?) In my interview with Mr. Ryan Jessup at his farm, I was assured
that neither he nor his wife made any attempt to tell their story to anyone.
"We were a little leery at first to even tell the police," Jessup said. "It still
sounds a bit silly to me. But my wife was so upset. Near hysterical."

Angela Jessup saw the elephant as it left their barn and, according
to her account, it was carrying something it its trunk. She said that at
first she thought it was her young son, Connor, who apparently was the
only one in the family to have seen the elephant close up. "He's actually
taken all this quite well," Mrs. Jessup said, "but then five year olds like
a lot of attention."

Young Connor is probably the only one who feels that way about
the attention. Chief Brophy is still expressing both dismay and concern
over the leak of information. "There were all kinds of hot shot reporters
from television and newspapers at the Jessup's place almost before I got
there. I guess elephants are big news. I just hope it doesn't turn out to be
a big nuisance."

According to Mr. Jessup, that is already the case with the reporters.
"They're one h--l of a nuisance. They're everywhere, with their cameras
and microphones. They're disturbing the whole routine of the farm, the
livestock and all. Why there's some nuts out there in the field right now
taking pictures of cow pies. And this slick city woman who wants me to
wear a straw hat and bib overalls while she interviews me. I've never
worn any of that kind of stuff."

Mrs. Jessup expressed some concern about the emotional effects all
this would have on her family. She said that they hadn't really had the
time to think about the danger aspect of having such a large creature at
large around their farm.

"Everyone seems to be treating it as if the elephant was just another big friendly cow on the loose," she said. "It's a big joke to them. Like the time that Beedle family from over near Farley spotted those UFO's...come laugh at the hicks and the whole world will laugh with you. Laugh at you is more like. It's no laughing matter to us. No one seems to think that we have any feelings. It's like we're stupid or something. Who cares what happens to us when they all leave here? I am just so thankful that the baby, Bentley Michael, slept through it all. Who knows what those wild things could have done if they discovered him? They could have snatched him right out of his crib."

And no one seems to have the answers to that or to where the elephant in question will show up next. (Hold on to your peanuts, fellow Americans). But one small mystery might have been resolved. The object that Mrs. Jessup saw the elephant carrying away from the barn is believed to have been the body of a chimpanzee that is also missing from the same aforementioned circus.

Little Connor Jessup reportedly had not seen the chimp, but according to his mother he not only saw the elephant but, judging from the size of the mess in her kitchen, fed the elephant very well. Perhaps in the future it would be best for all concerned if young Connor heeded the timely words on the tee-shirt he was given by someone: PLEASE DO NOT FEED THE ANIMALS!

CHAPTER TWENTY-THREE
Missing Link

"I'm sure that's Moe's cap the little boy is wearing in the picture," Amelia said without taking her eyes off the newspaper photo of Connor Jessup, who was all smiles and cute as a button with the Bears cap resting on his mop of blond hair. "Moe must be...dead," she said matter-of-factly. "I must resign myself to it. He'd never leave that cap behind. Never. He loved it so..." Her voice wavered and trailed off at the end.

"Perhaps he didn't leave it behind," Louise said. "Perhaps he had no choice, because he was carried away before he could retrieve it."

"I just don't know anymore." It came out softly through the tears.

"I do...Slade does..." Louise stopped herself.

Amelia's gaze wandered from the newspaper to Louise. "But whose side is he on?"

"He's on the side of the show. Which puts him on our side, dear Amelia. Like it or not, we're all in this together. What's good for the show is good for us all."

"But how does Moe fit in?" Amelia stared at Louise who in turn stared at the rear of the vehicle in front of her.

"Quite well, if you can find him before the crazies do. There are fools who are probably out there this very instant shooting off their guns and Lord knows what else." Louise watched the lines in the center of the road as well.

"I should think that's exactly what Slade would want. In fact, I've been sitting here thinking that he was probably the one who let the information leak to the papers about the escape." Amelia wadded up the paper in her hands.

"Not for the reasons you may have in mind," Louise said without missing a beat. "The circus, our little world, is very vulnerable. You know what bad press can do. Underneath all the hoopla, we're just ordinary working stiffs, trying to make a buck. But we can't allow the outside world to see or know that. For them we have to be outrageous, to do outrageous things. Yet, even there, there is a limit. Not too normal or too outrageous. We balance our lives accordingly, partly from within, partly without. If the newspapers and television are going to do stories on us, we might as well turn them to our own advantage. It makes our lives so much easier. It's all in the timing, and who better then a group of circus performers to pull it off?"

"I still don't see how any of this can possibly matter to Moe." Amelia said, staring out the window at the soggy scenery rolling by her.

"Well, our odds of finding him should improve considerably now that we're moving the show closer. That's something, and you're going to have to learn to take what there is whenever you can. Things aren't always as clear cut as we'd like them to be. No easy answers for us, in black and white." Louise looked from the wheel to the woman beside her. "For more years than you've been alive, I've been looking for a reason...something to make life worthwhile, not just seem it because I can attach some metaphysical nonsense to it. There, at the beginning, or here, at the end. It's the in-between with which I am more concerned."

The long caravan of trucks and trailers and assorted vehicles rolled along through the rain in fits and starts, but Louise never lost her train of thought, although to Amelia it did seem to veer sharply from its course.

"When I initially joined the sideshow," Louise continued, "its sole purpose was to shock and mortify the audience. Only, it was the freaks who were really mortified by it all. They were your usual assortment of fat ladies and tall men and so on. But I took that collection of oddities and deformities and worked it into a unified theme: *The Evolution Of Man.* It was a rapid transformation, one our ragtag little group badly needed. So there was no instant when someone could point and say, *there* was the transitional point. *There* was the time and place where the Monster/Man became Homo Erectus, or *here's* where the Tattooed Lady grew hair over her body and joined the ranks as one of our distant cousins. We simply manufactured the major roles and only now are we beginning the long and arduous task of filling in, in order to give a clear picture of the entire ensemble..." Louise could not be sure when she first realized that she had lost her audience and was just talking to the tune of the windshield wipers. Her opening confession fell on closed ears, with no absolution forthcoming.

The pickup glided around a curve, and Amelia pulled her window up tight against the splashing rain. She hated the thought of Moe out there in that foul weather. How would he keep dry? And keep from becoming ill? Was he mortified? In pain? They were disturbing thoughts to which she had no answer. But wasn't suffering a sign of life?

*

Every bump brought a reminder of life's rocky roads to Amelia. She decided then and there that when they found Moe—and she was becoming more and more convinced that he would be found alive—she was finally going to stand up to Slade and demand more from herself and for Moe. They *were* the show. She would take the act elsewhere if she had to. That was going to be her ace-in-the-hole. Slade would never let her go, for he knew that no else among his trainers could handle the chimp. She would insist on top billing. She would demand more bananas. She would force him to fork over more and more money for costumes for all the chimps in the act. She would become a headliner just like her parents. Then she would show them all a thing or two. She would no longer be a big, fat failure. If she had to she would take Moe on the road—on the road to Hollywood! Bonzo had nothing on her smart, hairy companion. He was King Kong in a size petite dress. Oh, how Moe hated that dress. She smiled to herself and made a mental note not to insist on his wearing any more ladies undergarments. Perhaps that's why he had run away in the first place. She was giving the poor little guy mixed signals. He was losing the real ape inside. Whatever Moe wanted, Moe would get, and in turn she would reap the benefits of his happiness by getting him to perform like a champ. It would be a win/win situation. All she had to do was stand up to Benjamin Slade.

"Why wait for Moe to return?" Amelia thought out loud. "I can confront Slade for the two of us and take control of our fates." She sat up a little straighter, prouder, finally feeling that she could pull her own weight. "Fortune never favored the coward."

CHAPTER TWENTY-FOUR
Fiddleheads

Bazil completed the grave by delicately piling loose dirt and leaves atop the body.

Moments before, he had peeled the squashed carcass from the roadbed and carried it to the edge of the woods. Moe watched the entire proceedings in silence, waiting until Bazil moved away from the opossum's gravesite before speaking. "I hope you're that considerate of me when I'm gone."

"It's your own fault, you know," Bazil answered. "No one forced you to eat all that junk."

"Junk..? It was having to eat all them leaves and other green stuff that poisoned my system against decent food." Moe rubbed his stomach.

"Nonsense. And you know it." Bazil uprooted some greenery and laid it on his tongue. "Eat some of this and you'll feel much better. You just suffered a mild relapse. But you'll survive. Eat, and let that stomach ache be a lesson to you...domesticity is fine as long as it's in moderation."

"Don't tell me. Let me guess...the Monster/Man?" Moe feigned sticking his finger down his throat.

"The road is much too long to keep placing yourself in positions that come to cause you so much pain, Moe."

"No, Bazil, life's too short to keep telling yourself you're not going to eat that last donut."

However, Moe finally did as Bazil suggested and rooted around beneath a covering of ferns. He pushed the leafy fronds aside, and each time he uncovered a young plant, he snapped it off near ground level. After collecting a handful of these, Moe settled back against a rock to dine.

The young plants were of the bracken family, sometimes called pasture brake, or simply brake because they grew at the edge of fields or roads. Another common name for them was fiddleheads due to their resemblance to the tuning end of a fiddle. They had a mucilaginous texture somewhat like asparagus and were quite edible at this early stage, but once matured they became poisonous.

*

"I see she's up to her old tricks again," Slade said. He had joined Louis, making the two of them an exclusive audience to Amelia, who was busy rehearsing her chimp act.

"I merely appealed to the part of her that drives us all," Louis said."The ego. Judging from our latest notoriety, the people will want to see elephants and chimps especially."

"I guess that cop did us a favor." Slade smiled from only one side of his mouth.

"The great Curry strikes again." Louis used the other side of his to form a grin.

"That's what worries me." Slade's frown was a permanent fixture on his face now, leaving deep imprints around his mouth and at the corner of each eye.

"My mother always told me, one day your face is going to freeze that way and that frown of yours will be there forever." Louis stared over at Slade. "Has yours?"

Slade ignored the remark, rather, he said, "It's Curry. He has the power to make us or break us, what with him leading our way into these...backwoods cesspools."

Louis laughed. "He likes to think so...What's the matter, Benjamin, am I rattling your ego? You don't particularly like Curry, yet you look at him and see yourself twenty years ago: an enterprising, ambitious young man who's outgrown the enterprising and ambitious old man for whom he labors."

"That don't bother you?" Slade asked, then answered Louis' shrug. "Well, it should, because he's the one person around here you don't control."

"Doubt truth to be a liar; but never doubt my power." Louis turned away and watched the chimps with renewed intensity. "See those two there? The smaller pair?"

"Yeah...they look all right." Slade caught Louis' smirk. "You trying to tell me..."

"They're the offspring of the six. Those chimps might not have turned out very intelligent, but it takes little brain power to copulate. And even less to bear children. Humans do it all the time. You should know that. We started with some of their unfortunate offspring." Louis reflected for a moment before continuing. "I thought it best, you know, just incase Moe doesn't decided to return to have a backup plan. Amelia doesn't have an agenda. At least not yet. So, perhaps stop pushing her toward one."

Slade huffed, puffed, but kept silent.

"Our little lady doesn't think of herself or her own happiness. It's all about Moe, or at least it was. Now I'm hoping that it will be all about the twins."

"I should have been told about those two chimps." Slade watched the two with more interest himself.

"Ignorance is bliss, but it's also your own fault. All you wanted from me were results, not explanations, and certainly not details. I went along with you and rushed things with those six chimps because our doubts are traitors, and make us lose the good we oft might win, by fearing to attempt. Well, the only good that appeared to have come out of that was that elephant destroying them."

"I always wondered who placed those cages too close to that pond," Slade said. "Was it---"

Louis ignored the accusation. "I wasn't betting on those youngsters to set things right either, so I simply didn't bother to mention about their births, except to Curry who was about to replace all six of the dead chimps. We worked it out that he purchase four chimps the same age as the two offspring That way I could check their maturity and progress against more *normal* conditions."

"Does she know anything about this?" Slade indicated Amelia with a nod.

"No, she had Moe." Louis smiled self-assuredly. "But soon it won't matter who knows, unless they want to take advantage of a new breed of chimpanzee who's not only intelligent, but will remain a workable size throughout its adult life. That little discovery of yours should put your name back on the right people's lips. Now, doesn't that sound more pleasant to you?"

"And what do you get out of all of this in the end?" Slade asked.

"The right to tell whomever I want."

*

"...If I remember right," Bazil was saying, "the Monster/Man was referring to humans at the time, but the lesson should do as well for animals. Remember that little boy? The one in the barn? He took us for what we are---or should I say he took me. You persisted in slinking around, hiding from him. You should have let him bring you food. He wouldn't have harmed you."

"I left him my hat," Moe said.

Bazil studied Moe, who was idly munching on the fiddleheads. Bazil added, "Now adult humans can be a different story. An entirely different story. Take those two who yelled at us from the window back at the farm. They might've harmed us...it's the way they look at us. They think they're so good. Superior. So if we're not exactly like them then we must be bad. Inferior. If only they'd try to get to know us. But they're afraid of anything that's different. And soon they'll train their little boy to be the same way. To think the same way. To act the same way." Bazil shook his massive head. "Too much domesticity."

"Damn, I really loved that hat." Moe was currently in a world of his own.

"Love is like fishing, my friend," Bazil said. "It's always about the one that got away."

Moe was not swayed.

Bazil twiddled his trunk as he looked across the road. "They probably organized a bunch more of their own kind to come after us."

"There's no getting away from 'em," Moe said, rejoining his friend on the road. "They're everywhere. Soon there won't be any space left to grow, no place for any Memories End. I have a theory though. How they can be stopped. For the good of everyone else, they have to start killing some people off. Thinning the herd---"

"That's horrible." Bazil lapsed into a singularly horrible memory of his own. He was standing alone at the very edge of the pond, the chimp cages sinking into the sunset. He was trumpeting wildly but there was no one rushing to the rescue. "How could anyone live with that?"

"Easy. If it's done scientifically. You kill off whole families. Like that one at the farm. Then no one's left to care."

*

In a small meadow later in the day, Bazil stood mesmerized by the dancing antics of two dragonflies. They swooped and circled along the meadow grasses, stirring up the inhabitants of the undergrowth. As the insects came up to inspect the reasons behind the clamor, they were picked off with elegant precision by the two dragonflies dancing a deadly ballet.

Moe, on the other hand, was jabbing a pointed stick into the ground. "So, this place you're looking for, do you think it's like Oz or Wonderland?" Moe hoped that Bazil could read between the lines to find the cynicism planted for his benefit.

"I do not think I know those places,"Bazil said in all sincerity.

"How about Neverland?" Moe plowed forward.

"I believe Memories End is its own unique place in this world." Bazil closed his eyes and he was there. "Like nothing we've ever seen before. No cages. No chains. No hooks."

"Oh, I see it now," Moe said. "It's dreamland."

"I guess you just won't understand, Moe."

"Seeing's believing, big guy."

"But I think you'll be surprised when we get there."

"If," Moe stated emphatically. "Never forget that there is always a big *if, and* or *but* in there somewhere."

"If or and, maybe, for you," Bazil snickered. "But I already got the big butt."

Moe looked at Bazil and they both burst into uncontrollable laughter.

"You're going to be a big hit when we get there, you big oaf," Moe said with tears streaming down his face.

"Hey, Moe, you said when: *When we get there.*" Bazil trumpeted loudly.

"I did..?" Moe was rolling on the ground. "I must be as crazy as you."

When the laughter subsided, Bazil asked, "Moe, tell me about those other places."

"What other places?" Moe was trying to work out a slight stitch that had invaded his left side from all the laughing.

"Oz. Wonderland. Neverland." Bazil liked the sounds those names made upon his tongue when saying them.

Moe was slowly brought back into reality. "Just three more places that just don't exist."

Bazil was convinced that he liked the laughing Moe a lot better than the cynical one.

*

In the evening, Moe once again made his bedding from the branches and leaves that were strewn upon the ground after the storm. He lay there restless and grumbling. The full moon above was shining down like a beacon and lighting up their hiding place for all the world to see. He was just about to give a shout to the heavens to turn down that blasted light, when he heard Bazil say, "How do you think the angels get to sleep when God leaves his porch light on?"

Moe didn't care. He grumbled something beneath his breath, and tried to beat a soft spot in the leaves to lay his head. Nothing seemed to work, and he was beginning to resign himself to another sleepless night when he heard the singing. It was soft and low, and not too unpleasant.

Eyes closed, Bazil was swaying and singing:

"Looks like the night is here to stay
And the rain won't go away
Will we ever see the sun
Well, a little rain never hurt no one

Tomorrow is another day
Tomorrow the rain will go away
Maybe tomorrow we'll see the sun
But tomorrows never come

Down around the trees
Where it's always safe and warm

Hidden in the reeds
In a garden grows the last rose"

Moe fell asleep somewhere between the fourth or fifth time Bazil repeated the words to the song. He slept and began to dream.

They were running. Running in the woods. Running away from the mob of angry humans. All of them, every man, woman and child carried torches, pitchforks and rifles. Their bellows of ugly curses and hatred drowned out the sweet chirping of birds and the soothing babbling of brooks. Moe looked back and saw the mob gaining on them. He knew right then and there that they were finished. The journey had come to an end, and an unpleasant end at that.

But then the light broke through. It filtered down from the trees. No, not from the trees, from the heavens above. It was guiding them through the forest, and away from the crowd. Moe knew in an instant that the light was meant only for them. The humans could not see it. Therefore, they could not follow. The light led them to a garden, the like of which Moe had never seen in any lifetime. It was beyond description, for mere words could not do it justice. There was light, warm and inviting. There were trees, tall and strong. There was fruit, plump and plentiful. There were animals, safe and thriving.

He looked all around and could see no circus tents. No long trailers in the dust. There were no cages, chains, bull-hooks or confinement of any kind as far as the eye could see. The animals were free. They were fat and sassy and happy. And they all seemed to be as one with this place. This paradise. This home.

Moe awoke from the dream with an aching in his heart. He looked to Bazil , who had stopped singing sometime when Moe was in dreamland, and was gently swaying with his eyes closed. Moe had a pretty good idea what the big lug had on his mind. But he was not quite ready to confide in Bazil about what he had...*dreamt*.

He was not quite ready to admit that maybe, perhaps, just maybe there was a Memories End after all. He fell back to sleep and, try as he might, he could not find that place again in his heart.

*

Moe left Bazil asleep in the meadow. The chimp was on a mission to retrieve the one thing he believed he could not live without in this or any other world. They hadn't traveled too far and if he could just be in and out with no unforeseen troubles in between, he would be back and napping before Bazil even knew he was gone.

Moe backtracked to the farm. He scurried unseen to the barn. Fortunately the door was left ajar, and Moe entered with only the moonlight streaming through several upper windows for guidance He searched, but he could not find the tattered belongings he had left behind. Most disappointing, his cap was nowhere to be found.

Moe exited the barn in a bad mood and with only one thought in his mind: the damn kid. He scampered across the lawn and took the front porch steps in a single bound. He tried the door but it was locked. Moving along from one window to the next he found them all sealed up tight. There was no way of getting in from the ground floor. These folks were snug in their cage and had taken all preventive measures against intruders of the night. But they didn't know jack about Moe. For him, where there was a will, there was a way in.

Moe backed off the porch for a better view of the second story of the farmhouse. The only light was rather dim, exiting through the blinds of the room in the left-hand corner, but he spotted it and took off in a hurry. With a leap to the drainpipe and a scurry up to the gutters, he was on the roof in seconds flat. On all fours he made his way to the room with the light.

Moe peeked inside, adjusting his eyes through the window pane to the soft light in the bedroom. He found the shape on the bed.

The boy had kicked off the covers and was hanging precariously on the very edge of the bed. Moe thought of the contortionists at the circus: how they twisted their bodies out of shape and then sprung back good as new. This kid had potential. The room was filled with the usual gadgets, games and thing-a-ma-bobs of a typical boy's room. Moe spotted the comic books upon the floor and made a mental note as to what to take along with the cap. *The cap*—where was his cap?

Moe scanned the entire room and came up empty. He was about to make a second survey when he saw it, hanging from the corner bedpost right above the sleeping kid's head. Moe tried the window.

LOCKED!

Moe swore out loud and then placed his hand across his mouth. The kid stirred gently. Another turn and he would be on the floor, awake and screaming at the hairy beast at his window. Moe thought for historical authenticity he should really be hiding under the kid's bed. He waited for the child to settle back into dreamland, and then his fingers traced all along the outside of the window. Not a crack or a seam out of place. There was nowhere to dig his fingers into the wood and make an open space to reach within and *pop* the lock and the latch.

Moe looked back inside at his cap. His precious possession—so close but yet so far. A determination like no other came sweeping in on him as he grabbed hold of what little was available on the window and the sill and started to *pull* with all his might. He used every ounce of strength within him to try to budge the unbudge-able. The only thing that happened was that he lost his grip.

Moe somersaulted across the roof, slid for about five feet on the slate shingles, and tumbled over the top. He reached out to try to grab hold of the rainspout but he missed. He fell off the roof and hit the ground, landing straight into a bed of roses and all their spikes. The entire incident had become a thorn in his side.

Moe regained his footing and his dignity. He pulled a few thorns from his fur, but nothing was as badly bruised as his pride.

He hated to admit it but he was defeated. He knew that he'd have to leave that precious part of him behind. Dejected, he shuffled along the side of the farmhouse. Someone would have to pay the price for this failure.

Moe left a small gift for the family on the front porch where he was sure that they would find it. He would have liked to bag it and set it afire, then watch from a safe distance as one or more of the occupants inside tried to stomp it out, but he had neither time nor his Zippo lighter. Besides, his antics on the roof caused another light to shine into the night from an opposite, upstairs bedroom window. He had been found out.

Moe didn't like being so crude, but after all, they left him little choice. He was feeling kind of wild at this moment in time. He also wanted the humans to know that there was a price to be extracted for the cap.

Moe made his way back to the meadow without further incident. He settled in with a heavy heart and a long sigh to match.

"Find what you were looking for?" Bazil asked without stirring.

"Shut up."

*

The next afternoon Moe was sitting beneath a huge oak tree, with the incessant buzzing of bees above his head, and wondering to himself if he could really make a home for himself somewhere in these woodlands. One thing he had come to notice more and more of in these woods was that most of the critters in the wild were either in pairs or scurrying along with kits or cubs. Even back at the circus he knew that the other chimps paired off within their cages. Hell, even ol' Baz had Bernice and Pinky as companions, if he wanted. Moe, for the life of him, could not recall ever being part of a family, unless one was to count Amelia, and he wasn't one to do so. His birth was shrouded in mystery, at least that's what he liked to tell himself. He never knew either one of the chimpanzees that were responsible for his being brought into this world. No hugs or kisses or fawning over the newborn. All he could remember, as if in a dream, where harsh bright lights suspended from a ceiling, his wrists and ankles strapped down on a small, uncomfortable bed, and needles being stuck into his arms. He could still hear the *hoots* and *screams* within the darker recesses of his mind, and he believed at times that perhaps it was he himself that was responsible for those self-same hoots and screams. Then one day it all came to an end, all the pain and emptiness, and he was brought into the world of humans, animals and circus lights. For the very first time he was cradled in the arms of another being and, at the time, it felt good. Or at least it did not hurt. Moe really didn't like dwelling on the past. Sometimes too painful—other times just boring. He was one for living in the present. And speaking of the present, something was *drip, drip, dripping* down upon his head. He looked up toward the top of the tree and saw a huge honeycomb dangling precariously out on a limb. It was the honey from that comb that was drip, drip, dripping on him. The chimp smacked his lips and decided to play the little thief that he was and steal the sweet nectar right from under the noses-- *'do bees have noses'?*, he thought, as he scampered up the tree.

Moe only saw a few of the buzzing bees circling around the limb. He hoped that perhaps the workers or drones were out and about gathering more juice for the comb. He shimmied out to the very edge of the tree limb and began to inspect the prize he was about to abscond with in a moment or two. He reached out and took a furry pawful of honey and *slurped* in down with wanton abandon. It was sweet and sticky and--

--the first bee stung him right below the right eye.

Moe swatted at the pest and sent it spiriling downward into the oblivion below. The diving bee must have sent out some sort of signal to the others for they began to buzz and swarm and attack.

Moe, in defense, took hold of the honeycomb, swatted at a few of the buzzing pests, and dove down into the mossy mess beneath the oak. He hit the ground running, with the angry bees in pursuit.

They flew at his eyes, nose, mouth and any other extremity that was exposed and vulnerable to stinging. For some reason he could not ascertain at the time, Moe would just not let go of the honeycomb. It was in his possession and he was not about to give it up. Not until almost his entire body began to swell. There was no telling how many stingers were now lodged from ass to elbow in the little primates regions. The appendages on his paws could no longer hold their firm grip on the object of his obsession. He had to let it go. With tears in his horribly swollen eyes, he dropped the honeycomb and hightailed it into the shadows of the woods. A few bees kept up the chase, but only for show, they soon circled back to the rest of the hive.

Moe limped and shuffled to a small stream, looking at the stingers and the damage done. He didn't even recognize himself. He washed away some of the pain, but there was more than enough to linger well beyond his hurting pride. He decided to find his was back to Bazil and accept whatever snide remarks or 'I-told-you-so's' were forthcoming from the pedantic beast.

Moe waddled in on Bazil swaying gently in the cooling breeze of the late afternoon. "Dob sab ab worb." The chimp wasn't sure how to work the words out of his swollen tongue.

Bazil nodded as if he understood. The big fellow did not say a word.

Moe sat off to the side and began to pick the stingers out of his flesh and fur. It took him the rest of the afternoon and into early evening before he finished.

A restless sleep followed, and he wondered if at some point in his upbringing, if someone from his non-existent family had told him or scolded him for trying some sort of mischief in his young life, if that would have eased him into thinking that stealing the honeycomb from right under the noses of the bees was such a great idea. Then again, all he could think about before he fell fast asleep was: *'Do bees have noses'?*

CHAPTER TWENTY-FIVE
It's A Jungle Out There

HUNTERS SHOT
by Martin Mulberry
County Call Staff Reporter

Since it was made public three days ago that an elephant was loose in the area, four hunters have been shot, including a boy of fourteen. He was shot in the right foot when the .22 caliber rifle he was carrying discharged accidentally. His injury is not listed as serious and the same diagnoses have been handed down for the other three men.

Hollis Turner, 36, of South Street, Fairmont and his brother Harold, 34, of R.F.D. 6, Fairmont were both struck by the same bullet. A spokesperson at Fairmont General Hospital said that the bullet passed through Hollis' buttocks and lodged in Harold's thigh. Both men are listed in good condition.

The closest to a critical, perhaps fatal, injury was sustained by Thomas Varney, 45, of nearby Winston. He was hit in the forehead by a bullet that apparently had ricocheted off a rock before striking him. "I don't know if I heard the {actual} shot or the bullet hitting the rock," Mr. Varney said upon his release from the hospital. He was still wearing a large bandage on his head. {The bullet} only broke the skin some. But left a pretty good sized welt. I guess I was lucky. I was far enough away from whoever shot and from the rock he hit, so I figure the bullet flattened some and slowed quite a bit. I guess if you're gonna be shot, that's the lucky way." No arrests have been made in any of the mishaps.

In addition to the gunshot wounds, the hospital reported numerous injuries related to the heightened activities in and around our local wilderness areas. There have been reports of pulled muscles, broken bones and sprains; also bee stings and dog bites; and an outbreak of poison oak and ivy. One man went so far as to complain that his foot had been crushed while in his sleeping bag when he was stepped on by a rogue elephant.

It has been further learned for you by your intrepid local reporter that the elephant's traveling companion and partner-in-crime is one "Moe" the chimp. His owner and trainer is one Amelia Boone, of the once-famous family of wire-walkers, the Death-Defying Boones. Look out, Amelia---fame (or will it be infamy?) lurks. The entire district waits with bated breath to discover the whereabouts of your little escape artist and his ten-ton co-conspirator.

Although much of this may seem humorous to those of us who are following these misadventures from our homes, several of the local women are taking it very seriously. They have moved themselves and their children into the city and vowed not to return to their homes until the elephant is caught or destroyed. Temporary shelters have been set up in some of the local churches and the Red Cross is on hand with donuts, coffee and other assistance.

Chief Desmond Brophy is another one who is not laughing. "We've been fortunate so far; no one's been seriously injured. But how long can we go on trusting our luck? We haven't lost anyone, but we're investigating reports of livestock being killed. Cows mostly, but someone apparently mistook a large sow for an elephant."

He may not have been amused but Chief Brophy could not hold back a slight smile when he revealed that someone shot a Volkswagen Microbus full of holes. "The d--n thing was parked along Morgan's Creek at the time. Unfortunately, it was painted white and light blue—close enough in color and size to the beast, and just as hard to drop."

Unfortunate as well is the lack of new information coming out of all these incidents. There's a lot of acreage out there into which an animal even the size of an elephant can disappear, and most of the land is covered by thick forest. "We can't say he's in there yet," Chief Brophy said, "but if he is, I don't know how we'll get him out. Maybe we can get his handler from the circus to stand at the edge and call him." He went on to say that he had a call from a handler at the circus, a man calling himself Blackie (given name Robert Morrison) who is very familiar with this particular elephant. The man has offered his services should they be needed. "He said all he needs to bring the beast to bay is something he called a 'Peavey Hook'," Brophy said. It's also called a "bull-hook". For those of you not in the know, it's an iron-pointed lever with a hinged hook near the end. Sounds like a medieval torture device of some kind. This reporter would not want to be on the receiving end of that thing.

Or, if that fails, and Sabu the Elephant Boy is no longer available, perhaps Tarzan will come to our rescue, as he did a few years ago when he visited our annual Outdoor Exposition. That particular year, Jock Mahoney, avid sportsman and former Hollywood stuntman and King of the Jungle, was our special guest and his appearance made the show a tree-rific success.

One of Jock Mahoney's movies was 'Tarzan Goes To India" in which he used the famous Tarzan yell to save a whole herd of elephants. How could one such a creature resist? AH AH AH AH AH!!!

CHAPTER TWENTY-SIX
Survival Of The Fittest

Arthur Curry completed another circuit of the circus grounds. The intermittent periods of rain had not discouraged nor dampened anyone's spirits. At least the rain had washed the you-know-what off his shoes, he reflected. The crowd was large and enthusiastic, yet Curry had gone relatively unnoticed in spite of wearing his finest finery. It was an indication the crowd, and its fashion sense, was drawn from beyond the local burgs.

"There's some money out there," Curry said to Louis at the entrance of the sideshow.

"You thinking of selling out?" Louis asked.

"I don't think they're in a buying mood just yet. But any selling is Slade's business. Does that bother you?" Curry straightened his silk tie.

"I haven't really thought about it," Louis answered.

"Well you should---think about it."

Curry started to walk away but stopped when Louis said, "Don't start anything you can't finish."

"Me? I didn't turn the vultures of the press loose." Curry pointed an angry finger at Louis. "Now, can you stop them from making this show a valuable commodity? Can you blame Slade if he decides to sell your little collection there right out from under you?"

"Anyone in his right mind knows that this sort of fame is short lived. It lasts as long as the story is kept fresh in the people's minds. Who'd be stupid enough to buy under such transient conditions?" Louis smiled in that smug way he knew got under Curry's thin skin.

"When I said there was money out there, I didn't say it was smart money. There's some yahoo out there offering fifty thousand dollars for Bazil—dead. He wants to stuff the body and display it in his dentist's office. That cop, Brophy, is having a hell of a time keeping that quiet."

"Apparently he's succeeding very well." Louis lost the smile but kept the smugness.

"Oh, he's a slick old dude. He gives me these *useless* bits of information, so I'll think I'm still in his confidence. But he doesn't trust me. He's convinced I spilled the beans to the press. You're making it tough for me to do my job, Louis."

"You think you'll still have one if Slade sells out?"

"You'll have to ask him." Curry moved away and lost himself in the crowd.

*

Louis called Slade aside while the Big Top was filling for the first performance.

"Curry tells me you've had a few offers," Louis said.

"What? To run me out of town?" Slade felt like laughing but kept his face straight.

"No. The kind that has you walking away free and clear. Only you and I both know it doesn't work that way...and Curry must have figured we'd have this conversation. So what's his angle? What game is he playing?" Louis went on questioning himself in silence for a few moments, then summed up, "He's up to something."

Slade's worry lines deepened. "Not another exposé. That friend of yours, that dwarf. He took ten years of my life with him when he disappeared. I never knew if or when he would show up again and spill his guts."

"That was more than a year ago. And I told you then that he had no intention of *freeing* anyone but himself." Louis let his mind slip to an image of the little man.

"Yeah, but worrying is the only thing I do well these days. Like I've been worrying about the reporters that've been snooping around here lately. What if they want to do a story about the side-show?" Slade was sweating despite today's cooler temperatures.

"No problem. Manuel will handle it; he's very articulate. Much the same as August was."

"That's him. August Pure---something or other. Ever hear from him?"

"No," Louis said curtly. "Manuel knows the part. He can give the reporter the rundown---or run around. Show them the make-up. The theory behind the show. It's doing quite well in fact. Curry's right about one thing---if we can find a fool, the whole show will bring a good price."

"You suggesting we sell and disappear like August the Pure dwarf?" Slade found that practiced smile.

"Ask Curry."

*

Moe felt a whole lot better in the morning as the swelling was sub-siding. That is until he watched the black speck as it turned cir-cles in the sky. He fought off droplets of rain to keep tabs on each three-sixty that brought the speck steadily downward, until it spi-raled into the shape of a hawk. Moe tried vainly to interest Bazil in the drama that was about to unfold, but the elephant was truly gray lately. In spite of the weather, which meant plentiful food and rolls in the the mud, Bazil had grown into a solemn giant.

Moe couldn't figure out the melancholy, particularly since they were nearing Memories End, so from his little nest at the edge of the small field he switched his attention to the hawk's prey. It was a medium-sized rabbit that had inched its cautious way to some sweet young clover. The rabbit's ears swiveled continually, but it was apparent to Moe that they weren't picking up any sound from above.

Up there, the red-tailed hawk was now visible for all to see, but only until it completed a final swing of the area. Then it plummeted, arrow-like, toward the hapless rabbit. At the same moment Moe sent a projectile of his own: a rock that landed in the vicinity of the rabbit. The rabbit made a short turn, which turned out to be long enough to dis   turb the hawk's delicate calculations. The bird clutched air with one taloned foot and only gained a temporary foothold on the rabbit's flank with the other. The squirming prey came loose the second it was lifted off the ground.

Moe watched the brief encounter with interest, but as the rabbit scurried away Moe caught the scent of blood and became uneasy. He was even more unsettled when the hawk banked toward him. Moe ducked out of reflex, but the dive never brought the hawk near enough to be any real threat. Yet Moe was certain there was vehemence in the hawk's piercing shriek.

"Did you see that, you big gray beastie?" Moe said to Bazil, his eye still skyward.

Bazil looked up from his foraging but said nothing.

"I saved that rabbit's life," Moe continued, "and all I get for it is a bird trying to snatch my eyes out."

"I don't think you did either a favor." Bazil seemed to be there and elsewhere at the same time.

"Well, well, it talks. Or is that you? Perhaps there's a little dwarf in there---or seven little ones---pulling your strings?"

"What good it is for the rabbit to live now? It will forever have the shadow of death hovering over it."

"Who's talking about the rabbit? It's me I'm worried about." Moe checked the sky again. It was empty except for the increasing clouds that promised more rain. "He wants *me* now...what, no answer to that? How about the Monster/Man? Doesn't he have an answer for everything? Come on, ask him for me?"

Bazil turned his back on Moe.

"I don't get these mood swings of yours," Moe said to Bazil's backside. "One minute you're singing---the next you're in mourning. Haven't you learned to let go?"

Bazil kept his memories to himself. He knew from listening to his diminutive mentor back at the circus that memories were really road maps to one's own soul, showing you where you have been and guiding you to where you want to be. But lately, Bazil had begun to question his own memories, and whether they deemed him worthy and sacrosanct enough to enter a place such as Memories End. He had his doubts.

*

After introducing the first act Slade slipped out the back to have a smoke. Curry was waiting for him with a question. "Did you see any familiar faces in the crowd?"

Slade took a minute to enjoy the cigar. "I can't believe that I still have a trailer full of these bad boys left. Ever since that--- What were you saying?"

"Anyone in the crowd you recognized?" Curry sounded annoyed.

"Prospective buyers no doubt." Slade exhaled with pleasure.

"Louis sure works fast." Curry nodded contently now.

"Just what the hell is going on here?" Slade suddenly lost interest in the cigar.

"Nothing," Curry said. "I was just stating the obvious. Louis took it from there. Probably has a guilty conscience."

"I seriously doubt if he has one at all. So I wouldn't play games with him. With Louis sometimes I get the feeling that I'm dealing with both Dr. Frankenstein and the monster at the same time." Slade checked to see if the cigar remained lit.

"Knowing Louis, I think he'd prefer Mary Shelley or James Whale." Curry saw the references sail over Slade's top hat.

"I get the feeling more and more that we're all just marionettes. He pulls the strings, and we dance." Slade took a puff but it had lost its appeal. "I'm getting pretty sick and tired of dancing to his tune."

"Then maybe it's time to change the record," Curry said. "Okay, like I was saying, there *are* some people here from the big shows tonight and there'll probably be some offers. Maybe not even serious ones, but there's no reason why you can't use them to your advantage. I came here to work for you---not that fat so-and-so. I'm not even sure I can accurately call him a son of a bitch."

"Well I'm sure of one thing," Slade said, pitching the half-smoked cheroot aside and checking his watch. "Any legitimate offers will be for individual acts, not the whole show, and that leaves both of us an out. Our only shot at immortality is to keep the show together. Louis is doing us a favor by keeping us around. He could attach his sideshow onto any big operation. You'd be surprised what people won't see when enough money---or just the thought of it---is waved in front of them."

"We've both been hanging around Louis too long," Curry said. "And so has Amelia. You think he has something cooking with her?"

"Such as?" Slade looked around for the cigar, regretting the waste of a good smoke.

"If I've read the reporters right, she's going to become a big number because of that ape. And Louis might have the inside track." Curry stepped back and crushed the cigar under his heel.

"I'll have to ask him." Slade gave up on the treasure hunt as Curry began to walk away. Slade asked after him, "Do you understand any of what Louis has been doing?"

"We're the opposite sides of the same coin. I manipulate with a handshake and a promise, he uses science and a Petri dish. The biggest difference is, when I slip up it costs us plenty to redeem ourselves. He slips up and he just kills the mistake and moves on to the next."

"Both of you are costing me dearly."

"You get what you pay for." Curry slid back closer to Slade. "To me he's no better than a witch doctor."

"And to him you're no more than a snake oil salesman." Slade looked Curry straight in the eyes.

Curry didn't blink when he said, "That's still a step up from a politician or lawyer. More important, what am I to you?"

"You're both pains in my ass," Slade replied without hesitation.

"Do you really want to go into Louis' lab, look under the veil and peek into the darkness? Haven't you ever read Nietzsche?"

The blank expression on Slade's face gave Curry his answer.

"If you gaze too long into the abyss---the abyss gazes back into you." Curry turned and hurried away. "Be careful you don't become one of those monsters yourself."

Slade watched the advance man walk away and kept his eye on him all the way to the Midway, where he blended in with the crowd.

"Just what I need, more psycho-babble and mumbo-jumbo." Slade stalked away in the opposite direction.

*

Amelia cornered Slade near the Big Top.

"When Moe is found I demand--"

"No."

"I want the two of us to--"

"No."

"His incentive would be for more--"

"No."

"I will up and leave with--"

"Not your property." Slade turned from her and began to ease himself away from the conversation. "Anything else?" He stooped to light a cigar.

Amelia wanted to cry but she knew she needed to show a brave face and stay strong. "You know full well Moe won't work with anyone else but me."

Slade blew smoke rings around her.

"This conversation isn't over yet."

"Hell, looks to me like it never got off the ground." Slade huffed and puffed. "Kind of like you and your wire-walker days."

The last jab hurt her. She was letting Slade get away with it and away from her.

"I want to talk about it now." Amelia sounded stronger than she felt.

"What would you like to talk about?" Slade turned with a sneer. "The elephant in the room? Oh, wait, we can't talk about the elephant in the room because the elephant is no longer in the room. He is gallivanting off in hell's forty acres with that god-damn monkey of yours." Slade was right in Amelia's face, invading any space that she had, making her feel uncomfortable. "So, young lady, you are in no position to bargain for anything. You're lucky to still even be here. If I had someone else who could train those other chimps your ass would be on the same road as those two runaways." He knew it was all bluff. He didn't have anyone else and she knew it. And nothing in this place really belonged to him any longer. He was just waiting for Louis or Amelia to leverage that knowledge against him. This, he was certain, was just the first volley.

"And what if, when Moe returns, we just slip off into the night again?"

He was right. Second volley.

"That would be stealing."

"Moe belongs to me now. You know it. I know it."

"Right now I'd say that little ape belongs to the wind. If he returns he's caged." Slade hated it when the hired help tried to rebel. "And you are out of line."

Any bravado that Amelia had built up was slipping away from her. She didn't say another word as Slade turned his back and strode off.

Amelia walked the walk of the living dead as she slid past the Big Top and into the crowd. The show must go on. She held onto the only thing she could at this time. Once Moe was found and back among them, she would have more of the upper hand against Slade. If she didn't perform, then Moe didn't perform. "Let's see how he likes that," she told herself. She was far from convincing.

CHAPTER TWENTY-SEVEN
Genesis

A *MONKEY SHAVED*
(First Of Two Parts)
By Martin Mulberry
County Call Staff Reporter

W.S. Gilbert, a showman in his own right, once wrote: 'Darwinian Man, though well-behaved, at best is only a monkey shaved!' This is hardly the place to argue the validity of that statement; but last night, after the circus sideshow closed, one ape/man shaved. Or to be more precise, he peeled off his beard, revealing the man beneath. His name is Manuel, no last name, at least not one he was willing to give up for this reporter.

"I had one once," he said, "but it was bigger than I was. I couldn't carry it around, or live up to it, so I dropped it." Something else he dropped was the veil of illusion which surrounded the sideshow. "We supply the make-up---as you can see my natural beard in hardly worth mentioning---and the audience brings the imagination. The only thing mysterious about the show is the fact that it consists more of a theme than a series of disjointed peep shows. But that's really more unique than mysterious."

The theme of the show is evolution, a touchy subject in our class-rooms nowadays, especially in this enlightened (or UN-enlightened) neck of the woods, but one that clearly spells money for the performers. "What it comes down to," Manuel said, "is survival. Call it 'of the fittest' if you like, because as can be seen most of us freaks are well suited to it. In fact, it's the only thing that suits most of us."

Manuel refused to speak of how he had come to fit into this particular niche in life, or of the misfortunes, other than the obvious physical ones, that brought the other performers to the circus sideshow to live a life strung from small town to small town, and from performance to performance, without even the illusion of freedom that the rest of us must have felt at the thought of running away to join the circus. The smell of grease paint, the roar of the crowd. Elephants. Lions. High wire acts. The fat lady, the world's tallest man, and the dwarves.

"That's what the people expect to see," Manuel said, "and perhaps it's why they're disappointed at first. Because instead of the run-of-the-mill freaks, they get to see what might well be a piece of themselves. Not that it's bad or that they don't like change. In fact, change is what makes the world go round. That, and the reliance on clichés. People would feel much better about change if it evolved into the image and likeness of you-know-who---but there's always some little freak of nature coming around to mess up the picture. To play with their minds and say 'not so fast'."

Manuel grins widely and often when he speaks. He enjoys what he is doing, especially when he is being part of a little controversy, to use his pun, which goes to show that he doesn't take himself seriously. Therefore, he never has had to develop a thick skin like so many of us. For some reason or another we come to believe that we have been afflicted by some inadequacy which opens us to ridicule and criticism. Often these shortcomings are nothing more than illusions or something as minor as pimples or a few extra pounds. These all fade in the light of Manuel's burden. He can peel off the make-up of his act and joke about losing his last name, but he can't set aside the fact that he is a dwarf. He is a four foot adult and the outside world makes very few concessions to size. In fact, bigger has always been thought to be better.

"I am a pair of brown shoes in a tuxedo world," laughs Manuel, as he removes the make-up and replaces it with a brave face.

Right here in the Fairmont area there is a proposal for a large shopping mall which would undoubtedly change the face of the landscape *as well as the business community. Those who would like to see the mall become a reality say it's the best way for the area to share in the convenience known to more metropolitan sections of the state. Of course, there's always a gamble that the venture would prove a boon to Fairmont, but it's a sure thing that the mall's construction would forever change the look of the land, much the same as the interstate did ten years ago. Local residents surprisingly have put up less of a squawk about the mall proposal then they have about what the sideshow proposes.*

"As I previously stated," Manuel said, "in the beginning the show was nothing. Then Louis, our re-creator, came along with a vision which in fact kept us all from drowning in self-pity. With his help, we made a complete break from the past and a whole new world opened to us. And we attracted all manner of new freaks to the show. The general public still took to referring to our kind as 'special people', but I believe that concession was made in order to relieve their consciences rather than ours. We are freaks but we're more like normal people than anyone would care to admit. Us included. We had the new-found freedom, but something was missing. Until my dear friend, August, joined us."

August is one August Purefoy, and the subject of the second half of this article. He played the part of the Monster/Man with the old show but as Manuel said, "He made us see that there was and is a bit of the beast in all of us." And that's where the real problem begins.

End Of Part One

CHAPTER TWENTY-EIGHT
Roadside Show

It was a quiet drive along an old, yet scenic, road which paralleled the interstate for a few miles before bending away sharply and cutting through a section of ill-kept houses and dying businesses. Prosperity had followed the new super highway, but, according to Amelia, she and Louise were chasing a wild goose which wasn't about to lay any golden eggs.

"I still say it can't be Moe." This was the third time Amelia brought up the subject.

Louise's answer was the same as usual. "We have to cover all possibilities."

"It still doesn't sound possible that someone out here could have Moe. Even if it did say so in the advertisements. Otherwise the police would have checked it out already...and you did say they were working with Curry." Amelia stared straight ahead, locking her gaze on the haze of the road out in front of the pickup.

Louise slowed the truck, leaning her large head out the open window of the driver's side to read an old, weather-beaten sign along the roadside: **GAS FOOD ZOO** 1 Mile Ahead.

"And they aren't even anywhere near here." Amelia looked off now in the direction of the slowly disappearing interstate. "What if they find him and we're not there?"

"What if this guy has him? Have you ever seen one of these places?" Louise pulled her fat head in out of the wind and suffocating heat.

"No." Amelia sounded dejected.

Louise smiled to herself and remained silent until she exclaimed, "This must be the place."

Tiny stones kicked up and pinged off the metal of the truck as she turned into the parking lot and maneuvered into an empty space. The only building on the grounds served as a combination gas station and general store with living quarters on top, and fronted the roadside zoo. The interstate was responsible for the usual lack of interest in the facilities, but Moe and Bazil had turned a lot of heads since their escape and a few of those heads were looking down the little-traveled dirt road once again.

"Why are we here? Really?" Amelia asked as she pulled her wet and sticky blue blouse away from her back. "You can't be seriously thinking this guy has Moe. Or if he did, could keep him."

"The story I heard piqued my curiosity. The elephant charging through the place. Knocking over the cages, an injured monkey left behind." Louise opened her door and a fresh blast of stagnant, roasting air hit her.

"Monkey..." Amelia hesitated at her side of the seat.

Louise pulled her substantial girth from the truck and stood in a small dust cloud that was settling around the tires. A reluctant Amelia had finally removed herself from the passenger side and joined her. While walking to the side of the building, they could see that there weren't many spectators, but two persons together around there could be considered a crowd. The owner/proprietor soon proved that to be the case. Three was definitely a crowd. The man was tall and painfully thin, as was his graying beard. His clothes and skin looked to have retained, for the past century, most of the dust and dirt kicked up by some long-past twister. He had set up a small table and a chair for himself at the gate to the chicken-wire enclosure, and Louise approached and placed a dollar bill in front of him.

When he made no move to accept it, Louise said, "For the two of us."

"Yes, indeed," he said through many missing teeth, again without reaching for the money. "That elephant almost kilt me, but I can laugh about it now. The big clumsy beast. Say, either of you know what they call a calypso-singing elephant?"

"Pardon..?" Louise said in dismay, but Amelia figured it was an attempt at a joke. Having no answer, she said nothing.

"What do they call a calypso-singing elephant?" The toothless grin remained.

"We don't know," Amelia answered after a brief, awkward silence.

"Harry Elefonte...Get it?" He laughed; Amelia smiled in spite of the fact that she was beginning to perspire heavily.

Louise nodded and pushed the dollar closer. Still the man made no effort to collect it; he only stifled his laughter long enough to ask. "Why...why don't elephants drive Volkswagens?"

"I couldn't care less," Louise said, patting her mouth with the back of her hand. "Here's our money. I trust there's no extra charge for the floorshow?"

She moved toward the gate, expecting Amelia to follow, but Amelia was waiting for the punch line.

"Your mother's a bit irritable," the man behind the table said.

"Huh?" Amelia was watching both Louise and the man.

He motioned with his head, where the receding hairline was moving back far enough to declare its secession from the front of the scalp, in Louise's direction. "Must be the heat."

"I suppose," Amelia said, tugging at her collar. "But why don't elephants drive Volkswagens?"

"Oh," he laughed hardily. "Because they don't have enough trunk space...get it? Not enough *trunk* space." The man stretched his hand out in front of his face to simulate an elephant's trunk. "I got a million of them."

Amelia smiled politely and stepped off after Louise. "I better catch up." She passed through the gate and made a quick survey of the area. The animal cages were arranged in a circle around the perimeter of the wire. Each cage was marked, although some of the printing on the signs had long since become obscured by the harsh elements.

Amelia voiced her discomfort as soon as she stepped alongside Louise, who said, "You didn't appear to be opposed to the ill-humor moments ago."

As if in spite, Louise insisted on lingering at each cage. Whether rattlesnake, horned-toad, coyote, or fox, there was little if any movement from any of them. The only thing that rose from the cages was an oppressive odor of decay, feces and death.

"The so-called ape is probably in the last one," Amelia said, trying to hurry matters along.

"You know," Louise said, "these poor pathetic creatures are a lesson to us all. In fact, they're probably a lot like most folks. If you open up all these cages, it's doubtful that any of the occupants would get up and leave."

Amelia stared at the inanimate ball of fur of which she was unable to make heads or tails. "That's because they're all dead."

"And others mournfully within the gloom of their own shadow walked, and called it death." Louise tried hard not to take a breath.

Amelia shuffled silently after Louise who was moving more rapidly now and didn't bother to stop at any cage except the last. Amelia pointed and said, "Even the spider monkey is dead."

"Only the spirit, Amelia dear. Only the spirit." Louise had seen enough.

In the truck, heading back to the interstate, and feeling worse for the experience, Amelia said, "What do you think hit that place? It certainly wasn't an elephant."

"Greed. Boredom. Hubris," Louise replied. "In a few years, if the zoo and the man are still standing, he'll come to believe that it really was the elephant and not his own lack of imagination that almost *'kilt'* him. But can you really blame the man?"

"That place was a disgrace. The man should be in jail or, at the least, out of business." Amelia watched the headlights of the truck shine like slivers of moonlight along the highway in the waning hours of daylight.

"He doesn't know it. Probably never will see it himself," Louise said watching the same lights as Amelia, "but he's in the same cage and under the same conditions as the animals. Like most people in life he's spent all his dreams like so much small change. There's nothing to be said. There's nothing to be done. It's life and it's just that way."

"I don't know what's more infuriating, his passing himself off as running a legitimate zoo or us giving him money to legitimize the whole shameful business."

"It can be said," Louise said, "that it is no longer 'In God We Trust.' The new motto is: 'Just Make A Buck.'"

"Somehow I feel that by doing what we're doing we've become a part of the man's conspiracy." Amelia took her eyes from the road and stared at her reflection in the passenger side window of the truck. She was uncertain as to whether she liked what she saw staring back at her.

Louise didn't say as much to Amelia, but she wondered if the naive young woman knew just how close she was coming to discovering the truth. She was under the spell right now of a different conspiracy, but the roadmap was right before her, and it wouldn't take her long to connect the dots. Perhaps with a little push in the right direction from her conspiratorial companion in the driver's seat.

They drove the rest of the way back in silence.

*

Walking through the woods, both Moe and Bazil were somewhat amazed, then dumbfounded, and finally saddened and sickened by all the dead remains of animals, both on the roadsides and in the woodlands themselves.

"Freedom may not be all it's cracked up to be," Moe said, averting his eyes to a deer carcass that had been gutted and left to rot in a ditch.

"It's a high price to be paid, that's for sure," Bazil answered as he proceeded to kick some dirt and leaves upon the remains. It was a burial of sort, but with an ulterior motive. He didn't want to look at the decaying body a minute longer.

"Everything out here is all about survival." Moe plucked some leaves from a nearby branch. "Life and death. Life and death. Nothing more, nothing less." He tested the leaves, tasting them. "I don't know which I've started to see more of: road kill or the leftovers from some other animal's dinner."

"The first is just a case of bad luck," Bazil said, standing over the mound of leaves. "The other is just nature being nature. That's why I don't think you should have interfered between the hawk and the rabbit."

"Now he tells me." Moe tossed the terrible tasting leaves aside.

"The Monster/Man told me that with every blessing in life comes a curse." Bazil rocked back and forth in the moonlight.

"What's that supposed to mean?"

"The rabbit lived. So, for now, the balance of nature has to be satisfied. For that to occur, something else has to...die."

Moe grumbled and picked up a rock. "Meaning me." He threw the rock as hard as he could into the woods. They never heard it hit. "I wasn't having enough trouble sleeping at night as it is. Now you saddle me with this." Moe craned his neck for a quick glance into the sky. Nothing but the moon and a few dark clouds met his gaze."The next rabbit I see I'll just ask to commit suicide. Nature balanced, pure and simple."

"I don't think it works like that," Bazil said, looking skyward himself just as one of the dark clouds tried to persuade the moon to tone down its light.

"Well, then you, the Monster/Man, the rabbit and the hawk can all go to hell." Moe sat down in a huff and turned his back on Bazil.

"We're all chained to the natural order of things. There's just no escaping that." Bazil felt a sudden chill wash over him, and a sharp pain stabbed at his side. For a moment it felt like he had been shot—a premonition perhaps, but most likely gas. In the end only time would tell.

Morning, or maybe just hunger pains, brought a renewed vigor to Moe. He went out foraging for anything that looked or smelled even slightly edible. He found some sweet onion grass and what he believed to be some wild mushrooms. He ate them, digested, and didn't keel over in any pain or discomfort, so he continued to forage for supplies.

On his way back to Bazil, whom he had left fast asleep beside a small stream in the woods, Moe took to checking the skies at every turn in the trail. If nature needed to be balanced, and he was that balancing act, he was going to make certain that all plans for his inevitable demise were met head on with a full stomach.

"I do my best thinking when I don't have to worry about being hungry," Moe said to no one in particular. "I do my very best thinking when I can follow up a fine meal with a good cigar." Moe wondered if there was a cigar tree around or if they, perhaps, shot up from the ground like a root. He knew they were made out of tobacco leaves, and that these leaves grew from plants, and that plants grew wild all around him in these woods. So far, no luck.

Moe was brought out of his reverie by the familiar sounds of a trumpeting elephant. The warning sounds of danger filtered in upon him through the trees. Moe dropped everything he had gathered in the way of foodstuffs and darted in the direction of the call.

Moe found the small stream but Bazil was nowhere in sight. He looked all around, following the swatches of light from the early morning sun as it filtered down from the trees and flittered along the trail. Moe saw the huge shadow before he saw the real thing. He found Bazil on the other side of a huge boulder.

"What are you doing here?" Moe asked.

"Did you see it?" Bazil's shaky voice was barely above a whisper.

"See what? Hey...are you hiding from something?" A slight laugh escaped Moe's throat.

Bazil chanced a peek at Moe, but he would not come out from behind the large rock to talk to him face to face. "I woke up and you were gone. I heard something rustling in the weeds. Thought it was you. Then...I...saw...it."

"Saw what?" Moe looked into the high grass and under-growth just beyond the boulder. "I don't see a--"

The tiny creature let its head bob out from beneath a leaf, sniffed the air, and darted back for cover. Before Bazil was aware of anything else, Moe was on the ground and laughing.

"That's...that's what...you're afraid...of?" Moe was covered in leaves and dirt as he got to his haunches and stared at the big baby behind the boulder. "A field mouse."

"You don't understand, Moe," Bazil said nervously. "Even back at the circus, they were everywhere. In the hay, in the feed, in the tents. I had to watch my every step. It was torture trying to sidestep everything in fear of hearing that tiny *squeak.*"

"To him you're the size of a house," Moe laughed. "Look at it from his prospective."

In the blink of an eye Bazil got the chance to do just that. When Bazil turned, the tiny field mouse was sitting atop the boulder and staring at him. It took a moment or two for the fear to register from the tip of Bazil's tail to the top of his head, but when it did, he trumpeted to the very heavens and took off running. The boulder shook, and so did the mouse, as it scurried away into a hiding place of its own. Only Moe was left standing in the spot where the two polar opposites had been.

"Wait, you big lug!" Moe shouted after the fleeing form of the proboscidean. "It's gone."

Either Bazil didn't hear or didn't care, for he just kept running. His feet pounded the trail, sending up huge clumps of dust and foliage and filling the forest with the sound of unnatural thunder. The birds in the trees took to the sky, and the smaller creatures on the floor of the forest took off in any direction they deemed safe from the rampaging beast.

Bazil tore up entire trees, roots and all, and they cascaded to the ground with a powerful *thump!* Moe was inclined to yell *'timber'* every time a tree was uprooted or smashed to bits by the fleeing gray giant. Moe was fast on the heels of the elephant, while Bazil was picking up a full head of steam but moving blindly through the woods.

Moe heard it first: the splashing roar of a river. He could tell without even looking just what Bazil was heading for. By the time Bazil became aware of the same thing, it was too late. He tried stopping. He tried putting on the brakes and skidding to a halt. At first he thought that his feet might dig deep into the dirt, keeping him from tumbling over the precipice. But he was wrong, dead wrong, and he fell.

The big brute felt a sudden calm overtake him as he heard the soothing voice of the Monster/Man from somewhere deep inside his head, or maybe his soul. *"It is not where your story begins that matters most, Bazil, but where it ends."* These were memories that he did not wish to forget. Nor was it the time or place where he wanted those memories, or his story, to end.

Moe arrived at the precipice just in time to see Bazil sailing through the air. He followed the long trail of skid marks in the dirt, and it led him to the very edge of the hillside. Moe looked over the edge and saw the huge elephant make a huge *splash* in the water, then cast his eyes downstream. Moe's worst fear came to fruition when he saw the unmistakable end of the trail at the edge of the river. Bazil was heading straight for it.

The waterfall cleaved the river in half. One side was roaring rapids, the other a steep fall into oblivion. Moe could no longer see Bazil. The gentle giant was underwater and not coming up for air. Moe ran alongside the river bank screaming out Bazil's name, to no avail. When Moe ran out of real estate he halted and prayed. It was then that he saw Bazil.

Bazil's trunk came poking out of the water just above the roaring rapids. For a second or two, it seemed to hang there, and then the entire elephant emerged. Bazil bobbed in the water, turning and churning in the waves. For a moment or two, he was in suspended animation, floating somewhere between water and air. And then, once again, he fell.

Moe quickly abandoned the hillside and raced as fast as he could toward the lower portion of the river. He tore through the undergrowth, the thorns and brambles cutting and tearing at his fur and flesh. He had a single-minded purpose, and no amount of pain or blood was going to stand in his way. Finally arriving, he looked up to the tremendous roar and slope of the falls. The icy cold water rolled over the top, toppling at least fifty feet below into a pool filled with jagged rocks.

Moe raced up and down the banks of the river. He searched the shoreline and the nearby woodlands, but he found neither hide nor hair of Bazil. How could that massive beast just disappear from sight? Moe had no idea how deep the water was at the bottom of the falls. Perhaps Bazil was now lying in the deep end, eyes and mouth closed, trying desperately to hold his breath.

Then it happened. The water roiled slowly at first, as if a large bubble was trying to make its escape from a much smaller snout. And then that bubble burst free of the river and so did Bazil. His trunk came out of the water and sprayed the entire area closest to the bank. It just so happened that Moe was standing there at that exact moment, and the icy chill of the spray hit him with all its might. He was sent rolling backward, only coming to a stop when the trunk of a mighty oak intervened and halted his trajectory. His head hit hard and he slumped to the ground at the base of the tree.

Moe stood, a bit dazed and confused, and stared toward the falls. Out of the river walked a waterlogged and dripping wet Bazil. The elephant shook his ears, and trumpeted mud and moss from his trunk. He stood on four unsteady legs, his eyes trying to focus on the woods just beyond.

"Moe...is that...you..?" Bazil spit out the words and a gallon of water. "My God, now I know how those poor chimps must have felt."

Moe made his way to the riverside, rubbing his sore head all the way, stopping a few feet from the elephant. "Are you all right?"

"I think so," Bazil said on rubber legs.

"I think you may have broken the river," Moe said upon examination of the big beast. "Do you realize how absurd this all is?" Moe tried hard to side-step all the *drips* and *drops* of water that were falling from Bazil. "It's like an entire house being felled by a single termite."

"I can't... help it...Moe," Bazil replied, with a nose full of mud. "Those little things scare the beejeesus out of me."

"It was a field mouse, Bazil, and you're a freakin' tank." Moe expressed himself with a kick of dirt toward the big, wet beast. "I guess we found your Kryptonite."

"My...what..?"

"It's the one thing here on earth that can bring down Superman." Moe sat down on dry land, backing up until he was out of range for any sudden outbursts from Bazil's trunk. "That's what I miss the most about my old life, a good smoke and reading comic books. The freaks had piles of them just lying around in their trailers. I guess they identified with all those heroes...or villains."

The sudden *screech* in the sky above brought Moe to his knees, and, tucking his arms around his body, he was soon huddling on the ground in a fetal position. His moans and groans were barely audible above the roar of the waterfall. He muttered about being too young to die, and the balance of nature and, perhaps, chickens coming home to roost.

Bazil looked to the sky and saw the speck of a hawk just above the tree line. He looked back at the pitiful Moe and stood guard, watching over the trembling body of his companion. "We sure make quite the pair."

*

"You know, Moe, I think I saw my entire life flash before my eyes back there."

"And..?"

"I don't know."

"You sound disappointed."

"It's not that. It's just that I didn't see Memories End through it all. What do you think it means?"

"How should I know. That place is your dream, not mine. I happen to think I reside here in the real world."

"You mean where a chimpanzee and an elephant are the center attraction?"

"Don't be a wise ass, Bazil. Hey, big fella, are we having second thoughts or doubts of some kind?"

"I just thought that I would have seen a sign or perhaps been given a direction, that's all."

"I don't think you're gonna find it on any map."

"What if it's all for nothing, Moe?"

"Welcome to my world, Bazil."

"He always said: 'To keep the faith not matter what'."

"He being the man who would be monster? If I had to go through life as someone called the Monster/Man I don't think I would trust in anything I saw, heard or smelled. Let alone have faith in some fairy tale land. But, who knows, Baz ol' buddy, maybe someday we'll all grow-up to be like him."

"We can only hope, Moe."

"I was being sarcastic."

"I was renewing my faith. The world is held together by just one thing."

"Duct tape?"

"Hope."

"Oh."

"Do you remember what his name was?"

"You, an elephant, are asking me, a chimpanzee, to remember something for you? Now I've heard everything. Let's see, I think is was Badinski Lovejoy. No, maybe it was Holier-Than-Thou Pureheart. Not quite. Oh, yeah, August Purefoy. Why?"

"I just wanted to remember him for who he truly was."

"He moved on. I suggest you do the same."

"I don't think I want to leave you, Moe."

"I ain't going anywhere, big fella."

"I think I am."

"Sounds to me like you're movin' on, Baz."

"I will see you again in Memories End."

*

A day later Bazil stood at the edge of a small clearing and watched a multi-colored group of butterflies fluttering from wildflower to wildflower. Their dance was mesmerizing to the big beast, and he wished that he could be as light of foot as they were of wing. He closed his eyes and swayed to some unheard music only beating within his big heart. It was a welcoming respite from his harrowing and terrifying tumble from the falls. He opened them again when he heard a series of low growing noises coming from the opposite side of the clearing. As the butterflies took to wing and disappeared above the treeline, Bazil saw two bear cubs lumbering into the field of flowers. They were oblivious of the grey giant across the way, and he meant to keep it that way. It was only when Moe arrived that things began to go sideways and dangerous.

"What you gawking out, big guy?" Moe was carrying a walking stick and making a line through the dirt behind him as he moved toward Bazil.

"Those two small things playing in the field."

Moe took a gander and held the stick behind his head, letting it come to rest upon his shoulders. "Those are bears, Baz, we used to have some trained ones at the circus once upon a time."

"I don't rememeber them."

"They weren't with us long. I think they were sold off to pay for some other human acts." Moe spit upon the ground. "Got to get your priorities straight. We are all expendable." Moe made a move toward the open field.

"What are you doing, Moe?" Bazil seemed a bit agitated.

"Just going to have a little fun."

The chimp was off and running before the elephant could stop him.

The cubs, a male and female, were busy gorging themselves on the juicy, sweet fruit from a mulberry bush when then stopped to take notice of the strange, hairy creature, something they had never laid eyes on before in their neck of the woods, approaching them. They were both wide-eyed and a bit in awe of the antics of the beast. He was twirling the stick he was holding over his head, changing it from paw to paw, then throwing it into the air and catching it on the way down. He only stopped performing when he was standing just a few feet from his young audience.

"Once a performer—always a performer," Moe said with a flare. "I see you may have heard of the *'Mighty Moe'*." He took a long, deep bow in front of his audience of two.

The cubs just stared, mulberry juice dripping down the sides of their mouths.

Bazil was staring as well. He had a bad feeling welling up inside him, and it wasn't just a nervous stomach this time. He wanted to call out for Moe to return toward him and that they should be on their way, but he didn't want to frighten the two small things.

"I am a star. The one that draws the crowds from miles around." Moe was in his element. "I have performed for kings and queens, for paupers and peasants, and I have found no difference between the two." Moe took a quick bite of a handful of berries he plucked from the bush. "I hope you don't mind, but performing always makes me famished." Moe was now doing his own staring. "Perhaps I can interest you two youngsters in learning a trick or two yourselves."

The cubs looked to each other, and then back at the chimp. They kept themselves quiet and still. Moe had an evil thought embedded in his brain at that very moment when he saw the lion tamer cracking his whip and then was a silent witness to the elephant trainer using the *'bull hook'* on Bazil and the other elephants. But he could not bring himself to be that cruel. He wasn't that human.

"And now," Moe went on, "for my next trick."

Bazil saw it before Moe. He was about to trumpet out a warning, but it was too late. Bursting out of the tall undergrowth was a massive bear. The mother of the cubs. She was all teeth and claws and anger. Moe was wide-eyed with fright as the huge beast lunged forward and straight toward him. The only thing that saved him was his walking stick. It was still clutched in his right hand, and when he turned ever-so-slightly, the weapon caught the big brute square in the jaw. The large female stopped in her tracks, and this gave Moe the chance to run for his life.

Moe skittered across the field and did not look back at what was gaining on him. And what was gaining on him was over a thousand of pounds of fury. The bear was growling and snarling at the top of its lungs as Moe was screaming at full capacity. The two cubs stayed in place at the mulberry bush, watching their mother chasing down the strange creature that they had found a little bit amusing.

Moe hunched over on all fours and ran like the devil was giving chase, and in his mind that is exactly what he was thinking. At that very moment he wished he knew a prayer or two to say to save his life and his soul. How he wished he would have given a better listen to what that pious little man was trying to teach his big ol' buddy.

Speaking of big ol' buddies: Where the hell was Bazil?

Moe looked up to see the huge gray beast of burden just staring out across the field from the safety of his stance along the edge of the meadow.

Moe was running and shouting now, "Help me! Bazil, do something!"

The elephant just stood his ground and waited patiently right where he stood. He saw as the bear was closing in on the much smaller and helpless creature running for its life among the wildflowers. Bazil was breathing easily, calming himself, and readying himself for what had to be done. He remembered the Monster/Man teaching him how to calm himself down after his bad memories would flare up and send his heart racing and his soul to aching. Breathe. In and out. In and out. Bazil closed his eyes, breathing as he was taught. When her opened them he saw as Moe raced across the field and straight past him. He heard the chimp cursing him up and down, but he didn't move a muscle. Bazil turned from watching Moe disappear in a flash, and braced to confront the bear. Just as the massive beast was about to attack, Bazil lifted his trunk and trumpeted as loudly and as fiercely as he possibly could. He let out all the breath he had stored up in his huge lungs and the sound it produced was ear-splitting, and the mighty roar stopped the big bear in her tracks. She skidded to a halt just a few yards from the edge of the clearing where the elephant stood. It had never in its lifetime come across such a magnificent beast as this. The bear and the elephant just stared one another down.

Then, a rather strange and wonderful thing happened. The bear was backing away, but not before making a slight bow toward the other creature. Bazil reciprocated with a bow of his own.

The elephant stood at the edge of the field and watched as the mother bear returned to her cubs. The three of them lumbering off gently on the opposite side of the woods and being swallowed up by the trees. Bazil turned to face an angry and inconsolable Moe.

"You...you...you..." Moe was much too furious to complete a simple sentence.

"You're welcome," was all that Bazil said before walking away.

CHAPTER TWENTY-NINE
Evolution

A MAN SAVED
(Last Of Two Parts)
By Martin Mulberry
County Call Staff Reporter

The gaudy poster read: "See the MONSTER/MAN. The Missing Link. Proof of our evolution from the apes." The price of admission was a half dollar and what you saw was real.

"Physically, August Purefoy, the Monster/Man, would have stood out in any crowd. The terrible deformity took care of that," Louis Smith, the creator/owner of the sideshow, said. "Perhaps that's what brought him here, the need to simply fit in. But soon that became impossible because there was more to August than met the eye."

That more, according to Manuel of the missing last name, first became apparent once the sideshow completed its transformation. August was enthusiastic about the change but he became increasingly disturbed by those in the audience who expressed revulsion at his participation in such a spectacle. At first, he believed that people were finally able to see him as a human being, and not as an object of pity or disgust. It was only the show they were objecting to. They were judging him on their own level, by their own standards; but as it turned out it was their standards which were really on trial.

"There were some shaky times," Manuel said. "When he was just the Monster/Man, no one objected too much or even bothered to ask his opinion on the matter. But later the critics came out of the woodwork, accusing Louis of exploiting the less fortunate, those who had little, if anything, left except a need to have faith in something or someone. Well, August never believed that for a minute and it was then that he began to speak up, much to everyone's surprise."

"In a sense he was defending himself by defending the show," Louis Smith said. "He had faith that the new premise was a step forward, a conscious effort on part of all the performers. He saw to that. If someone didn't understand the ramifications of the change, he had the gift of communication on any level."

He believed that if you had a true faith in something then nothing on God's earth was powerful enough to destroy it. And that explained his distress with the critics. He realized that their criticism was based on half-truths, misinformation, myths, and some outright lies, but it had all the earmarks of a true belief just the same...except when it came time to reason with it.

According to August and the others, there was no way of defending the show against the criticism. It became a matter of shuffling some dates, canceling others, and skipping some towns altogether. *"It was for the best,"* Manuel said. *"There was just no way of dealing with those people. It was August who first realized that the ones who screamed and protested the loudest about evil and corruption were the ones who had the least faith. They screamed to cover their lack of faith and the fact that if they ever stopped shouting, someone might hear the sound of their beliefs falling apart, because they were built on such weak foundations in the first place. Then there were the usual death threats and 'burn in hell' bombasts that were all par for the course."* Ignore them as best you can, but sleep with one eye open. And he went on to say that they were even run out of one town with torches and pitchforks. *"I felt like we were in some monster movie."*

In the beginning, at the start of the new twist in the sideshow, they were at the height of their popularity, and this led to the inevitable hate-

speech and attacks by every preacher, priest and do-gooding bible-thumper on the face of the earth. The crowds dwindled, and so did the threats. And the show continued in low key obscurity and into backwater burgs whose residents didn't care about ascension of man or the devolution of mankind. They just wanted to see the freaks that made them feel a bit better about themselves. As long as they were segregated from the circus and the family crowd, no one seemed to care. But now, with the news around the world about the escape of the animals from the circus (to which the sideshow is currently attached) it is feared by some in the show that, "this will bring the nuts out of the woodwork once again."

August Purefoy's foundation—his birthplace, upbringing, and life before the sideshow—is another example of the mystique that surrounds the circus folk. Even his name may have been a stage prop, a convenience for the rest of us. Louis Smith admits the mystery is quite often part of the act, but in some cases it's merely another way of leaving the past behind. Out of sight, out of mind. But as Louis says, the fascination for outsiders is the same in either case.

For him, the circus, the sideshow in particular, has always been an exciting and stimulating place, even while he was growing up in a small town similar to our own fair Fairmont. "It amazed me that people like that could even exist," Louis said. "I was raised to believe that you were one of two things: either naturally good or inherently evil. But it was difficult as a youngster to distinguish between the two." I got the hint that perhaps Louis Smith came from fire and brimstone stock. "Everyone looked and acted pretty much alike where I lived. And if they knew about my, unusual to say the least, circumstances at birth, I don't know where they would have thought I fit in." Mr. Smith paused here for a moment as if a vivid, and perhaps painful, memory clouded over his dissertation of all things passed, before he continued, "Then I entered the circus and its sideshow. I guess I first went there looking for some sign. Of madness, I suppose. Or acceptance, I'd hoped. Because my father always said that, 'whom God wishes to ruin, he first drives mad'."

But instead of madness, Louis found, to use his paraphrase of William Shakespeare, that there was more to the world than found in his father's simpleminded philosophy. It seemed such a waste of time and life to build a fortress of presupposition and then defend it against everyone, instead of trying to understand how what you believed might relate to the world at large. It was this new philosophy of Louis's, so similar to August's, that bound their friendship; but like all things great and small that too came to an end.

"August became so tied up with the show. He so identified with it and convinced the rest of us to do the same. When the outsiders planted the seeds of doubt about the legitimacy, call it morality if you want, of the show, he took it personally," Manuel said. "His whole idea about not digging in behind your beliefs at the exclusion of all else came into play here." It had been long since rumored, either started by pure gossip or a rival show, that the Slade Bros. Sideshow was somehow manipulating its freaks. They were not so much born but re-born. I must say that while wandering through the Sideshow grounds at night this intrepid reporter did get the sense that there was much more here then met my keen eyes. The freaks were all staring at me as I was staring back at them. And I got the feeling I was really the odd man out. There certainly were a few oddities among them that I had no idea what they may have been. But upon questioning a few, and upon receiving the umpteenth cold shoulder, I got the feeling that their silence was more one of simple survival then keeping untold secrets. I also got the distinct feeling that they may have been getting paid, rather well, for that silence. One of the sources, that asked to remain anonymous, said that if I wanted the real story of what was going on behind the scenes, I should look no further then that monkey who was on the lam. There was something very 'unnatural' about that creature, I was told in hushed tones and whispers. He even freaked out the freaks. It was as if, my source said, that ape could understand every word you were saying. I may look into all of this one day, but for now, by the time I could find out anything worth mentioning, the circus would be long gone, and who knows what may have become of that odd little chimp. It would be quite a scoop if we were now on the cusp of some radical genesis of the next evolution. Not the far out stuff of mainly Science Fiction novels

any longer. However, it must be stated that nothing has even been proven, nor brought about in any court of law. The freaks never talked much and it went no further than just that---all talk. This reporter wonders if, somehow, Mr. Purefoy found out a bit too much about these rumors and rebelled. Or, perhaps, he was a willing participant and could no longer live with the knowledge of what they were becoming. But that's just one man's opinion. "August found a cause," Manuel went on the say, "and the thing about causes is---they can get you killed."

As was often the case with the interview, Louis Smith completed Manuel's thought. He said that, "August Purefoy never truly doubted the validity of the show. His problem was the influence he held over the other performers in the sideshow. He felt as long as he was present the others would be unable to make up their own minds about the validity of the show and the roles they were playing. He wanted them all to have, at least in their own minds, free will. Even if he came out and asked them to do it, it would still be his doing. It was a definite dilemma. It tore at him, stirring up much the same feelings that had been aroused by the critics." In the end, for August, it came down to what was best for the show, and what was best for him. Old newspaper reports that this reporter was able to dredge up only mention a few incidents, such as an arrest for drunk and disorderly, and another for wanton destruction of property. It seems that a Mr. August Purefoy, of no fixed address or occupation, was charged with stealing the baby Jesus from a church Nativity scene just before Christmas a few years back. The charges were dropped when an anonymous benefactor bailed him out and paid the church for all damages to the Nativity and peoples' Christmas Spirit. The last report ever filed on the man only mentions that a diminutive person was seen leaving the same church a day or so after the incident of the theft of the statue and Purefoy's release The man apparently left behind a number of fliers to the 'Evolution Of Man' sideshow event at the Slade Bros. Circus.

"Call it fragmentation, or the fear of it. The fear of being torn apart. So you rail at your tempters, be they your critics or your admirers, as was the case with August," Louis said. "He was damned if he did and

damned if he didn't, at least from his point of view. And that's the only one that mattered. So he did what he thought was best. He disappeared."

"It was all very much in character for the little man with a heart of gold." Manuel said. "Now you had the choice of believing that he was abandoning you. But as it turned out, his absence didn't weaken his effect on us; it strengthened it."

Manuel found one thing rather amusing upon relating it to me. "I often saw August talking to that elephant. You know, the one that ran away. I overheard him say once to that big beast that no matter what happened, they would find one another once again. He only hoped that, when that miracle day arrived, the elephant would remember him."

When asked where August Purefoy might be and if he might ever return, Manuel answered without hesitation. "I'm not really sure if he's dead or alive. My wish is that if the great man died, he died peacefully in his sleep. And I also wish to believe that all the horrible things he had to endure in his brief life, and all the terrible scars inflicted upon him and the memories he carried, have finally, mercifully, come to a humane conclusion. I also heard a rumor that he was born into wealth and that he was set to inherit. Who knows, we may find out someday soon that he owns this whole shebang." The new Monster/Man paused for a moment, tears in his eyes, and said with one final thought, "Perhaps he's gone to heaven. Or to use August Purefoy's phrase: Memories End."

CHAPTER THIRTY
An Ant In Theory

John Ciardi wrote: "An Ant In Theory? A Giraffe in Blueprint? Ten thousand doctors of what's possible could reason half the jungle out of being." Or so the Monster/Man had tried to explain to Bazil. But it was now left to Bazil alone to try to reason away Moe's unreasonable fear of the hawk that Moe insisted was following him to balance the nature of things that he, Moe, had "screwed beyond recognition."

The frightened chimp was wrapped up in a tight little ball on the hard earth, whimpering softly. He refused to move. He refused to eat, drink or talk to Bazil. The elephant had thought to himself that perhaps Moe was singing his "death song" not unlike a Native American brave would do before battle. The Monster/Man had delighted in telling Bazil stories about the old west and the history of this country. Bazil did not feel that all the stories worked out for the betterment of those who had been here before him. Life was harsh and hard back then, and it did not seem to get much easier or better as time went on.

Bazil decided it was time to change tactics with Moe.

"Do you remember snow?" Bazil asked.

No answer from below except for groans.

"I remember one time, years back when I was still a calf, when we were traveling north. Way up north, if I am not mistaken. I looked out the tiny window of the railroad car that housed us, and I saw it. Snow. It was white and pure and wonderful. I wanted to get off that train as fast as I could and play in the snow. Everyone else looked and acted miserable around me in the close quarters of the car, but I had a window seat. I can recall that the train came to a sudden halt, quite disconcerting for the rest of them. But I also remember that the jarring motion of the sudden stop jerked the latch on the railroad car, leaving it slightly ajar. No one else in the car moved an inch. Either they were too frightened or too cold to explore the new world around them. But not me. I was up for the challenge. I nosed my way to the door, and nosed my way through what was left of the lock. In a minute or two I was free. I leapt from the car and landed in the snow. Let me tell you it was everything I hoped it would be and ten thousand times better. It was cold. It was wet. It was flying every which way. And I loved it. I wanted to run away and keep running until I reached the mountains in the distance where I had heard that, even in the midst of a summer heat wave, they never allowed the snow to melt. Just think of it, Moe. A place where you could play in the snow forever and ever and never see the end of it. That was something to see. That would fill my dreams for a very long time to come." Bazil looked to the ground to see if Moe had moved. He had not. "I promise, Moe, that there will be snow in Memories End."

If Moe was listening he showed no signs of caring.

Bazil moved forward with his tale. "It was also the first time that I had a taste of the 'bull-hook'". Bazil didn't want to go there, so he went somewhere else. "Everyone else stayed on the train and stayed in their places. For as long as I live I will always remember that time I spent in the snow."

"I'm about to be torn limb from limb by sharp talons and he's talking about frolicking in the snow." Moe spoke without moving.

"I am happy to see you're still among the living," Bazil said. "And I wasn't only talking about that."

"You could have fooled me."

"I was trying to say that, there has to be a reason to just keep going." Bazil took himself back to that moment on the train. "All the other animals there did not move. They did not participate. I have the memory. What do they have?"

"The memory of you acting like a jackass?" Moe still had not moved from his fetal position.

"Get up and move, Moe. Participate." Bazil began to slowly wander off.

The elephant meandered slightly from the path and headed into the woods. With one hopeful, backward glance he saw Moe still lying on the ground. The hope faded from his thoughts but Bazil had a feeling that he was still heading in the right direction. He looked to the sky and saw no sign of the winged predator surveying for his prey. When he brought his eyes back to earth, he nearly stumbled and had to make a quick left turn, for Moe was standing directly in front of him.

"What happened to the hawk?" Bazil asked.

"I told it to piss off." Moe made a rather unfriendly gesture to take in the entire population of the sky above. He stared hard at Bazil. "Was that story of yours even true? Did it even happen?"

"And if it didn't?" Bazil replied. "The lesson's still the same."

"I know one story about you that is true, big fella, and I don't know how far you'll have to go to outrun those memories." Moe skipped ahead at a much lighter step.

Bazil didn't know if Moe's aim was to be cruel, but the barb certainly hit its mark. Those dark memories came flooding back like an unyielding stream, and Bazil knew that he'd have to face them again before Memories End.

*

A huge throng of reporters were camped out in front of Amelia's trailer. The place was no longer her refuge or fortress of solitude, so she sought that peace of mind elsewhere. The story that the two highly intelligent and resourceful chimps that had taken over the act were hers to train and teach, as was the wayward chimp Moe, had begun to make its rounds around the periphery of the circus and the towns where they were booked to perform. She had no idea how the story spread, like a prairie fire, and caught the attention of everyone. She only knew that it did not come from her. She would have preferred to do her job, collect her pay, train the chimps and, last but not least, find Moe. She sought out the peace she now craved and the seclusion that had been forced upon her at the sideshow.

Louise was waiting for her as if anticipating Amelia's escape to the last place that held out sanctuary for her. It was a different view of the backstage and another view of the sideshow participants that Amelia didn't know if she was quite ready for. As she met with Louise, and the larger woman took her by the arm, they began to stroll among the more permanent structures attached to the sideshow tent, housing the living quarters. As a rule, Louise never allowed anyone to enter here and see the breakdown of the show's facade, but she made an exception, this one time, for her friend.

Amelia saw Manuel, the new Monster/Man, who had replaced the man she now knew was August Purefoy, as he hung out his laundry to dry on a makeshift clothes line strung up from one tree branch to another. It seemed like such a mundane task for a powerful performer. She also saw several of the 'Family Of Man---Neanderthals' seated together around a fire in a barrel, toasting marshmallows. A man, woman and two children, all with sloping foreheads and hairy faces, seemed to her to take their work very seriously. She also caught a glimpse of a very tall, bearded woman who bared a striking resemblance to Abraham Lincoln as well as the usual assortment of folks: Gator Slim, the man with the alligator skin; the world's tallest man and the world's smallest woman; sword swallowers and glass eaters, whose practicing made

Amelia turn away. These performers had remained even after the sideshow had taken on a different meaning and tone. They had lasted this long, and they were sure that they would be here when the times, and show, had changed once again. All in all, it was not the sort of picture she had expected to see.

"Is something wrong, my dear?" Louise asked. "You look rather pensive."

"I'm just happy to see such a contrast between here and that roadside horror." Amelia felt bad for even comparing the two.

"You were, perhaps, expecting cages instead of homes?" Louise sympathized. "Contrary to popular belief, we do not eat our young nor do we keep the majority of the freaks in locks and chains or fermenting in alcohol." Louise's slight shiver went unnoticed.

"I didn't mean to sound disrespectful, Louise. I'm sorry."

"You are forgiven for your... short-sighted point of view. But, after all, you are only human."

Amelia felt ashamed and walked with her head slightly bowed, fearful to make eye contact with those she felt she may have offended. This downward view did offer her a rather unique perspective into what may have been happening here, and throughout the years, as she glanced at a half-burnt piece of paper, the remains of a letter, upon the ground. She could make out several words among the smudges and ash, capitalized for effect and handwritten in red, such as: Abominations. Spawns Of Hell. Grotesque. Death. Die. Dying.

After this she felt even more ashamed of herself. They were nothing like the letters that she had begun receiving lately, mostly from school children from all around the country telling her how lucky she was to have a pet monkey. Amelia shook herself free of the shame and returned her attention back to what Louise was saying.

"I cannot say that we here ever really get used to such preconceived notions of how we live or how we should react," Louise said, still giving Amelia the visitor's tour. "But I can say with all certainty and some history, that we have all come from a world that has always felt the need to...put us in our place." Louise was on a roll and decided to elaborate. "My own life, growing up, was not one that you would want to emulate, dear child. My father was a self-proclaimed preacher and drunkard. My mother was but a wisp of a woman who bore the brunt of the man's sermons and fists. At a very young age I learned the only chance I may have at any sort of life was to rebel. The fundamentalist upbringing was meant to smother me and drive forth the demons of pure thought. I would not allow that stultifying atmosphere to control me then, or now, nor to shape my way of thinking or behavior. I caught the eye of another black sheep relative, my Uncle Philip, who saw something in me akin to the prodigal progeny. He sent me, against the ranting and raving of my father who at first thought it such folly to indulge my freakish whims, to the very best schools, and I did well as long as my purposes aligned with those institutions and my benefactor. I studied medicine. Law. Politics."

Louise squeezed Amelia's arm a bit tighter as they passed by a makeshift shed with a huge padlock upon the door. Louise did nothing to even acknowledge the existence of the place. Amelia didn't have much time to think of it at all, as Louise was quick to continue and follow her own train of thought. The smell emanating from beneath the door was one that Amelia could not place although it struck her as something quite familiar, medical in origin but deathly in practice.

"Humans are a somewhat enlightened species," Louise said, "Quick to acknowledge the less fortunate but just as quick to forget them. It's an adopted trait which allows us to survive, and to reserve our thoughts for the future. And I am proud to be a member of the first species on this planet that can choose its future."

Louise stopped and took hold of both of Amelia's hands. "You have that opportunity now, sweet Amelia. You can choose to run and hide or you can choose to embrace the fame which the circus now holds forth to you while shoving aside the infamy."

"What are you saying?" Amelia was too scared to try to free her hands from Louise's strong hold.

"I am saying that the first thing you must do is face those reporters who have descended like a pack of vultures at your doorstep."

"But I'm too afraid."

"Of what?"

"Of saying the wrong thing."

Louise slowly moved in and embraced a shaking Amelia. "It's your opportunity for exposure, dear. All you have to do is simply tell them what they want to hear." Louise backed away slightly and took Amelia's chubby face in her hands. "Or you can choose to expose us all."

Once again Louise took hold of Amelia's arm and began to lead her back toward the locked shed. "Let me show you a little secret about our humble circus and sideshow, my dear."

As Louise was unlocking the shed, she took one last opportunity to let Amelia know her thoughts concerning the younger woman's fears.

"Do you know what frightens more little children than any threat of a boogieman in the closet or a beast beneath the bed?" Louise paused for effect, not an answer. "It is a simple prayer, my dear."

"Now I lay me down for sleep,
I pray the lord my soul to keep,
If I should die before I wake,
I pray the Lord my soul to take.

"Now you try getting to sleep after that." Louise let a slight laugh slip forth. "And the worst part of it all is that you don't even have the comfort of hiding under the covers to protect you from it." She made sure she still had a captive audience. "It is fear that keeps us from achieving the impossible."

The door to the shed swung open and Louise reached in and turned on a light. The older woman held the door so that Amelia could decide if she wished to step over the threshold or not. The sickly smell of something fermenting took hold and Amelia stepped back slightly, but then her curiosity took an even stronger hold and she ducked inside.

"This is where the miracles come to life," Louise stated softly, "or die before fruition."

*

Bazil could not for the life of him remember how the performance had gone that night. He performed his routine by rote, balancing on his hind legs, placing all four of them upon the huge ball in the center ring, prancing and dancing around, weaving in and out among the trainers and handlers. He thought he left the center ring, to the thunderous applause, as usual. He knew he must have been led along to the'side of the trailers and wagons, where he would have to wait to be watered and fed. All of this was a blur to him now, for all he could recall with any certainty and clarity was what happened next. He did not wish to remember but he knew he could never forget.

Blackie, the man with the yellow teeth who spit tobacco juice into a Styrofoam cup he carried with him everywhere he went, was in a sour mood. He was looking for someone to take it out on and the nearest scapegoat was tons of docile pleasantness and gentle persuasion, two things that the angry handler had had enough of. His offer for a raise had been turned down, Slade saying that as soon as the box office picked up, so would the workers' wages. And he was sick and tired of shoveling elephant shit. The man searched through his trailer for just the right instrument to vent his frustration and vehemence, and found it in the bull-hook. He grabbed the thin wooden handle and went off in search of his victim.

Bazil was tearing through what was left of a pile of hay. He was hoping not to find any surprises with his meal. The last time he tried to eat in peace, he began to nibble on some hay, and the tiny squeak nearly scared him half to death. He never saw the mouse but he kept a wary eye open at every meal from then on. Bazil looked up and saw the line of chimp cages near the pond. He could not recall any other time when the cages were set so close to the water or so far from their handlers. He did not like to look at these particular specimens. They were not like Moe. They were a different breed altogether. Their fur was in patches, and some were even bare to the skin from constantly scratching and biting at their own flesh. Their eyes bulged from loose, runny sockets, and they screamed, hooted and cried constantly. Most of the time, mercifully, there was a large tarp covering the cages, but not this night. The row of cages was left coverless, the pitiful occupants free to gaze at the stars or scream into the night.

Bazil did not see the menacing shadow behind him until it was too late, and when he felt the stabbing pain at his heel there was nothing he could do but wince and lift his left foot. The bull-hook was already wrapped around his right hind leg and digging into his flesh.

"Where do you think you're going, ya big dumb brute?" Blackie smiled through the yellow teeth and twisted the bull-hook spike deeper.

Where the hook was implanting itself, there had once been a deep wound, then a scar, and now a searing pain. It must have hit a nerve, for Bazil had never felt pain like that before in his life. Excruciating. Pounding. Relentless. He trumpeted and turned, swinging his leg to the left and his large trunk toward the rear. He saw the man holding on as tight as he could to the bull-hook, and heard the barrage of curses filling his ears. Bazil kicked out with his free hind foot and caught the man a glancing blow to the chest. Blackie let go of the torture device instantly and was sent flying back into the shadows. Bazil heard the trumpeting cries fill the night, but it took him a moment or two to realize that it was he, himself, that was screaming. He saw the blood pouring forth from the open wound at his heel and he panicked. He swung the embedded bull-hook back and forth, the pain beginning to dull his senses, till he was finally able to free himself of the hook, handle and all. But it did not free him from the pain.

Bazil did the only thing he could think of at that moment---he ran.

Either he did not remember that they were there in his line of sight, did not care, or was blinded by the pain, but he ran straight for the chimp cages. He hit them with the full force of a rampaging freight train and the unstoppable locomotive didn't stop until the cages were thrown high into the air, sending them straight down the small incline and sailing into the freezing cold waters of the pond.

Then Bazil stopped on a dime. He heard the frightening, sickening cries and hoots of the captives in their cages, and looked to see the line of chimps sinking before his startled eyes. He trumpeted loudly. He ran along the bank of the pond and searched the ripples of the water. In the pounding pain of a heartbeat, the cages were gone. They sank beneath the water and never surfaced. The screams of the dying chimps were drowned out by the whooshing sound of the cages filling with frigid water.

Bazil stood on the edge of the pond and watched the bubbles, the last dying breaths of the malformed chimps, rise to the surface. He wanted to scream. He wanted to plead with whatever gods there were to raise the dead. He wanted to exchange his life for theirs. No one answered. No one rushed to help. No one watched the chimps as they died. He wondered if any one, besides him, even cared.

Later that night, four other handlers roped and then chained Bazil to a post near the back of the compound. It was thought best to let the beast settle down and be alone for the rest of the night. It was the worst possible thing that they could have done to the poor, grieving elephant.

Sometime later, Bazil awoke to a soothing sound at his ear. He was being petted and whispered to by something much smaller and lighter than himself. He opened an eye and saw the dwarf atop a wooden ladder, crying and talking to him.

"It wasn't your fault, big fella. It will be all right."

Bazil still felt a stinging pain at his heel, but when he looked he saw that it had been cleaned and bandaged and cared for with tender, loving care.

"I know what they did to you, Bazil. It's a shame. A crying shame. A majestic king like you brought to his knees by the unmitigated stupidity of humankind." The Monster/Man was weeping into the night.

Bazil let the man cry, pet him, and talk his soothing talk. He somehow felt that the dwarf needed it more than he did himself, so he just let the friendly little man go on and on with his prayers and pity. He just wished he would save a little for the lost chimps.

Bazil would always remember that kind little man. He came often to just talk or sit with Bazil. Bazil didn't always understand what the Monster/Man was saying, but that didn't matter much. It wasn't so much the words but the way the man had of saying them that meant the most. One other thing that Bazil knew would remain with him into forever was the perfect picture that August Purefoy had painted for him of Memories End.

The last thing that Bazil could recall about the man, the very last time he came and sat and spoke to the elephant, was that he was leaving. He said that it was time for him to move on and explore new and interesting possibilities of this world—or the next. And he suggested to Bazil, in no uncertain terms, that the elephant find somehow, some way, to do the very same. He asked Bazil to do him one big favor. He asked Bazil to never forget him, and said that when they met again, somewhere in Memories End, he hoped that Bazil would know him, for he was convinced that he would not look the same as he did at that last moment they talked.

Bazil wanted to tell the Monster/Man that he would know him anywhere, at any time, for it wasn't the little man's looks that he would never forget, nor the stature of the man. It was the size of the man's heart. That big, strong, loving heart would beat a perfect tune inside Bazil's soul for eternity. It would be the one thing he would not---could not---ever forget.

Bazil found Moe picking at a large termite mound with a long stick. "Are you ready?"

"Ready for what?" Moe asked, withdrawing the stick filled with termites.

"Memories End."

*

Amelia ran from the shed in tears. She swung open the door and it slammed shut right in front of Louise. A few seconds passed until Louise opened the door and stepped from the entrance. She turned, locking the door.

When she backed away to leave, she was surprised to see Amelia standing there. The younger woman had a look of disbelief on her face and tears streaming down as well.

"What made you think I would want to be part of any of it?' Amelia heard herself screaming.

"I just thought you deserved to know the truth," Louise said quietly. "What you intend to do with this knowledge is now entirely up to you, my dear."

"So it's all a lie?"

"Not quite. I manipulated the nature while you provided the nurture."

"Why? How? For what purpose?

Louise let the other woman catch her breath, settle her nerves, before speaking. "Do you really want to know?"

Amelia turned away and then stepped back. "How many failures?"

"Too many to keep track of."

"And where are they all now?"

"Secrets buried along the highways we have traversed."

"Do you even care?"

"More than you know."

Amelia took a few tentative steps backwards, then turned to face Louise one last time. "Why me? Why did you give Moe to me in the first place?"

"I thought that would be obvious, my dear?

"Not to me."

"It's your heart. You have one of gold. You would not let me or Moe down, and now it's the same now with the twins. You have the capacity for so much more, Amelia dear. I offered it to you in a little bundle of fur and hope. You have yet to prove me wrong."

Amelia wiped the moisture from her face, expression turning stern and determined. "This is the end. No more experiments. No more needless torture or deaths just to satisfy the coffers of this circus and sideshow."

"You have my word," Louise said, "but I urge you to think of the consequences to you and Moe."

"I will go to the police. I will go to the newspapers. I will expose all of you." Amelia was fully charged. "If I hear of one more of these...these...--" She slipped away without finishing. She was certain that Louise had received the message.

Louise didn't say another word as she watched Amelia make her way through the back lot of the sideshow. With a few steps of her own, the shape and stride of her gait began to change, and it was not long before Louise completely suppressed herself and took on the traits of her alter ego.

It was Louis that walked the rest of the way through the grounds.

*

Bazil lumbered along lazily through the heat of the noonday sun. His belly was on empty but his mind was a jumble of thoughts. Moe slept fitfully atop the giant's head, waking in fits and starts with a hoot and a holler to the sky. They had started out a few hours ago, and every five minutes thereafter Moe asked, "Are we there yet?" It was funny the first fifteen times, but wore quite thin, until Moe rested in peace.

Bazil halted before a grove of large dogwoods. Something was amiss. His trunk rose slowly, sniffing for the one scent that did not belong in the woods, and he found it.

"What is it?" Moe asked, rubbing the daydreams from his eyes. "Why have we stopped?"

"Smoke." Bazil slowly began to tremble.

To Moe it felt like the low rumble of a train, but he hung on. He stood up to get a better view of their surroundings. Then he saw it, trickling about the trees in a slow, grayish swirl. Despite one recent rain, the ongoing drought left the forest in peril. A discarded match or unattended campfire were sure harbingers of disaster. Somewhere out there in the flashy grass on a roadside or in dry boughs adjoining a pitchy, sparking fire, disaster finally struck.

The acrid smell descended upon them and the sweet singing of the birds in the trees came to a choking halt. Small furry creatures were underfoot, but Bazil had no time to worry about them. He fixed his trunk and his gaze upon the woods just beyond where he stood. It didn't take long for him and Moe to spot the first signs of the flames. The fire crept through the undergrowth and headed straight for the dogwoods.

"What do we do?" Moe sounded the panic alarm. "We'll have to turn back."

"How far?" Bazil asked, his eyes on the approaching flames.

"Till we're out of the line of fire."

"I don't want to go back, Moe. I think we're closer than we think to--"

"To what? Death? Being burned alive? You ever smell roasted monkey? It ain't pretty."

Bazil took a tentative step forward toward the smoke. "I think I can make it through. I've seen the firewalkers do it. I've seen the lions jumping through flaming hoops."

"That's because someone's cracking a whip near their asses." Moe did not like where this conversation, and Bazil, were heading.

The smoke was already upon them in the trees and the flames were not far behind.

"Well, do what you're gonna do and get it over with," Moe screamed into Bazil's left ear.

Bazil moved out from the dogwoods, the heat of the fire already blistering their bark. He bent down with his tusks and began to dig a trench into the ground surrounding him and the trees.

"What the hell are you doing?" Moe decided to scream in the right ear in case the left had gone deaf, but Bazil wasn't listening in either one.

"Just trying to save the trees." Bazil dug deeper and deeper, trying to hold back the flames as best he could.

"Just get us out of here, Bazil." Moe was kicking at the elephant's side. "It's hard to breathe."

Moe was right and Bazil knew it. They both began to cough uncontrollably, with eyes stinging constantly from the smoke, and Moe felt a migraine building on both sides of his temples. It was getting pretty difficult to breathe with all the thick, gray smoke surrounding them.

"I...can't...breathe," Moe was choking on the words, "and my...head feels like...it's about to...explode."

Embers were biting at fur and skin on the both of them.

Bazil reluctantly left the trees to nature and slowly began to rumble forward at a trot. He picked up speed in the next few seconds, but halted suddenly when the way he was going became blocked by a wall of flame. He turned back, pirouetting with balance and grace in the midst of chaos, and headed in the opposite direction. But that direction was closed off by the conflagration of trees. There was no other choice, so the big guy spun around and headed straight for the heart of the fire.

Moe could only think of one thing to add to the situation: "Shit."

Moe hung on for dear life as the elephant rolled along the edge of the flames. The yellowish-orange tentacles were reaching as high as an elephant's eye, but Bazil just ignored their sizzling bites. Moe could smell burnt flesh and hoped to high heaven that it wasn't his. He had both arms wrapped around his nose and mouth, but his eyes stung from the soot and ash that rose from the burning foliage at Bazil's feet. How the beast could keep on moving when the ground around him was as white hot as searing coals, Moe did not know. The big brute had a one track mind— and that track was leading them toward certain death.

They both heard the ugly *crack* of one of the trees on their path, and upon looking up they saw that an enormous oak was leaning their way. The tree was completely engulfed in flames, roots and all. Moe screamed and placed his hands over his eyes. Bazil shifted to his left as the oak fell, glancing off his hind quarters and sending a burst of burning wood shards over him and Moe. Bazil danced out of the line of fire, as Moe furiously shook off the angry sparks from his fur and slapped out the dazzling flames.

Just then a pair of cardinals fluttered down from the treetops and landed upon Bazil's back. The birds stared at Moe and he stared right back. He gave them the heave ho with the back of his hand and a shout, "Get your own elephant."

Bazil's eyes glazed over and he trumpeted loudly. Moe had just enough time to grab a handful of the elephant's ears when Bazil burst across the field of fire and headed toward the far edge of the opposite woods. Moe had one eye on the ground and the other on the fire, as both swept by him at tremendous speed. He had the feeling that he was in a whirlwind, and as they shot on by, the flames were trampled out by the fleeing beast. When Moe took a glance back, he saw the grove of dogwoods being eaten alive by the fire. He closed his eyes and hung on, along for the ride.

When Moe opened his eyes again, Bazil had slowed to a crawl. They were both singed and a bit blistered, but alive. Moe's fur was smoking, as was Bazil's tail, and the chimp spit into both of his paws so as to quickly douse a small glowing ember that alighted on the top of the elephant's left ear. Moe slid from the the hot seat and sprawled out upon the cool earth.

"That was fun," Moe said. "Let's go back and do it again."

The chimp looked up to see the elephant staring straight ahead. The big guy's eyes were wide and worried.

"What now?" Moe got to his feet and followed Bazil's line of sight.

CHAPTER THIRTY-ONE

Bridging The Gap

A lazy flowing river was snaking its way through the landscape on their left, and the dry land to the right of them was rough with rocks, and boulders the size of Bazil's head. The smoke and fire was far behind them. Bazil somehow knew that there would be one last obstacle to overcome before they reached their destiny. He just did not know what it would be. And he certainly did not think it would have anything to do with water again.

"What's wrong? Moe asked.

"Water. It always seems to come down to water," Bazil replied. "I am still paying a heavy price for my sins. This will forever be my memento mori."

"What's the big deal? You can swim, can't you? At least we can wash off all this soot and shit."

"You don't understand, Moe. I have had all I can stand with water and drowning and---"

Moe made his way to the edge and dipped a toe. "Warm. Bath time." He turned back to the timid elephant. "Think of it this way, Baz, before you can reach Memories End you have to be baptized."

The big brute refused to move.

"We just walked through the gates of hell and now you're gonna tell me you're afraid of a little water?" Moe threw his hands up in disgust.

Moe paced from the edge and came to a halt near a large fallen tree that nearly spanned the river. It landed about five feet short of the opposite shore.

"Looks like a natural bridge to me," Moe said upon returning to Bazil's side. "Do your stuff. You know, balance on one foot. A hop, skip and a jump and you're on the other side. Think of that tree as just one big, stupid ball in the center of the ring that they expect you move to move and get those massive mitts of yours atop and roll."

Bazil wasn't buying any of it. He was done performing.

"We could build a raft and float free and easy down the river like Tom and Huck. True, we'd have to knock down half a forest to build one to accommodate your wide girth." Moe was laughing.

Bazil was not amused.

Moe's laughter turned a darker shade of bitter. "Or how about the time they put a pink tutu on you and made you prance and pirouette around the stage? Just use those memories to get your big ass across the goddamn water." Moe was adamant.

"Only if you brought your matching dress." Bazil flicked his trunk at Moe.

"Touché."

They stood together in the sunshine and tried to come up with one good thought, one good plan between them.

"I'll go back a-ways and see if I can find another place where we can cross." Moe patted the big beast on the nose.

Bazil was grazing peacefully by the river when Moe came leaping down toward him from a overhead tree.

"You're not going to like it, but, well, I found us another way 'round the river." Moe was less than enthusiastic, which Bazil picked up on almost immediately.

"What does it entail?" Bazil asked.

"You won't have to use your tail at all," Moe jumped down from a branch and landed successfully on the ground. "A month ago I would have probably fallen flat on my face."

"I meant, what's it going to take to get across that?" Bazil swung his long trunk toward the river.

"A bridge."

"A what?"

"A bridge. You know, that thing-a-bob that people use to get from one side of a thing to another."

"Did you inspect the trestle?"

"The what now?"

"Did it look sturdy to you? Did it look like it could hold the weight of, ohhh, let's say---me?"

"How am I supposed to know."

"Did you cross it? Did you go back and forth and---"

"Look, I said I'd find you another way across the water and I did. If you recall, it's not me that has the problem with that river. It's you. I can be on the other side and on my way to Memories End in a heartbeat and a jump."

"Maybe I'm like that person that the Monster/Man told me about. The one that wandered in the desert for years and years."

"This ain't the desert and the damn Monster/Man ain't here with us. Now, are you coming or not?"

"Like that man, perhaps I am not meant to enter the promised land."

"Look, ya big mug, ain't none of us promised anything in this life. We scratch, we crawl, we bite and we bleed. And where does it get us in the end?"

"Stuck in a rut at the river's edge."

"Exactly, my friend. We have two choices here, Bazil. One: Stay and live out our lives on this side of paradise. Two: Cross the damn river and find Memories End." Moe stopped pacing and opened up his arms, as if pleading or pledging some sort of promise to Bazil. "I must confess, big guy, I never for one minute believed in that place of yours. I'm not sure that I do now, even after all this time on the road with you. But you believe. And that's enough for me. And if you believe, then nothing should stand in your way of achieving your dream. What is Memories End to you, Bazil? I'll tell you what it is to me. It's the next meal, a cool drink of water, a warm female. It's out-running that silly hawk while not getting too far away from the things I really care about---" Suddenly, a picture of Amelia flashed before Moe's eyes, and he was startled for a moment.

Bazil kept silent, waiting for Moe to continue.

"You can't allow those bad memories of yours to force the good ones from your mind, Bazil. You seem to be forgetting all that the Monster/Man told you. I thought I could outrun my fears, but I know that that hawk will have as little trouble crossing the river as I would, to follow me to the other side. Fears and all. But there's really nothing worth staying here for or going back to. There's only the bad memories awaiting me, and you, back there, Baz ol' buddy. At least, if we cross, if we go on, there's a good chance of forgetting. I have made my choice. I am going to cross that bridge. The rest is up to you."

Moe turned and scrambled back into the tree. Bazil stood and watched him leave, but did not make an effort to follow. He was still digesting the words that Moe fed him. They tasted both bitter and sweet. Bazil knew that the truth usually was.

*

The suspension bridge looked both formidable and foreboding to Bazil. It was wooden. The trestle, steps, the planks that held it all in one piece were worn, tattered, weather-beaten wood. How many years they had supported this sorry excuse for a bridge, he could not tell. The ropes that were tied and swung from one side to the stringer a hundred or so yards in the opposite direction, looked incapable of holding the deck aloft, let alone anyone stupid enough to try crossing to the other side. What it was going to do when a pachyderm-pedestrian the size of a building was crossing would be anyone's guess.

Moe scampered across easily, making it to the other side without incident. He scurried back and said, "See, big fella, nothing to it. Come on, give it a try."

Bazil stared at Moe and the bridge. "This is a test. A test of my resolve. A test of my faith. A test of my--"

"--patience." Moe tossed his head to one side and grunted.

Bazil took one small tentative step forward onto the first plank. The bridge began to sway, creak and groan. So did Bazil. "This isn't going to work, Moe. I'm too big, the bridge is too small. The spirit is willing but the flesh too much."

Moe got behind Bazil and began to push. It was like a flea trying to move a tractor. The chimp cursed and punched, and then walked to the front and took hold of the elephant's trunk, all to no avail. Bazil was a boulder, an unmovable object whose gravity had landed him at the edge of the trail and refused to budge another inch. He may as well have been frozen in time.

"Where's that faith as great as a mustard seed to move this mountain, big boy?" Moe was huffing and puffing. "What must the Monster/Man be thinking of you now?"

"It's no use," Bazil said. "You may as well go on yourself, Moe. Find Memories End for the both of us. Make yourself a home and a life there."

Moe sat down on one of the wooden planks of the bridge. "Should I come back from time to time to see how you're doing? Maybe plant some flowers around you so you resemble a garden gnome instead of a big, dumb brute?" Moe rose and began pacing in front of Bazil.

"I'd like to cross, you know I want to, but I just don't think it's possible." Bazil pleaded.

"So you're just gonna give up? Sit down and give in to the impossible? This ain't the Bazil I've come to know and love."

Bazil stared at Moe as if seeing his little traveling companion in a new light.

"Oh, hell, you know what I mean," Moe said as he gave the big beast a friendly punch in the side.

Bazil backed up slightly, reviewing his options, "Perhaps if I can get a running start at it." He moved back further and further as Moe leaped to his left, balanced upon the side of the wooden railing, and watched with some interest.

Bazil trumpeted lightly, pawed the ground around him, closed his eyes and began to chant: "I can do this. I can do this. I can--" Bazil opened his eyes and bolted straight for the bridge.

He stopped dead in his tracts right before he hit the first rung. "---not do this."

Moe leaned over the railing and spat off the bridge. Leaping down from his perch, Moe tipped his invisible cap to Bazil, and began to move across the bridge. He hadn't even noticed that he was now using his front appendages to speed across as well as his back legs. For all Moe's navel gazing, he hadn't paid much attention to the fact that he was acting more like an ape than ever before in his life. Nature was taking its course and he was going with it.

Moe reached the other side in a flash and looked back to Bazil, who was still stuck. Moe was about to speak, but all he could think of were few choice curses. He let them stay in his thoughts instead of making it clear what he thought of Bazil, the bridge and Memories End.

Moe disappeared from Bazil's sight in the next moment. The discontented elephant wanted to shout out that Moe should wait for him, but he knew it was a sham---all bluster and no bite. Who was he kidding? He's wasn't going anywhere near the place where all his dreams could come true. He was stuck on the other side of hopes, dreams and paradise, with bad memories and no prospects. Bazil turned away. He was inconsolable in his misery and grief. He was just a big, dumb, stupid---

---he heard Moe screaming from the other side of the bridge.

"I found it! It's there! It's just over the rise!"

Bazil turned to see Moe returning, the chimp racing across the bridge as if it were on fire.

"It's beautiful. It's wonderful. It's everything you dreamed it would be." Moe was still shouting when he landed about two feet from Bazil. "You got to see it, Baz. You won't believe your eyes. Come on, I'll show you."

Bazil was so excited that he began to move forward without thinking.

"I saw so many different animals that I couldn't even count them. And get this: they were all there side by side. No one pushing. No one shoving. No screaming or biting or going at one another like--humans. It's not to be believed, Bazil. That crazy old Monster/Man of yours was right. That son of a bitch knew what he was talking about. Get this, big guy, it was snowing. Snowing, and the sun was shining at the same time, and it was warm and wonderful. Now how do you suppose that could happen? Only in Memories End, huh? And you know what else? You're not gonna believe me when I tell you what else. The minute I got there, they all knew my name. And you know what the first thing they asked me was? Wait for it. They asked me---where's Bazil? Where's Bazil, how do you like that, you big goofball?"

Moe stopped and winked at Bazil. The big brute didn't even realize what he had just done. It took him a full minute or more to come to the realization that he had crossed the bridge. Without even knowing it he was now standing on the other side. He turned his massive head in the opposite direction and saw that huge span was weaving and teetering on the very verge of collapse, but somehow, miraculously, it withstood his enormous weight. Neither the bridge nor the elephant tumbled to their deaths. They were both alive, swaying with the incredible exhilaration of conquering fear and feeling so much more alive in this big, bright and beautiful world. Mere moments ago Bazil was at the crossroads, already beginning the surrender of his dreams to failure. He was under the impression that the bridge itself didn't want him to move forward and cross to the other side, so great was his commitment to remaining stuck. He was certain he heard the inanimate object breathe a huge sigh of relief when he decided not to cross. Now here he was on the other side and he didn't even know he did it. He wanted to bend down and kiss the ground. He also wanted to say a prayer and thank the bridge for allowing him to cross over and live to tell the tale.

He settled for a simple, "Thank you, Moe."

A few miles down the road, Bazil had to ask, "You didn't really find anything, did you, Moe?"

"What do you think, Bazil?"

*

Bazil's dreams usually led him to some dark place he did not wish to go. But this night the elephant gods must have smiled upon him.

Bazil was chained. He didn't have much of an opinion one way or the other about it. It was what it was. But as he stepped back toward a nearby tree to scratch an itch that was just now ascending from his back legs to his rump, the chain let loose and he was free. But free to do what?

Bazil ran. When he looked back, no one was following. In a few moments he found himself meandering through a field of warm and healing sunshine. He was neither hungry nor thirsty. He felt full of life. He was alone but he wasn't lonely. When he heard his name being called, he turned to see a familiar face.

The Monster/Man was seated upon a large boulder in an endless field of sunflowers. As Bazil approached, the man said with a smile, "You made it, my friend."

"Where am I?" Bazil asked.

"Where do you wish to be?" The Monster/Man answered, his face turned to the sun.

"Right here, I guess."

"Then, you have made it, my friend."

"I don't understand how I got here. Is this a...dream?"

"All life is a dream, Bazil. So, I suppose you could say that you are in a dream within that dream."

"But where will I be when this dream ends?"

"Back to the dream of life."

Bazil looked around him at all the beauty that shone from cloud to flower. "I just don't think that I belong here."

"You're here now, aren't you?" The Monster/Man asked.

"But I don't know if I can stay. Too many bad memories that just won't end."

"Forgiveness, Bazil. It's the only thing we can truly do for ourselves."

"Believe me, I have tried."

"Everyone believes that life has to be made up of a series of accomplishments--the bigger the better. But it's not true. It is the little things---like forgiveness. Hope, love and forgiveness, Bazil. One can spend their entire life trying to figure out the meaning of it all, but then there is the chance that one will miss what living is all about."

The dwarf leapt from his perch atop the boulder and began leading Bazil through the sunflowers.

"How can I truly forgive myself for what I have done?" Bazil asked.

"Just let go, my friend." The Monster/Man replied.

The elephant turned when he heard another sound coming from just beyond the field. When he glanced back, the Monster/Man was gone. He stood alone now in the sunflowers,, and he felt lonely. He was hungry, thirsty and tired. He wasn't ready for the dream to end and life to begin *again, but he suspected that he had little choice in the matter. He looked back to the edge of the field and saw himself, chained to a stake and waiting for something, or someone, at the end of this dream.*

Bazil awoke in pale, bleak moonlight. He looked for the chains, but realized that he left them far behind in dreamland. The only chains he carried into the waking world were the ones weighing him down the most, those still fastened to his heart and soul. The dream was already fading into memory, and the cold moonlight threw the landscape into stark relief. Bazil's thoughts were similarly clear. He knew that he had one more thing to accomplish in life before he could enter Memories End. It might be the toughest thing he ever had to do. He had to learn to forgive himself.

CHAPTER THIRTY-TWO
Center Attraction

"What am I supposed to do with this information?" Amelia sighed. The passage of time had not soothed her anger one bit.

"Whatever you wish, my dear." Louise walked alongside the agitated younger woman. "You now hold all the cards. Play them as you see fit." Louise moved to take Amelia by the arm, but Amelia pushed away and Louise let it go without contact. "Just remember that Moe is a very big part of this, as we all are. Even bigger in some respects. After all, he was my---*our* first success, besides some of the freaks who volunteered for the---show."

"And what about the failures?" Amelia asked.

"Best not to dwell on them, my dear." Louise's thoughts turned to Evangelina, but she quickly pushed them to the side. No room now for sentimentality or the needs of the one.

Amelia stopped in mid-stride and asked with all sincerity, "Don't you worry about the death threats? I saw the letters you tried to burn. More cover up, I presume?"

"It all comes with the territory, Amelia dear." Louise stopped alongside her. "Every free-thinker, innovator and revisionist has suffered the same fate through the years. We have been called heretics or blasphemers. We have been either burned at the stake or forced to recant and reverse our proven theories in the face of blind stupidity and religious fervor."

"You're playing with lives here. Living, breathing beings. How could you? What were you thinking?" Amelia turned away with tears in her eyes.

"I want to find the very essence of the soul and make it better. I will improve their circumstances and give it all a meaning in the end." Louise reached out to touch the younger woman's shoulder, but once again Amelia shied away from the human touch.

Amelia faced Louise once again. Anger replaced pity. "That should be left to God."

"God, at his best, is indifferent to the plight of his freaks. August was the only one who really understood what I was trying to accomplish here, but I believe that even he, in time, became a bit disillusioned with it all."

"With the many failures?" Amelia cut to the bone of the matter.

"Slade pays them, or their families, all very well for their services to the cause." Louise cut back sharply.

"And their silences." A moment of silence passed before Amelia continued, "Have you received your thirty pieces of silver?"

"You're quickly making me regret letting you in on all this, dear Amelia."

"You can always whisk me into your lab and transform me back into the docile little doll you think I am, if you wish." Amelia picked up the pace, avoiding the sideshow section of the grounds. "You're just like Slade. You two could be brother and sister for all I know." For a moment or two Amelia seemed to lose her way, not knowing a way out of the dead end she'd seemingly talked herself into. "How do you just expect me to keep quiet about things? Or do you just expect me to go along with it all?

Louise tried desperately to steer both the destination and the conversation to her side of things. "I hope you will consider all the ramifications and consequences of your actions before you act on them. Let me remind you again what it will eventually bring to you, me, the other two chimps now in your care, and especially Moe."

"You hold him over my head like the Sword of Damocles." Amelia looked all around her for a way out. Louise smiled smugly, and Amelia responded in kind, "I am not as stupid as you all think I am."

Amelia stood right up next to Louise and made the older woman blink first. "Like I said before, only, and I say *only* , if it all ends with them. Here and now. The twins and Moe and that is it. Freaks included. No more."

Louise nodded her head in agreement, and motioned for Amelia to lead the way. It was only after a few steps that Amelia realized she was being guided, once more against her will, toward her own trailer and the horde of reporters waiting for her there like a pack of wolves.

*

Somehow, despite overzealous reporters hungry for a story, Amelia was able to duck inside the confines of her trailer with only a few scratches to her elbows and ego. A moment or two later, Louise managed to slip in as well. Louise took a moment or two to take in the homey feel of the trailer. Her eyes settled on a large pile of unopened letters on the desk in the living room.

At first the letters came in a trickle, mostly from kids. There were a few letters about sightings: Moe was here last night, Bazil was there, and so on. The bulk of the letters were about how they wished they could have a monkey; all they had were dogs, cats, lizards and canaries.

They came in all sizes and shapes, some addressed simply *To The Monkey Lady---At The Circus,* yet somehow they found her. Soon, so did missives from the grown-ups, with all their indecencies: marriage proposals, wild propositions and lurid suppositions.

Eventually Amelia stopped reading them, but she couldn't stop their coming any more than she could stop the curious from congregating around her trailer. A few sold out shows with the twin chimps performing, and the wild antics of Moe on the run with the blasted elephant, made her a rock and roll idol with groupies, hangers-on and reporters camping out for any word from on high.

For reasons even she could not fathom, Amelia agreed to let Alex, the clown, fix her hair and makeup. She had to eventually and inevitably face the reporters at a scheduled news conference that Louise and Slade set in the Big Top, and fans were still mingling just outside her sanctuary.

"Why do they do it?" Amelia asked after she plopped herself, exhausted, onto the well-worn but comfortable sofa.

"They want a piece of the action," Alex said as he applied the finishing touches to Amelia's hair.

"It's sick."

"Not really...oh, there's a few of us sickies in every group." Amelia jerked her head to one side. "Now keep it straight, Amelia. And don't be so touchy." Alex patted the side of Amelia's hair. "There. And I hope you'll always keep a warm spot in your heart for us little folk...now come on."

"I don't think I want to go," Amelia said with a heavy sigh.

Alex chanced a look to the door, where Louise was still waiting for them by the pile of unread fan mail. "Maybe I should have added some pancake and a red nose," the clown said in ill-humor. Louise did not laugh, and neither did Amelia.

After another awkward moment, Alex looked outside. "There's no turning back now. You can't stay in here forever, no matter how safe and orderly it may seem at this moment. Besides, the public won't be allowed in the press conference."

For one brief instant Alex took hold of Amelia's hand, looking her in the eyes. She waited for him to say something, but he let the moment pass in silence, letting loose her hand.

Louise opened the door and said, "Come, Amelia, your ador-
ing fans await. As Amelia sidled past the much larger woman, she
heard a whisper in her ear. "Give them what they want, Amelia.
The onlookers and the reporters, they all want a piece of you, but
only give them a bit at a time. Make it easy on yourself, dear, and
let them believe they're getting exactly what they want." And then
Louise proceeded to bore a path through the converging crowd.

Some of the more brave and brazen among them pressed even
closer as Amelia appeared; then came the ones who reached out for
autographs, handshakes, or simply touches or nods of recognition.

Amelia shook, signed, touched and nodded without breaking
stride, but all the time she felt certain that disapproving eyes were
on her. She was sure that some of those eyes that glared were set in
the same heads that thought up those disgusting letters of proposi-
tion. The harassing mail was now reflected in hateful stares. It was
disconcerting to be undressed, to be lusted after, even by thought.

Louise caught a few of the nastier looks herself. A chill ran
up and down her spine and she suddenly longed to be on the road,
far away from these small-minded towns and their small-minded
populaces.

Amelia wasn't relieved until she and Louise switched positions, with Alex somewhere behind them and lost in the pack.
Amelia continued toward the Big Top while Louise dropped back
to block the entrance.

If anything, Amelia found less order inside the tent. Reporters of all ages and shapes, temperaments and notoriety scrambled
to engage her. She was reminded of a gaggle of clowns emerging
from a small car and rushing toward her in the center ring. Lights
blinded her, microphones were pressed at her face, and questions
assaulted her every thought and nerve.

Yet, somehow, through all the insanity and vanity, Amelia
managed to tell the story of her life to point present. How much
of it registered, or even was heard, was unclear, even after the sto-

ries appeared in the various media. When all was said and done, Amelia had had no reason even to appear at the press conference; the reporters wrote their own versions in spite of her account.

As for her future, she had little to say.

It was hard to know if she would go on if Moe were found dead.

The twin chimps were fine. Working hard.

No, I am no longer a wire-walker.

My mother and father were the famous ones. I'm just glad to have a job.

Yes, Moe is smart. Very smart. He's kind, caring, loving and---yes, I know it sounds like I am talking about him as...human.

No, no one from Hollywood had approached her. (The offers for movies or photo shoots were for lurid and revealing prospectors).

There were no plans for a book.

No, sorry, I can't get anyone Moe or Bazil's autograph.

She hadn't heard about the man who held up a bank wearing a monkey suit.

No, she didn't feel responsible for that type of thing.

Because there's not enough trunk space.

Yes, sorry, I had heard it before.

She did not put any stock in the rumors about the circus, the sideshow or her chimps.

Her hair and makeup were done by a friend at the circus.

Yes, I know---it shows.

No again to having heard about the parents who approached Slade Bros. about wanting to sell their deformed child to the circus sideshow.

It was not a plan of the circus to gain publicity by having two of their animals escape and run wild in the wild.

*

"Today's headlines are tomorrow's lining for their birdcages," Louise said. "Rather redundant, don't you think?"

"What was the purpose of all that?" Amelia did not wait for an answer. She was once again seated unhappily on her sofa in her trailer. "They didn't listen to a word I was saying. I could have told them every dirty little secret about this place, and all they would have bothered to print was that I was now getting big enough to throw my weight around---literally. The girl too fat for the high wire. What were you and Slade thinking?"

"Slade was thinking, use the press to our advantage. Free publicity---gold in the bank. The reporters, as usual, were doing their best to punish the monkey and let the organ grinder go." Louise stood at the open door like a vampire, awaiting the invitation to enter.

"They think I'm a joke. They think I let Moe escape to further my own career. Make a name for myself. What name?" Amelia felt like crying but she didn't want to give Louise either the satisfaction of an *'I told you so'* or a way in to try to comfort her. Amelia did not need Louise---she needed Moe. "All I have succeeded in doing is giving the newspapers ammunition to rally the countryside to go out hunting for--I'll never forgive myself if he is killed because of me."

"Moe is a survivor. He's bright, cunning, and a hell of a lot smarter than anyone that's going to come after him." Louise tried to sound helpful and hopeful.

"It doesn't take any brains to fire a bullet." Amelia got up and shot past Louise into the night.

*

Benjamin Slade was in a hurry, rushing through the grounds like a freewheeling tornado at Manuel's report that Louise was throwing some sort of a tantrum at the sideshow. They had heard glass shattering and things being thrown around inside the woman's private workshop, and now Louise was burning reams and reams of papers and notebooks in the huge fire barrel that was constantly burning backstage at the grounds.

Slade's only passing thought was that he was now going to have to deal with Louise. For one reason or another, not quite up to speed as to why, he had always dealt with Louis. He wasn't even sure what he was going to say to the woman. A nagging thought passed within him that Louise had been playing him, and along with him Curry as well, by making them deal with her alter ego. Manipulation was her game and she played it well, and she was playing them both like a fiddle, and they were always dancing to her tune.

Upon arriving, Slade let into the woman like the tail end of that self-same tornado. "Just what the hell do you think you're doing, Lou--ise?"

"Keeping my promise." Louise did not look up when Slade arrived, refusing to turn and meet the man's fury.

"Promise to who?" Slade was spitting fire himself.

Louise dumped large, handwritten notebooks in the smoking barrel. Grayish ash and tiny sparks escaped the flames and flew into the space just above their heads. "Whom."

"What the hell does it matter? I want to know just what you think you're doing here!"

"I made a promise to Amelia." For the first time in the brief, but heated, conversation, Louise turned to acknowledge Slade's presence. "I told her everything. She knows it all, and she hold all the cards."

"What the hell did you do that for?" Slade was still spitting sparks. "What were you thinking? She could sink us all."

"Or keep us afloat." Louise returned to her chore. She stopped to stir the ashes and then dumped a load of books and papers into the inferno. "She said she wouldn't say a thing as long as I promised her that Moe, and the twins, were the last of our--my--little experimentations for the greater good. I added that last part, myself."

"And you believe her?"

"I have...faith."

"And I have a migraine."

Louise held a rather large notebook in her hands, smoothing the wrinkled red cover with her fingers. "All my research up in smoke."

Slade reached over, trying to grab hold of the notebook fated for the flames. But Louise held tight, dragging her own hand, the notebook, and Slade's fingers into the fire.

Slade pulled back almost immediately, but Louise lingered just a little too long before dropping the notebook and removing her hand. The smell of burnt flesh and singed hair tickled Slade's upturned nose.

"You're crazy!" Slade screamed.

"You're weak." Louise replied calmly.

"Pack your bags, you stupid freak. You're finished." Slade began to walk away, turned, and twisted the screw. "I'll see to it that you never work in this line of endeavor ever again." This time Slade kept walking away from the fire and his last fried nerve, but not before swinging for the fences. "Why don't you go and join that miserable, misguided little dwarf of yours? Help him search for that fantasyland of his."

"August was twice the man you are, Benjamin, even at his height!" Louise shouted after the fleeing form of the owner. Louise watched for a moment or two more, then added in a much less harsher tone, "We're a dying breed, Benjamin. Can't you read the writing on the wall

"No. What's it say?" Slade spoke without turning.

"Make way."

"Make way for what?"

"Whatever's coming next."

Slade gruffly slid past Manuel on his way out of the grounds of the sideshow, and said with a grunt, "You're in charge."

Later that evening Louise, fortified with a few shots of liquid courage, set about the final phase of destruction. She torched the shed. She stood and watched it burn. It reminded her of a Christmas tree all lit up and burning cheerfully in the night. She had the sudden urge to hum a carol or two, but thought better of it. All her work, research, and dreams were going up in smoke and she didn't give a damn. She was finally free of the past. The acrid smoke surrounded her and choked off her thoughts.

With one last stab at redemption or closure, Louise began to burn all of Louis' belongings. The persona of the man within went in a sacrificial puff of smoke. She had never been baptized, but now she felt somewhat purified by the heat of the flames.

When her thoughts returned, she envisioned a place for herself somewhere far from here. The myth that August had always talked about sounded better and better to her in that one moment of clarity. What was the name of that place? It was on the tip of her tongue. Oh, well, no matter. It would come to her when she needed it most.

CHAPTER THIRTY-THREE

Memories End

It was a sleepless night for both Moe and Bazil. One tossed and turned, the other rocked and swayed in a restless, warm, dry breeze. It was an hour or more before sunrise but they were both thinking the same thoughts: may as well be foraging for food or hitting the trail. The chirping crickets and croaking bull frogs had reached their full crescendo a while back and were now reduced to an almost imperceptible din, leaving only a few stragglers still searching for an elusive and amorous mate this night.

"Moe, are you asleep?" Bazil asked barely above a whisper, not wanting to invade the eerie silence.

"How can I sleep with all this quiet?" Moe asked.

"Do you think we're doing the right thing?"

"It's a little too early in the morning, and a little too late into this thing—whatever it is—to be asking now."

"I just get the feeling that we're nearing the end of this journey."

"And that's a good thing, right?"

Bazil contemplated the question, and the stars in the night sky. "If we go back, show them we're sorry or something, maybe it won't be so bad."

"Having doubts once again, big fella?" Moe kept his eyes closed but his mind was wide open. "Feeling a bit forsaken by the Monster/Man, are we? Would you like the burden of finding

Memories End to be lifted from you? Your Garden of Gethse-
mane moment?"

"No. I was just thinking that it may not be what I thought
it was going to be." Bazil reeled in his thoughts from the heavens
and landed them back on earth.

"Things seldom are, big guy." Moe managed to open one eye
upon the silhouetted form of the elephant. "Just have to wait and
see. Who knows, it may be paradise after all." Moe closed his eye
and turned his back to the night.

Bazil surveyed their surroundings and decided to let the peace
and quiet wash over him like a soothing blanket. Tomorrow would
be another day, and whatever was going to happen, he was certain
of one thing: it was going to happen no matter what he thought or
did or expected. He had no control over what was awaiting them at
sunrise. He tried to picture, one last time, the image of Memories
End within his mind, but all he could see was the empty night. He
started to gently sway with the warm breeze, and waited for the first
signs of glowing light to appear on the horizon.

*

Amelia heard the early morning commotion on her way to the
cook tent for some breakfast. She turned a corner in time to see
Curry with Blackie and several other men. All the men, except for
Curry himself, were well-armed and bore deadly and dangerous
attitudes. They piled into a nearby truck and drove off. As they
passed, she heard Blackie say, "There's only two ways to deal with
an elephant that's gone rogue: chain it up or put it down."

Amelia decided to skip breakfast and made her way straight
toward Louise's trailer. As she entered, she found its occupant in
the throes of packing.

"Are you leaving?" Amelia asked, standing just inside
the doorway.

"I've been told to vacate the premises," Louise said, placing some books inside a waiting box.

"Slade? Because of what you told me?" Amelia sounded worried.

"It's been coming on for months now, dear. No need to shoulder the blame yourself. I think Benjamin has always seen me as a rival. He was looking for an excuse and I gave him one."

"Where will you go? What will you do?"

"Places unknown. Things as yet undreamed." Louise said in a rather contemplative tone. "I have lived two different lives for too long now. I think it's time I try one at a time for awhile."

Amelia stood silent at the door, while Louise continued to pack.

"Was there something you came to see me about, Amelia? Or will this be good-bye?" Louise stood with a rather large hardbound book in her hands.

Amelia had to think for several seconds before she could even recall why she had come to talk to Louise. Remembering, she said, "Something may be happening. I saw Curry and several men heading out on the road. They had guns and they were in a hurry."

"I know. They found what they have been looking for. I heard the Forest Service broadcast over the radio just a few minutes ago. Curry must have gotten the call from them." Louise placed the book to one side and stared at Amelia. "I guess we'd better follow."

*

The morning brought a fresh commotion to the forest. Bazil paced nervously and Moe scurried up a nearby tree when the strange sounds reached their ears. The peace was broken initially by the raucous cry of a pheasant, and then the sounds of hidden creatures scuffling through the dead leaves—commotions not so out of the ordinary when he and Bazil passed through any given area in the woods, only it always took just a little time for both the dust and the local inhabitants to settle. Now the animals had more than enough time to quiet down, yet still the disturbances continued further down the trail.

The first thing Moe saw from his lofty perch was a herd of frightened deer, perhaps ten in all, leaping, twisting and pirouetting their way across the open trail and into the safety of the thicker woods. Moe couldn't make out anything more, except the faint wisp of an old familiar scent: man.

Moe looked down to Bazil and said, "They're coming this way."

"It doesn't matter, Moe," Bazil replied calmly, settling himself beneath Moe's tree. "It's already too late."

Moe turned in the direction the deer had taken, figuring that was what Bazil was referring to. From what Moe could see, they both were standing at the edge of a deeper forest. "Anything could get lost in there," Moe said, "even memories."

*

Inside the pickup the air was stuffy and silent, except for the radio and the female country singer crooning a tune with words that struck straight at Amelia's disenchanted heart.

> *I have danced to your tune for far too long*
> *You held the strings as I played along*
> *I am here to say that those days are now gone*
> *I will sing and dance to my own song from now on*
>
> *I always let you have the say*
> *I always let you have everything your way*
> *I am here to say that today that is going to change*
> *In my own voice, I will make my own choice, come what may*
>
> *Take some time to think it over*
> *But don't take too long*

'cause by the time you've thought it over
I will be gone

I have heard all your words before
I don't need to hear your words anymore
I can hear all those words as I walk across the floor
None of those words will bring me back through that door

When she had heard enough, Amelia reached over and put the song out of her misery. The silence was once again refreshing but also reflective. "You took me to see those pathetic animals at the roadside zoo so it'd be easier for me to see Moe in a cage," Amelia said as they drove down a back road.

Louise only smiled.

"And you think Slade will keep him alive, and me alone?" Amelia bounced with the pickup, wondering what would give out first: her nerves or the pickup's shocks.

"Of course," Louise said. "Moe will be waiting for you by the time we get there. You already know what big news he is...and you are. Soon you, Moe, and the twins will be superstars."

"We haven't come very far in the way we treat them, have we?" Amelia said.

"How so?"

"In medieval times they used animal skins to write their books and illustrations," Amelia winced at the thought. "It's called vellum. In some books the fur and hair of the animals are still visible and there for the touch. How cruel is that?"

Louise felt her hands sweating as she gripped the wheel. "It's a form of preservation, I suppose. Perhaps a more fitting tribute to the animals than slaughter houses and rendering plants."

Amelia almost wept at the thought. "I should be there... when they get him. I don't trust that one called Blackie." Amelia glanced out the window at the thick forest before them on the service road.

"Nothing you could have done, my dear," Louise said while trying to steer them in a straight direction. "It was really just luck that someone found them. The drought has caused the Forest Service to man all its fire watchtowers in the area. One of them spotted Bazil instead of smoke. Like I said, pure luck."

"I hope it holds...for Moe's sake." Amelia looked longingly at the driver who was still staring directly at the road ahead. "The luck."

"Moe's lucky to have you, Amelia."

*

Moe descended to Bazil's back and Bazil ambled off at a slow gait.

"Soon, we'll be with the Monster/Man," Bazil said.

"That's what I'm afraid of." Moe kept his eyes focused on the trees ahead but his thoughts to the men behind them.

"You have nothing to fear from him." Bazil weaved around a small set of boulders on the path. "Nothing at all." Bazil began to flap his large ears, creating a soft the breeze by which to guide his thoughts. "This will be a day to die for."

*

"What's going to happen to the elephant?" Amelia asked.

"Someone has to pay for the damages," Louise answered. "Unfortunately, both Bazil and I fit the bill."

*

As they slowly moved forward, Moe kept a constant vigil over his shoulder. He still could not see what had his hairs on end, but he and Bazil had yet to penetrate the woods far enough to escape the wind carrying the disturbing noise. It had the sound of an ongoing spectacle, like the overly rambunctious and blatantly ex-aggerated parade of performers leading off each show at the circus.

Bazil seemed unaffected by any of it, even after Moe's atten-tion began its slow shift to the front. Bazil continued to follow the meandering course set by the narrow advancing trail, making speed and progress rather slow. This gave Moe the opportunity to leap to the ground without them stopping in their tracks.

Moe landed on all fours and scampered off in a more direct line, unaware that his actions also speeded up Bazil. Moe left the trail, dodging trees in his path and only halting when the bright-ness of the morning sun warned him of an open space ahead. The hairs on his neck bristled at the slightest hint of wind coming from behind him.

The clearing turned out to be a firebreak, cut into the thick vegetation in a long swath perhaps thirty yards wide. From the safety of an edgemost tree, Moe could see the hill that rose to his right.. To his left, a slight decline led to a small creek, then up the slope of a second steeper hill. He didn't care for any of it. The easiest, most obvious point to reach from the path he and Bazil were following, or were being funneled into, was a trap.

*

"I'm not sure I follow?"

"It's really not that difficult," Louise said. "It's just that you've lived in a world of your own for so long, Amelia, all the time thinking that to put on a show all that you had to do was step in the center ring." Louise looked at Amelia as they walked along a small trail in the woods. They followed the frantic activ-ities of the birds in flight and the scurrying animals underfoot. "But you've recently seen otherwise---you've sampled some of the price you'll have to pay. Well, the same goes for the circus and sideshow in general. In every one of these little towns along the grid of a map there are always *unusual* and sometimes *outrageous* demands by local officials and businessmen to be met. Egos must be salved and pocketbooks must be augmented. Without this the show *doesn't* go on."

"Why are you telling me all this?" Amelia was sweating straight through to her undergarments.

"So you know who to deal with and how." Louise blazed the trail just ahead. "I won't be available to hold your hand or sidetrack Slade and his cronies any longer. Curry will want this—Slade will expect that—and a hundred more will be standing in the wings to see you falter. I won't be there to pick up your pieces, my dear."

"I just want Moe back." Amelia felt like crying but the sweat and gnats were already stinging her eyes. "I don't care about anything else right now. I know everybody has to pay to play. I know everyone must leave a little blood on the floor. Nothing is free, not even freedom."

"You say all the right words, but do you believe them?" Louise asked. "I want you to know what you're getting yourself into if you stay."

"Are you asking me to go with you?" Amelia looked a bit shocked at the prospect. "I won't leave Moe or the others."

"Just be prepared for what comes next, dear," Louise said as she turned.

Amelia forged ahead of Louise on the trail, scaring up a small flock of wild turkeys. Amelia did not want to think about *what comes next.* "I guess I'm just not like you. I guess it will never be the same for me."

"It never was."

*

Moe was about to turn back when he was surrounded by commotion. Men with guns popped up along the opposite sides of the firebreak at the very same moment that Bazil broke free from the tree line. Moe had just enough time to recognize one of the men as the elephant handler with the ever-present *bull-hook* and angry face. This time the man was carrying a rifle. Moe heard the first volley of shouts as the shots rang out, but in his attempt to stop Bazil, Moe was bumped aside by a huge leg. Then the shadow of unconsciousness descended on him and he heard or saw very little for the next few seconds.

In those seconds, Bazil moved steadily forward, into the face of the gunfire. The shots were coming from several different angles; most missed, but more than a few hit their mark. He rambled tall and unwavering for some fifteen yards, slowed for another five or so, and finally halted near the far edge. One man with a rifle was awaiting him there: Blackie. The man's dark, evil eyes matched the sneer of his stained, crooked teeth. Blackie stood directly in the path with his rifle pointed at Bazil, but Bazil never moved any closer to the far side of the forest.

Critical distance is the certain distance within which animals will attack. Beyond that distance, the flight distance, an animal will retreat. Bazil did neither one. The elephant stood in the clearing for a long second, staring straight ahead at the bull-hook man. Blackie knew that he had no time to run. The two-ton killing machine was poised to trample him to death, and he was determined not to go down without a fight. He would have his pounds of flesh. The man stared into the eyes of the animal and something there, inside those huge, rheumy eyes, stirred him for a moment—but only for a moment. He waited as long as he dared...and fired.

Instead of charging, Bazil raised his trunk in the shape of an S above his head. Then he lowered both trunk and head as all four of his legs caved in on him at once. *For one brief shining moment he saw it just behind his huge almond-colored eyes. No, not sight, something else. A wonderful feeling deep, deep down. A Paradise of pure grace and beauty washing over him and helping him to forget. Trees, tall sweet grass and elephants that went on forever and forever and forever. He had finally shed his name and come to the end of all his terrifying memories. Then there was nothing, and in that nothing there was peace. In that perfect peace he found forgiveness. It was the end he had been hoping for, and forever in this place just outside of time he would now be dreaming of...* The big beast flopped down in a heap, blood pouring from numerous holes in his wrinkled and wizened flesh. In the end, Bazil just let go.

"A heart filled with hatred is left only to contemplate and seldom commiserate but never to tolerate a soul so full of love." August Purefoy aka The Monster-Man.

*

Amelia heard the gunfire and screamed. She took off running in the direction of the shots as an uneasy calm settled back into the forest. Death had come to claim a prize today, a price to be paid for the balance of nature, she was certain of that. Louise watched her disappear further up the trail, and decided that running in the woods, in all this heat, was nothing but folly for her. She would arrive in time to pick up the pieces one more time. This was something Louise was sure she was not going to miss once she left the circus.

*

Curry stood alongside the other men who had all gathered around Bazil's body.

"I thought elephants always went off to die in some elephant graveyard or something," one of the skinnier men said.

"Nah. That's just a myth," a second, heavier-set man replied. "This here's just a big, dumb brute."

Blackie kicked at the body of the elephant a few times, just to make sure. "He had me dead to rights but he didn't charge. The big, stupid beast could have kilt me."

"You're all wrong about this one." Curry stated as he began to walk away. "Wrap things up here. That elephant is now...irrelevant."

The other men remained to study their kill.

"This one's big and dumb maybe," Blackie said to the others, "but certainly not empty. What the hell are we gonna do with two tons of dead elephant?"

The skinny man ran his hands along the large tusks. "Should we take these as souvenirs?"

The men all posed for pictures around their kill, all smiles and bravado while some turkey buzzards began to circle above.

*

Amelia never made it to the scene of the kill. She was just about to enter the clearing when she saw him huddled among some of the thicker underbrush in the forest. She approached with both caution and care, gently whispering his name over and over. Moe did not respond. He made no attempt to move or acknowledge her presence. Amelia began to weep softly for now she was certain that he was dead.

Louise came up from behind but stopped a few paces from the both of them. She watched and waited, looking for any sign of life from either one of them. Amelia's tears gave her away, but the chimp lay motionless. Louise looked up as Curry came poking through the trees.

"Pack him up," he said without emotion. "Slade wants that one back home."

Louise wasn't sure if the man was referring to Amelia or Moe or both. She watched as Amelia gathered the limp form of the chimp in her arms, and carried him past her and back along the trail. Curry led the way, an advance man in every sense of the word. Amelia followed and Louise brought up the rear. She did not like this position at all but she knew that things had somehow changed—for better or worse—in the hierarchy of the show.

*

Moe was alive and well, a bit dazed and confused about what had happened in the woods, and how he was returned to the circus, but on the mend. Amelia watched over him and doted on him constantly. He loved the attention, and the extra rations of bananas. Amelia even somehow managed to secure him a cigar, but for some strange reason, one he could not explain at the moment, he didn't want it. When she wasn't looking he tossed it into the trashcan in her trailer.

Slade stopped by once or twice, not so much to ask on Moe's recovery but to make certain that the chimp would be well enough to return to performing sometime soon. Amelia wasn't so sure herself how he would react to the twins in the show, but Moe was behaving himself, at least for now, and that was good enough for her.

Louise came by to say her good-byes. She was leaving in the morning and wanted to wish Amelia the very best.

"I'm glad he's safe and back home," Amelia said to Louise. "But I don't know how to feel about that elephant."

"Bazil was doomed from the start. Ever since he killed those chimps—the ones that drowned in their cages—his days were numbered. But then again, so are all of ours." Louise felt a slight chill even in the heat of the early evening. "At least it's all over and we can all forget. Bring those bad memories to an end."

Amelia looked off toward the place where she had always been able to count on seeing the big brute swaying gently at stake. She felt a pang of sadness for the elephant.

"I think Moe has learned his lesson," Louise continued. "He knows he cannot survive as nature intended; nor will nature allow him to go back to the way he was: a chimp in man's clothing. If he wants to live, he must take the best from both worlds." She knew a little something about that herself.

Amelia let that statement settle in, wondering to herself if she agreed.

"Where will you be going?" Amelia asked in all sincerity.

Louise suddenly had the image of a Dixie cup being tossed and turned over and over along an empty highway in the wind. "Wherever I end up, I guess. A very wise little man once told me: 'If change is what you fear-then your fears will never change'. I no longer fear change." And she felt for only the second time in her life that she was really going to miss someone.

*

A knock on her trailer door brought Louise from her stupor. She was settling somewhere in between not quite enough to drink and a little bit too much. In the back of her mind she was hoping it would be Amelia, and she was not quite ready to have to settle for Slade. Yes—she was leaving. Yes—bright and early in the morning. When she opened the door she didn't recognize the tall, slim figure that stayed just to the shadows at the bottom of the trailer steps.

"What can I do for you?" Louise heard the slight slur to her own words.

"Blasphemer." The male voice was harsh.

"What?" Louise tried to focus on the image of the man and not the words.

"Abominations."

That word again. Only this time it hit her like a thunderbolt. Poor Evangelina.

"Spawns from hell." The vehemence was rising to the top of the voice. "The wicked shall rue the day they were born and the righteous shall smite down the nonbelievers."

"I think you have the wrong place, friend. There's a church about three miles down the road." Louise smiled warmly. She wondered for a brief moment if their God had had to suffer the same fate of ignorance and bigotry from the other creatures of Eden when they were finally introduced to man.

She did not see the revolver until it was too late. She had no time to call out or prepare. She just relaxed and calmly accepted her fate. The name of the mythical dreamland that August had mentioned once upon a time never came to her with her final breath. Her memories had failed her. Without its name she felt certain that she could not enter its heavenly bonds. The very last words to pass her lips were, "Sine Die."

The first bullet hit her and she went down like a bull elephant. The next five were just overkill.

"If change is what you fear-then your fears will never change." *August Purefoy aka 'The Monster-Man.*

CHAPTER THIRTY-FOUR
Rolling On

FREAKS OF NATURE
by Martin Mulberry
County Call Staff Reporter

Fairmont bids a final farewell to the Slade Bros. Circus and Sideshow. "And not a minute too soon," Chief Desmond Brophy said. "Ever since they rolled into this area they have brought nothing but trouble. I suspect that the next things would have been a horde of locusts, followed by toads and boils." To say that the Chief was glad to see the circus trailers' taillights would be an understatement. They did leave behind, besides the pockets of grassless fields and settling dust, two of their own. The elephant that had been on the lam for weeks was finally captured and, according to one nervous and unsettled resident of our fair town: "Put out of our misery". The other casualty was one Louis Smith. (A man that I had interviewed a few days past about the history of the sideshow and some of its "colorful" characters.) I also learned that the elephant's name was Bazil. Captured with the fugitive pachyderm, but unharmed in the hunt, was a chimp. (The same chimp that was thought to be dead in an earlier report, but now has been confirmed as very much alive and kicking.) He may have been the ringleader all along. The carcass of the huge beast went unclaimed by the circus. I guess in their opinion it had caused them enough aggravation in life, so why let it continue to cause grief after its death?

This reporter did learn that after some debate by the town council and local authorities, the body was turned over to the rendering plant just outside of Hobart. I talked to the manager of the plant who said, "We never had something this big before to grind up and spit out. I hope the machines can take 'er." When pressed as to what would be done after the grinding, the man was reluctant to give an answer, except to say, "Looks like some local dogs is gonna have some real gourmand meals for a long time to come." I think he meant 'gourmet' but the sentiment remains the same.

As for the body of Louis Smith, it, too, remained unclaimed by the circus. But no answer was given as to why. The one real conundrum was left to the local coroner to figure out. The man, Philburt Nash, said that upon examining the body for autopsy, (after all, Mr. Smith had been shot at close range under suspicious circumstances) he said he found some 'things' that were a real puzzle to him. "I ain't never seen nothing like this before in all my years. And I been doing this kind of thing for going on thirty years now." It would seem, and this is according to the coroner's report that I have before me while writing this article, is that Louis Smith could also be mistaken for: Miss Louise Smith. For when it came to filling out the gender section of the final autopsy, it seems that Philburt Nash was at a loss. The dead man was equipped with both male and female "parts." His superiors came to his rescue and suggested he just leave that part of the final report blank. "But I'm a real stickler for detail," Mr. Nash said. After thinking it over, and a few martinis later, he decided to fill it in as: "Freak Of Nature." Perhaps a fitting ending for the man (or woman) who ran the sideshow.

The body has been placed on ice in the morgue at the Coroner's Office, preserved but as of yet unclaimed. I will take it upon myself to see if I can run down any next of kin for Mr. (or Miss) Smith. I will not be holding my breath in the interim.

When asked by reporters as to the suspicious nature of the sideshow man's (???) death, Chief Brophy was rather hesitant and somewhat vague in his responses. "It's under investigation," was all he would say. "We have no motive. No suspects at this time." Thus ended the news con-

ference. He did not respond when asked why he let the circus move on if one of their own was left behind under such a cloud. My feelings are, the man just wanted to be rid of the nuisance that had invaded his territory.

As for me, your intrepid County Call Staff Reporter, I guess it's back to covering Feed 'n Farm Shows, the openings of new retail stores and gas stations, and the occasional human interest stories that I know you all have come to love and cherish. But I must say, for me, the last few weeks have been one h--l of a ride.

See you in the funny pages.

CHAPTER THIRTY-FIVE
And The Show Goes On And On And On And...

The obituary for the sideshow bill of *"The Evolution Of Man'* was written about the same time that Louise Smith died. The freaks were sticking together; they were a tight old crew. But Slade gave them neither a dime nor a damn. Slade's only concern was the circus and one of its more popular attractions. The publicity, good or bad, was dying down from the terrible incident in the forest, and the notoriety that was coming to be known as *"The Great Escape."* But the man was trying hard to ride those coattails as far and as long as he could, milking every bit of publicity (and money) from a fickle public.

"It was simply...wonderful," Manuel said as he ran his fingers along a set of keys. "It's getting better every time I see it." He had just made sure that Moe was secured in the cage and there was no possibility of escape.

Amelia smiled sheepishly, holding a bunch of bananas. It *was* a wonderful act, more than just another animals-going-through-their-paces routine. This one was fraught with danger, better than anything Amelia had envisioned--better than wire-walkers working without a net and making their paces through fiery hoops. It was danger right off the front pages; it was headlines; it was reality. And Moe had helped to create it. Now here he was re-enacting it, twice every weekday, six times on the weekends, including matinees. The twins would substitute for Moe when Amelia felt he needed a break.

Bernice, the circus's only remaining adult elephant, played the part of Bazil. She kidnaps Moe from the circus; carrying him off in her trunk. Moe escapes, seeking refuge in trees, which Bernice proceeds to uproot, until Moe is recaptured. They run into a small child whose life Moe saves by being nearly trampled himself, before being carried off again by the rogue elephant. Finally Moe outwits the brutish beast Bernice and lures it into a trap set by the humans. The audience approved as at every show their roars and applause filled the Big Top at the death of the mighty beast and the rescue of the hero (or heroine) in the end. King Kong had nothing on the mighty Moe.

Manuel glanced at Moe. The chimp was still in full costume, but he was holding tight to the bars and tied in a knot in a corner of the cage. His dress was pale pink and frilly—he made a perfect damsel-in-distress. "You're lucky to have him...I hope I don't sound too envious, when I really should be angry. He's making it difficult for the rest of us freaks. Just billing him as an Ape/Man isn't enough anymore. This missing link is out performing us all. Folks won't be very tolerant of us more placid freaks. I guess I'll have to start singing for my supper." Manuel jangled the keys a bit as he placed them around his belt. "So, how's the show going overall?"

"As well as can be expected, what with the crowds thinning out more and more." Amelia tried sounding hopeful.

"The writing's on the wall," Manuel said. "I heard about Slade's latest scheme, the *'name the twins'* contest for kids. How's that progressing?"

Amelia could no longer keep up the hopeful tone. "Larry and Curly seem to be the front runners."

"Why am I not surprised?" Manuel laughed.

"There's already too many clowns in this circus," Amelia replied. "Besides, I've already named them."

Manuel waited patiently for the answer.

"Louis and Louise." This brought a slight smile to her face.

"Seems fitting," Manuel said as he turned. "Well, I've got to go. I have a performance in an hour."

"Who are you tonight?" Amelia asked with interest.

"Just the Monster/Man. Someone to scare the kiddies." Manuel answered as he walked away.

Amelia watched until she could no longer hear the ringing of the keys at the little man's belt.

All this time, throughout the conversation with Manuel, Amelia had been trying to pry Moe apart with bananas. He paid her no mind---it was elsewhere.

At the first sound of the guns, then with the smell of blood, and finally fear, Moe opened his eyes. He was unharmed, but not unafraid. He struggled to his feet as he saw Bazil fall. A cry of terror, of anguish filled the air. It came from Moe's throat as reflexively as the broken branch appeared in his hand. He must have looked frightening and enormous as he crossed the clearing with his hair fluffed out and the club swinging above his head. He felt frightening; even if instinctively he knew it was all a bluff. For who else would know him as he was now; who out there in the world would care any longer...

"Come on, Moe." Amelia's voice trickled into his reverie. "Be a good fellow. Relax. And eat. We have another show to do tonight."

...But that's not the way it happened. Not the way it happened at all. He wanted to run to Bazil's side. He wanted to strike out at the men who brought the big guy down to his knees, and then to the ground. But the truth was, he never entered the clearing. He rolled himself into a tight little ball and hid from the world.

Moe left his memories behind in the field with his friend. Reluctantly, he let loose his hold on the bars of the cage and accepted the peace offering from the woman. But one thing he thought was imperative that he not forget was what the other woman had been saying about him. The part about taking the best of both worlds that had been offered to him. And he knew that if that life was going to be more than just simple existence, he must continue to keep those worlds separate, at least in his mind---tomorrow and tomorrow and tomorrow. At least until the time it would take to send him once again after Bazil to Memories End.

*

Slade joined Curry inside Louise's trailer. The bloodstains still covered the floor, the walls and some of the furniture. Her belongings were still stuffed inside boxes that cluttered up the rooms. She had burnt all of the male finery. The police tape had been removed and the crime scene cleared.

"We'll have to see about giving this junk to Goodwill or something," Slade said. "Know anyone that could use men or women's clothing in size extra-large?" He rifled through some books, judging them mostly by their covers. "Find anything interesting?"

Curry came out of the bedroom empty handed. "Looks like the freak took it all with him."

Slade opened a cupboard above the sofa and shifted back a step or two. "What the hell is that?"

Curry sidled up alongside and both men stared hard at something in a large glass jar.

"And what's that awful smell?" Slade quickly started breathing through his mouth.

"Smells like formaldehyde." Curry picked up the jar to examine more closely its contents. "Looks like something's been preserved in there."

Both men were at a loss to explain with any certainty what they were actually staring at. It looked a little bit like a doll dressed-up to resemble a butterfly, wings and all. Its eyes were closed as if preserved in a peaceful slumber. It was malformed, whatever it was, to their own eyes.

Curry handed the jar to Slade. "Maybe you can revive the sideshow with this."

Slade placed the thing back on the shelf, and was about to turn away, when he could swear he saw the eyes of the doll open.

"What the hell?" The man jumped back at least three feet.

Curry turned and saw Slade breaking out into a cold sweat.

"It opened its eyes. The damn thing is...alive." Slade choked back down his uneasiness.

Curry took a second look at the jar. The thing inside looked peaceful, eyes closed and unmoving, as if sleeping. "Maybe it's a sign."

"What sort of sign?" Slade asked with a shudder.

Curry had no answer. He stood looking back across the inside of the trailer. "There's nothing here."

Slade closed the cupboard door upon the thing in the jar and quickly opened a window on another subject. "Heard anything from that Sheriff pal of yours about the murder?"

Curry looked annoyed when he said, "He's not my friend. And not much to go on from their end of it all. I did hear that some of the freaks turned over some hate mail that Louis and the rest of them had been receiving for some time now."

"That's the first I'm hearing about that sort of stuff," Slade said with a worried look.

"That's because you're such a lovable fellow," Curry laughed but was not amused. "Some of the stuff, I hear, was pretty vicious. The usual condemnations about them being abominations to such God-fearing folks. Looks like they'll be following those leads, looking into that angle on things. But I wouldn't hold my breath. I don't think the mysterious death of one freak is going to be a priority to them. That Brophy fella was probably happy to see the ass-end of this circus moving out of his town."

Both men stood side by side in the clutter that surrounded them.

"You ever notice that one's life comes down to all the junk you've accumulated in a miserable lifetime?" Curry felt the need to suddenly wash his hands of the whole mess. "Just get me back out there on the road. It's the only place I feel useful."

"I was thinking we should maybe head up North," Slade said. "I think I'd like to see some snow."

Curry refused to be sidetracked any longer. He shuffled around a few boxes, wanting to leave it all behind him.

"Did you find anything that would explain what Louis was doing?" Slade asked. "The slightest little thing to help us revive his program? To help us survive for a few more seasons?"

"Everything went up in smoke. Louise saw to that when she lit up the night and burned down the shed. All that remains are those chimps." Curry headed straight for the door. He turned and said, "I don't think their trainer is going to let you near them." Curry left in a hurry.

Slade stood alone. The passing thought of fumigating or torching this place crossed his mind. He glanced back toward the cupboard and the ugly abomination within its confines. He shuddered once again at the thought of it, and slammed the door shut on the trailer as he left.

*

Robert 'Blackie' Morrison was drunk on success and a now empty bottle of 'sideshow hooch'. He had to hand it to the freaks, they gave him the creeps, but they sure could brew up a decent and potent batch of moonshine. He was cheerfully staggering toward his trailer to sleep the sleep of the righteous. He had now claimed that state of grace for himself having recently cheated death, and coming one step closer to almost believing in a higher power and some sort of divine intervention on his behalf. But what he had really learned was that every good christian soldier needed someone or something to hate. Someway to vent their God-fearing frustrations of guilt, shame and blame. And what better way then to unleash all the pent up animosity toward his fellow man with a difference of opinion and religion.

His muddled thoughts were taking him in a different direction than the usual befuddled route, picturing now that horrid little misshapen man that was named after the hottest month of the year. Oh, how he hated that ugly dwarf. That sanctimonious little prick even had the gall to try to get Slade to ban him from using the 'bull-hook' on the elephants. He had to plead his case to the boss for how was he supposed to keep the big, dumb brutes in line without a little pain and suffering. That pesky pint sized freak was always judging him, spouting out his silly platitudes as if his own shit didn't stink. It always made him chuckle when he saw that creepy little man and that giant killer rogue together. Seeing them side-by-side was well worth the price of admission. He was sure glad when that freak finally up and left the circus. 'See you in hell', were his only thoughts as the dwarf exited stage left. He was also equally glad that the big beast was dead as well. He had always surmised that that thing would someday be the death of him. But instead, for all its massive size and fury, in the end it had been nothing more than a coward. So easy to bring down. And now the last piece of the puzzle would be trying to get his hands on that hairy little monstrosity that everyone was fawning over since its return. Shouldn't they be saving some of that hero worship for him? After all, wasn't he part of the rescue team that brought the little shit home safe and sound? If it wasn't for him that hairy dumb ape would have eventually ended up trampled to death or eaten by that other big, stupid brute. Now, every time their paths crossed and that monkey made eye contact, it was as if he was being judged by some hairy magistrate. Those eyes would follow him, staring straight down into his blackest soul. It was as if the little ape thought he was to blame for it all. And what about all the others? They didn't even offer to shake his hand or pat him on the back for a job well done. And what about a raise in pay from Slade? Yeah, as if that was going to happen in this lifetime. What he should have done was taken the tusks, sold the ivory, and told them all they could kiss his own hairy ass.

He tossed aside the dead soldier, stumbling up the few rickety stairs of his trailer. He tried to switch on a light but the interior remained in the dark and so did he. Taking one unsteady step inside, Blackie tripped, twisted and fell unceremoniously upon his backside. But that wasn't the worst of it. He felt a sharp and piercing pain at his chest that demanded his drunken stupor's full attention. He looked down with non-believing eyes and gasped in horror as the spiked end of the 'bull-hook' was sticking out of his body. He was afraid to move, watching the blood flowing freely like a broken, cheap bottle of wine. All he could manage was a tepid gagging, as blood and bile spurted forth from the sides of his crooked mouth, while clutching himself in an attempt to secure the innards that were spilling out from some severed place somewhere deep inside him. Those vital organs just kept on coming, and he suspected they would until he was completely emptied.

He lay there with only one thought in his head: 'How the hell did this thing get on the floor, and now within him, in the first place?" His question went unanswered. But he knew that this had been set against him on purpose, for the modified weapon was wedged between several sandbags and propped up with the pointy end protruding. It had been there to greet him when he slipped inside the room. Someone had done this deliberately so that the Angel of Death could exact its revenge and balance the debt that was owed.

His bleary eyes closed momentarily, he searched himself for a prayer, but in all his years he never learned one that stuck for any length of time within his mind. He knew bits and pieces. Something about the 'Valley of the shadow of death', and something else about 'Jesus loves the little children', but he didn't think either one could help him now in his hour of need. When his eyes re-opened, more reflex then habit, he looked upward toward the heavenly ceiling of the trailer. He didn't see God but he thought he could make out a shadowy, small, hairy face looking down on him.

Blackie was about to cuss up a storm but found he could no longer summon up the words or the thoughts to sustain him any longer. He looked one last time around in the dark and could not find one thing to comfort him or speak to him of love or home. There were no tender memories here to recall or even to forget. It was all so empty and barren of life and dreams. He closed his eyes forever, unaware that the 'bull-hook's' spike had penetrated his darkest of hearts and set free his blackest of souls. As a last bit of some cosmic gesture of amusement the 'bull-hook' took away any rhyme or reason for his nickname. Karma was a bitch, and a vengeful and painful one as well. The monster known as 'Blackie' had slipped from this mortal coil without a bang or even a whimper. He was just gone and forgotten.

"Monsters are not born, they are nurtured, they are shaped, they are scarred and haunted and then they escape with their demons intact, and let loosed upon an unsuspecting world."

August Purefoy, The Monster/Man

*

One condition Amelia had surrendered to Slade was that Moe had to be housed in a cage at night. This seemed to bother her much more than the chimp, as he took to life behind bars much the same as he had his little brush with freedom. The despondent look on Moe's face every time the door was closed shut and locked hid the secret that he was just biding his time. Amelia felt so alone, and she thought that she was now a prisoner herself in her trailer without Moe roaming free within it.

Later, inside her trailer, Amelia discovered something lying upon the floor beneath her bed. When she picked it up to examine it, she found it to be a handmade flier. A wanted poster showed a crude, child-like illustration of a chimp and an elephant. In darkly set lettering the cardboard poster stated: *REWARD: For The Return Of Monkey and Elephant To Me: Peanuts and Bananas--- The Special Prize.* The poster also contained a phone number and R.F.D. Fairmont address.

Amelia chuckled and wrote it off as perhaps sent to her by one of the parents of the many children who were fascinated with the two escapees. It was only when she turned it over that she was in for a rather chilling surprise. There was something also handwritten on the opposite side. She did not recognize the handwriting, and she knew instantly that she did not write it herself. The only other one that had been in her trailer recently had been---No---it couldn't be---could it? He was smart. He was very smart. But---No---but that could explain all the comic books she had been finding over the months in the trailer. But perhaps he just looks at the pictures, she thought to herself. But maybe---just---maybe---

Amelia looked at the one word printed there and sighed. How could one word be fraught with so much meaning? The *M* and the *o* were perfect. Only the lower case *e* was written backwards.

Amelia was taken aback by what she saw. This changed everything she thought she knew about Moe. One thing was for certain. She knew now that she did not own him, nor did anyone else---for Moe owed allegiance to no one but himself. She folded the poster and stuck it into her pocket. She hadn't realized that while she was staring she had begun to cry. The tears stung her eyes as the word pierced her heart. She knew that this was just the very beginning. Moe was not compliant to her, to Slade, or to the show. He was going along because that is what they all expected from him. He was just giving them what they wanted, putting on a brave face and acting the fool. But Moe was certainly no one's fool. What they saw as surrender, he saw as opportunity.

She did not know the time, the place or the circumstances as to when it might happen, but she did know one thing was as sure as the turning of the earth. When the time was right, Moe would be gone, and he would not be coming back.

Just before allowing herself to be swallowed by self-pity a knocking came upon her trailer door.

For a fleeting moment she thought of Poe and his Raven, but she did not let herself be consumed by Gothic gloom as she opened the door. The last person she expected to see standing there was Alex Hornbill, sans make up. He held out one lone rose.

"What's all this?" Amelia didn't know whether to laugh or cry, so she did neither.

"I thought you could use some cheering up." Alex stood on the step outside.

"What makes you think that?" Amelia took a step back.

"Because we can all use a smile or two from time to time in our lives." Alex wiggled the rose in front on her. "Don't worry, it won't shoot water. It's real." He saw the skeptical look on her face. "Besides, don't you know a clown can sense unhappiness from miles away? May I come in?"

Amelia stepped to the side to let the man slip within the trailer.

"With all that's been happening I just thought you could use a friend and..." he handed her the rose.

She took it without a word. For the life of her she could not think of a single thing to say to the man.

"How are you feeling, Amelia?"

"Numb." She was trying to sum up everything with that one word.

"Every day we are given the opportunity to laugh or cry. The choice is between laughter or tears. It's up to us to choose how one would wish to live one's life." Alex held a brief smile. "Spare parts, along with broken hearts, are what make this world spin 'round."

"What do I have to be happy about?" Amelia could not find her own smile.

"You are alive in this very moment. You are still part of this world."

Amelia was trying to hold back tears.

"We are going to hold a memorial for Louise in the big tent. Just us performers. I'd like for you to be there." Alex briefly looked away, then back again.

"I don't know if I can." The woman fiddled with the rose.

"Think about it, my dear." Alex turned to leave then moved in closer and planted a long, passionate kiss upon her lips, whispering, "Barely a breath goes by that I do not think of you and what may have been." He headed for the door, leaving her with something more to think about. "We don't have to go through this all alone if we don't want to, Amelia." He stopped just before leaving. "Don't you think it's time to leave the victim routine for the show? You don't need it any longer in your life."

Alex's exit left her stunned. She thought of all the people she knew throughout her life, but then, had never really gotten to know. She held two fingers to her lips, and for one brief, shining moment she forgot about Moe, the twins, the show and everything but that kiss. Maybe, just maybe there could be more of those interludes in her future. Once more Amelia Boone was atop the high wire, and falling never felt so good.

∗

Manuel Ortega was slowly making his way back to his trailer. The weekend shows, one in the afternoon and then again in the evening, were beginning to take their toll on him. The contortions that he had to put his body through to transform into the Monster/Man always left him with not one inch of space upon his body that do not hurt. This time the pain was seeping deep down into the bone and making him one big blob of suffering. It made him think that perhaps this was why August had finally up and left the show. It had begun taking too much from him. Once again he hoped that the man had found the peace he deserved in this world. He, himself, was looking forward to a relaxing evening where he could let the adrenaline subside and the peace and quiet wash over him like a soothing balm. The pain would just about end when it would be time for the next show.

Upon reaching the trailer he saw a single light from inside and instinctively held his ground. Had he left that light on? Cautiously he walked up the two concrete steps and entered. He was surprised to see the visitor that was there to greet him.

Moe was seated on a chair and staring. Manuel had quickly noticed the chimp's attire: sneakers and jeans, a Bat-Man tee-shirt, but no cap. Moe had shunned them ever since his return from the road. The visitor gestured for the little man to be seated, and Manuel did so without hesitation. Both occupants exchanged glances, and then Moe reached behind him to produce two cigars. He handed one to the man and kept the other for himself. Manuel took the gift with a slight smile, and then from his own pocket he brought forth a Zippo. Leaning slightly forward, the man offered to light Moe's cigar first. Moe took in some deep *puffs* and the stogie burnt to life. Manuel sat back and flared up. They both smoked in silence, and then as a gesture of goodwill, Manuel handed the lighter over to Moe. The chimp took hold without hesitation. Only a slight grin gave away his acceptance. It would save him from having to steal it later.

Moe looked the little man up and down. He no longer had much faith in Amelia. She had the twins and other things on her mind. He was also growing bored of performing, and he was a bit ashamed at the lie that was being perpetuated every time he hit the center stage. What would Bazil think? But if he had to stick around for the time being, he was looking for a new partner-in-crime. His friend had the original Monster/Man to look up to and confide in, so Moe thought to give it at least a try with the new version.

"I was so sorry to hear about Bazil. He was a good ol' boy. He did not deserve what happened to him. I sure hope he found what he was looking for out there." Manuel spoke through the surrounding smoke. "Ain't it kind of funny how these things always seem to come in threes. First Bazil, then Louise, and finally Blackie." Manuel eyed Moe a bit more closely. "You wouldn't know anything about that last one, would you, Moe?"

The chimpanzee was too busy blowing smoke rings to answer or care.

"Ironic, wasn't it? And justified, if you ask me. I guess we all have it coming. One day we'll all have to kneel before the cross and tell the good Lord what we have done." It felt natural to be sitting there talking to the chimp. "Would you like some wine to go with that smoke?"

A few moments later Moe was puffing on the cigar and sipping some wine.

"How about some music to sooth the savage beast within?" Manuel reached over and turned the dial on a portable radio set on the table between them.

When he noticed the pile of comic books setting in the corner, Moe was thinking that there was some hope for humanity after all. Tomorrow he would be thinking about going or staying, but for now he was just kicking back and letting the Monster/Man entertain him. What would ol' Baz think about that?

He missed his friend, and he would carry his memory with him, but he knew that someday he would have to venture out there once again to find out what Bazil already knew, and all he would have to do was find just a little bit of faith in a place he did not believe in, as simple as that. One thing he did know for certain was, no matter what, Bazil would be there to welcome him home. That big, goofy, lovable elephant had faith enough for the both of them in Memories End.

EPILOGUE
All That Remains

The impeccably dressed little man with the sharp, clear gray-ish-blue eyes entered the Fairmont Coroner's Office and strode gracefully up to the front desk. The woman seated there, with the too-late-in-life blonde hair and loose jowls, leaned over the desktop to get a better look at the man.

"What can I do ya for, Shorty?" She said with a toothy smile.

The man let the rude remark slip past and replied, "I am here to see about the remains of my friend. A Mr. Smith."

It took a moment or two for the name to register, but then the dim light went on inside the head. "Oh, ya mean that crazy geek with the dual plumbing?" When the fashionable man did not answer, the woman continued, "People have been payin' us a pretty penny ta come see it---them---whatever." She could see that the man was not amused. "Okay, what do ya want done with that--- thing?"

"I would like the remains of Mr. Smith to be interred in the nearest consecrated ground."

"You want what now?"

"A Christian burial in a church cemetery. High Mass and full worship service."

"Your creepy friend would have wanted that?" The woman made a strange face.

"Quite the contrary," the little man said.

The woman took a good long look at him before she asked, "Say, are you the same guy they're saying saved that elephant from the rendering plant? What're you going to do with something like that?"

"Take him home." The dwarf took out a checkbook from his vest pocket, tore off one piece of paper, and handed it up to the woman. "I will pay for everything for my friend. This should suffice."

"Okay, I'll see to it, Mr.---" The woman scanned the signature on the check. "---Purefoy. Anything else I can help ya with there, Shorty?"

"Yes. Can you kindly point me in the direction of the circus?"

THE (Memories) END

From The Author

This book was written from notes, research and talks between myself and my brother Michael concerning this story. We were going to write this novel together. Unfortunately, Mike passed away before we had that chance. I went on to write several novels of my own, but always these characters, this story, and of course, my brother Mike were always in the back of my mind. (I want to believe that Mike went off in search of the real 'Memories End' --- and found it.)

I want to thank our friend Bruce Rosenberger for suggesting that I write that story, the one that Mike and I were going to do together, because, like Bruce said: "He wanted to read it."

Acknowledgements

Thank you to: Montag Press for taking the chance on me and my manuscript, my editor Kate Sargeant for demanding of me a stronger and better book, and my family and friends for all their faith, support and encouragement. It has been a long journey from there to here, and you have all shined your light down upon the path.

And a very special thank you to Ella Beedle (Mrs. B.) who always believed in me and my dreams. I got the chance to tell her this entire story, and I am very grateful for that. I am sure someone with a heart and soul so beautiful has found a special place in Memories End.

Gary Petras was born in the untamed wilderness of the eastern part of Pennsylvania. The reading and collecting of comic books shaped his early adventures into the literary world, and his own creations and musings helped spark his interest in being a writer. His works range from Super-heroes, to Fantasy, Fairy Tales, Horror and Mystery. From books for children, to young adult to adult, and he likes to believe there is something for everyone to be found in his novels. He is the author of the *Thorndancer*, *Small Heroes*, *Farrow And Blackstorm* Trilogies, *The Sisters Hood* novel, and for Montag Press: *Memories End*. He has also written screenplays based upon his published works, plus originals. He is also a singer/songwriter. An avid hiker, spending most of his free time in the woods, as walking helps his storytelling to take shape becoming novels, songs, and dreams somewhere along the path of life.